She Was in Marc's Arms Again,

and it was the only place she wanted to be. She didn't say anything, didn't want to talk, to think, to move. She just wanted to stay in the security of Marc's embrace, the only place she had ever felt truly wanted, truly loved.

Marc's hands stroked smoothly over her body and he kissed her cheek, her earlobe, her arching neck.

Say it, Megan begged silently. Please say you love me. Say it even if you don't mean it; make me feel special once again.

Marc cupped her chin, tilting her face toward his, but the words he spoke were not the words she longed to hear. "We have to talk, Meggie," he said, his voice ragged. "There are things I have to know."

JOANNA SCOTT
lived for many years on the East Coast, but now this teacher-turned-writer is quite happy with her home state of California. She is married and has one son.

Dear Reader,

Silhouette Special Editions are an exciting new line of contemporary romances from Silhouette Books. Special Editions are written specifically for our readers who want a story with heightened romantic tension.

Special Editions have all the elements you've enjoyed in Silhouette Romances and *more*. These stories concentrate on romance in a longer, more realistic and sophisticated way, and they feature greater sensual detail.

I hope you enjoy this book and all the wonderful romances from Silhouette. We welcome any suggestions or comments and invite you to write to us at the address below.

Karen Solem
Editor-in-Chief
Silhouette Books
P.O. Box 769
New York, N. Y. 10019

JOANNA SCOTT
Exclusively Yours

Silhouette Special Edition

Published by Silhouette Books New York

America's Publisher of Contemporary Romance

To Joe, who should have won
the Babe Ruth Award,
and to Linda, Jeff and Roy,
his blue ribbon family

 SILHOUETTE BOOKS, a Division of Simon & Schuster, Inc.
1230 Avenue of the Americas, New York, N.Y. 10020

ISBN: 0-671-53636-2

First Silhouette Books printing December, 1983

10 9 8 7 6 5 4 3 2 1

Map by Ray Lundgren

America's Publisher of Contemporary Romance

Printed in the U.S.A.

BC 91

Other Silhouette Books by Joanna Scott

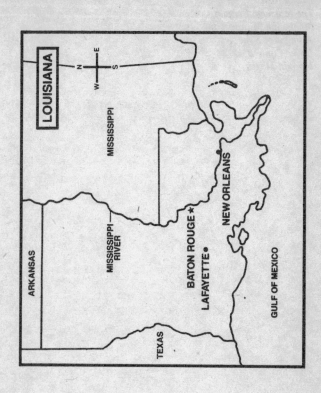

Chapter One

$\mathcal{M}$egan Mahlar walked beside her grandmother's new husband Tim, as he proudly introduced her to the other wedding guests. Most of them were long-time friends, members of the church her grandmother attended, so their typical response upon seeing Megan was, "Little Meggie? My, my, how you've grown. I never would have known it was you."

Megan cringed each time she heard the greeting, a concrete reminder that the shy, awkward girl she had once been still lingered within the sophisticated woman she had become. At Fremont Oaks, one thing remained constant, the feeling of not belonging, of being inferior, illegitimate, an outsider. But Tim was so elated that she couldn't let anyone know how she felt, and her face began to ache from all her polite smiling.

Her smile faded and her mouth went dry when Tim rested his hand on her back and led her to the man talking with the bartender at the end of the terrace.

Marc. Even without seeing his face, she knew it was him.

"Mr. Marc," Tim said, "look who's here."

Marc excused himself to the bartender, then turned toward them. "Well, Tim, how's the happy . . ." He stopped mid-sentence and his smile faded when he saw Megan. "Hello, Meggie," he said, in a resonant yet smoothly modulated voice that reflected the expensive education he had received at Louisiana's most exclusive private schools. Everything about Marc was expensive, sophisticated, tauntingly virile.

It required great effort, but she managed to return his smile. "Hello, Marc." Her gaze moved over him, comparing the man standing before her with the images secreted deep within her memory. The thick black hair and piercing blue eyes were the same, but the ruggedly carved features, always arrogantly masculine, were now harsher, more mature, with deeply etched lines around his mouth that enhanced his aura of dynamic power.

She longed to reach out and touch him, to close the distance between them, place her head on his chest and once again rest blissfully within the strong circle of his arms. *No,* she warned herself firmly, *don't do it;* don't destroy everything you've worked for. It's just not worth it. The man you loved never existed. He was a mere figment of your teenage dreams, sweet summer fantasies that vanished with the sun. Freezing her lips in a noncommittal smile that revealed none of her inner turmoil, she maintained an air of detached sophistication.

"What do you think of my new granddaughter?" Tim asked. "Isn't she something? And smart as a whip too . . . a college graduate . . . works for a fancy New York magazine."

"She's something, all right," Marc said wryly. "There's no denying that." His disdainful gaze moved over her curvaceous five-foot-six figure, expensively attractive in a V-necked taupe silk dress with a slightly flared skirt that swirled to just below her knees. He lingered on her long slender legs, clad in the sheerest nylon and lifted enticingly by a pair of high-heeled bone leather sandals, then he retraced his path with the same deliberate ease until their eyes met and his mouth curved in an insolent, knowing smile.

Megan felt the heat rush into her cheeks as she looked away and bit her lower lip. She knew he was remembering her as he had seen her last eight years before, naked, panting, writhing in his arms. He couldn't forget any more than she could; and now they were together again, face-to-face with their past. She had been a fool to return, even for her grandmother's wedding, even for the plum assignment her editor had declared "right up her alley." Some experiences were just too humiliating, too painful to relive.

"Tim," she said, struggling to control her voice. "You'll have to excuse me for a minute. I have a slight headache." Foolishly, she had thought things would be different, that the years spent in New York would have given her strength, but now that she was back at Fremont Oaks, she saw that nothing had changed and nothing ever would.

"Do you want me to get Nora?" Tim asked.

"No." Megan shook her head. "It's just the trip in from New York. I'll be fine once I take an aspirin. Tell Grandmother I'll see her in a few minutes." She forced herself to smile at Marc, then fled into the house and down the long hall leading to the bathroom, where she locked the door, leaned against the marble sink with its gold-plated fixtures and pressed a damp tissue to her throbbing temples. Breathing deeply, she looked into the gilt-framed mirror and tried to calm herself. It was useless, totally useless.

Walking quickly to the carved fruitwood vanity, she

plucked another tissue from the white and gold box, wiped her hands briskly, then crumpled the tissue into the Florentine wastebasket. Stop this, she told herself. Cut it out right now. It's ridiculous to get hysterical just because you've seen Marc Fremont. You're a sophisticated woman of twenty-six, not a naive eighteen-year-old.

Finding him there was hardly a surprise. Ever since she had agreed to return to Baton Rouge to attend her grandmother's wedding, she had known she would probably see Marc. After all, the wedding reception was being held at Fremont Oaks, the plantation that had always been his family home. She shredded another tissue between her fingers, then wadded it into a ball. You little fool, she chided herself, behaving like a starry-eyed teenager. Don't let him do this to you. You'll ruin everything, everything you've worked for; don't let that happen.

Returning to the vanity, she sat down and, tossing her head back defiantly, ran a comb through her long auburn hair. Slow, smooth strokes from her crown to her nape. Cool and collected, she told herself with each contact, cool and collected. That's the image you want, the image of success.

The fiery curls billowed around her now pale face, proving that she looked entirely different from the last time Marc had seen her. Then, her wavy red hair had been cut boyishly short. Now, it tumbled to her shoulders, lushly styled by one of New York City's most skillful hairdressers. And the sprinkling of freckles which had covered her short straight nose at eighteen was now almost completely concealed beneath a light dusting of carefully applied makeup. Her clear green eyes, always her most compelling feature, had been made even more striking by a touch of shadow and thick curling lashes. Equally noticeable was the defiant hatred flashing from those eyes, an emotion Megan had been nurturing since that degrading day eight years before when Marc's father had ordered her to leave Fremont Oaks.

Despite her determined efforts to put the past behind her, the demeaning remembrance undermined her confidence, and she wished she were a million miles from here, away from Marc and his father, away from the painful reminders of the humiliation they had caused her. Wishful thinking, she told herself. But enticing as the thought might be, you can't disappear, nor can you stay in here forever. You've been avoiding Marc for eight years and the time has come to stop; you can't run away anymore.

She straightened her shoulders purposefully, but false courage couldn't prevent her stomach muscles from tightening when her fingers closed around the doorknob; and the tension became unbearable when, walking out into the hallway, she saw Marc leaning against the flocked gold wallpaper, his arms folded across his chest.

"Feeling better?"

"Fine, thank you." So polite, she thought, like strangers, as if he hadn't known her more intimately than any other man, than any other person.

Marc too seemed to be assessing the changes that the years between had made, and when Megan saw the undisguised admiration in his eyes, a glowing sense of self-satisfaction melted her chilling apprehension and restored her confidence. Her efforts had been success-ful, and just this one moment of triumph made all her years of struggling worthwhile.

"Trying to avoid me, Meggie?" Marc asked, his manner a study in self-assured arrogance. "I wonder why?"

I'll bet you're wondering, Megan responded silently. She wondered too, because if she really had gotten over Marc, why was she so afraid to face him? Muscles deep within her tightened as her eyes locked into the penetrating blue of his. Eight years was a long time, but not long enough to erase her memories, passionate, erotic memories that could still make her blush and tingle with desire. Was he remembering too? Closing her eyes, she faced the past she had tried so hard to forget.

Megan's seventeen-year-old unmarried mother had died in New Orleans when she was born and her grandmother had brought her to Fremont Oaks. The spare hours of her lonely childhood had been devoted to escaping the reality of life by riding horses wildly and spending quiet sessions lost in the fantasy world of books. The written word had so intrigued her that she had wanted to become a part of that excitement, to be a writer.

When Megan entered her teens, Marc, eight years older than she, became her secret idol, the man of her dreams, a raven-haired fairy-tale prince come to life. Whenever he was home from school, she tried to be around him, but he was always too busy entertaining his sister Jacqui's beautiful debutante friends to notice the housekeeper's granddaughter. Still, Megan hadn't been able to stop herself from fantasying about him. She couldn't; he was her hero, her beau ideal.

Then one day Angus, the stableman, mentioned that Marc went riding every morning before breakfast, and Megan adjusted her schedule to fit with his. Marc thought they were meeting by chance, but she knew differently, knew she was pursuing him. It was the first time she had ever done anything like that; she was usually so shy. And Nora's attitude toward dating hadn't helped at all, since she absolutely refused to let Megan have anything to do with boys—no dances, proms, football games, nothing. More loneliness, more being different and apart.

After their first few meetings, Marc seemed to be expecting her, even waiting for her, but she couldn't be sure because when they were together, his attitude toward her was strangely ambivalent. Sometimes he seemed to think of her as a woman, yet on other occasions he treated her like an amusing little child—until—until that day when they stopped to rest their horses near the bayou and she convinced him that there was nothing childish about her.

She recalled the events of that day as clearly as if they had happened yesterday, and cringed at the memory of the naive eighteen-year-old she had been, so sheltered, so desperate for love and acceptance.

"I'm going to miss you," Marc had said while they studied their reflections in the brackish bayou water.

"Miss me? Are you going away?" Fear paled her face.

"No, but you are, aren't you? You did say you wanted to go on to college, didn't you?" His blue eyes deepened, searching her face.

Marc wasn't leaving. Relief pacified Megan's fear. Bending, she picked up a twig and tossed it into the water. "I want to be a journalist . . . to go to Columbia, in New York, but first I have to get a job and save some money. I can't expect my grandmother to pay for my college. She's done too much for me already."

"But you would want to go to college . . . if you had the money?"

"Of course I would. I want to make something of myself, to be important, wear beautiful clothes . . . be beautiful." Using the water as her mirror, she pulled her short auburn hair down over her ears and around her face, trying to make it look longer, more glamorous. She dreamed of a new Megan, a Megan who was not only beautiful, but also admired, loved, most of all loved. Her poignant sigh passed through every particle of her being, echoing through the bayou.

"You are important. And beautiful. Young and sweet and beautiful, don't you know that?"

"No." Tears welled in Megan's eyes as she listened to Marc's whispered compliments. She was so unaccustomed to them that they melted the protective shield that had always guarded her emotions. "No one has ever called me beautiful." She shook her head despondently. "You don't have to lie, you know the truth about me. . . . I'm ugly . . . bad luck too. My mother died when I was born. Nora had to raise me." The words tumbled out, a dam released. "If not for me, my mother wouldn't have died and Nora wouldn't have been so unhappy. Look at all the trouble I've caused." Covering her face with her hands, she began sobbing, deep, racking cries that she couldn't control.

"You poor kid," Marc said, gathering her into his arms. "What happened to your mother wasn't your fault." He cradled her head on his chest and began stroking her hair. "Don't tell me you've been living with that all your life." He hugged her tightly, protectively.

Sighing, Megan collapsed against him. At last someone who knew how she felt, understood her loneliness, her unhappiness, just as she had always known he would. She wanted to get closer to him, to touch him, to feel his arms around her. Looking into his reassuring blue eyes, she stood on tiptoe and pressed her lips gently against his.

Marc's arms dropped to his sides, releasing her. His lips were immobile, unresponsive, as tight and cold as a statue's. "Don't . . . you're unhappy, too upset to know what you're doing. You'll regret it later."

Megan turned away. She'd been a fool. Marc didn't really care about her, not in that way. He was just being nice to her. Tears streamed down her cheeks. Why did she have to ruin everything by kissing him? "I'm sorry. I shouldn't have done that. I don't know what got into me." Her voice was a sniffling whisper.

"No, Meggie, sweetheart, no. . . ." He turned her

gently toward him, drawn by the glittering brightness of her streaming tears. "Please don't cry." His arms tightened around her once again, clasping her to his chest. "I didn't mean to make you cry. It's just that . . ."

"You don't like me . . . in this way, I mean. It's all right. I understand. You're used to more sophisticated girls. I'm not pretty enough." Too embarrassed to face him, she shifted in his arms and tried to move away from him. "You don't even want to kiss me."

He caught her chin, cupping it and lifting her face toward his. "It's not that, never that. It's just . . . You're so young . . . so fragile and beautiful . . . yes, so very beautiful. Someday after you've gone to college and done all the things you want, you'll meet someone your own age, someone more suitable."

Rejection again, sensitively handled, but still rejection. She couldn't restrain herself, couldn't conceal her hurt. Humiliation was unimportant when compared with what she felt for Marc. "I don't want anyone else. And you don't have to lie to me. You can tell me the truth. Admit that you don't want me."

"I want you, Meggie . . . Believe me, I want you . . . more than I've ever wanted anything in my life. I want to hold you in my arms, to feel your body against mine . . ." His voice wavered. "But that's the problem. You're so young, I shouldn't even be speaking to you about these things. You've got your whole life ahead of you and it wouldn't be fair for me to ruin everything that's waiting for you. *You* haven't done anything wrong, Meggie. The problem is *me*. I'm a *man* with a man's needs and just kissing you isn't going to satisfy me."

He wanted her. Exactly what Megan longed to hear. She looked at Marc and her heart expanded like a blossoming rose. "I love you, Marc. I love you so much. I want you to make love to me . . . please." Her hands went to his neck, combing through his hair with a hungering urgency.

"We must . . . I shouldn't." His fingers tightened around her chin and he stared at her as if he couldn't decide whether to draw her closer or push her away.

By leaning forward ever so slightly, Megan made the decision for him, and Marc groaned helplessly as he pulled her closer and accepted her offer. Crushing her in his arms, he kissed her with a desperate hunger that she yearned to satisfy. Her lips parted, opening to his probing, and she answered his expert explorations with the tentative innocence of her own.

That first hour of bliss in Marc's arms had been followed by many more, making the next few weeks the happiest Megan had ever known. Marc had been a demanding yet considerate lover and had, after their first time together, taken precautions against getting her pregnant. He became her entire reason for existing, and her lifelong goal of college and a career now faded to nothingness because she was certain that before the end of summer Marc would ask her to marry him. But he hadn't, he hadn't done that at all. Taking a deep breath, she tried to clear her head and bring her thoughts back to the present.

She had loved him so much. Loved? Past tense? If only. Seeing him again had shown her that despite everything, the emotional ties between them still existed, still drew them together. The images of the past grew hazy and blurred. Megan blinked them away, blocking out the past and concentrating her attention on the older, even more dynamic Marc now standing before her.

As if he could read her thoughts, perceive that the potent temptation that had first drawn them together was as powerful as it had ever been, Marc's gaze moved boldly over her, his admiration flaring into sensuous desire. "You're more beautiful than before," he said, his voice low and husky, "something I didn't think possible."

"Oh ye of little faith," she said lightly, trying to brush past him. Keep it impersonal, she decided, as if he were merely an acquaintance, no one special.

"Don't toy with me, Meggie," he said, grasping her arm and drawing her to him.

"Let me go."

"Ah, Meggie." His voice grew low and husky. "Was that ever possible?"

"Marc, please." She fought to keep the tension from vibrating into her voice, but the memories were too strong; her tone was almost as sensuously husky as his. And memories alone weren't causing the weak longing that rippled from her stomach to her legs; much as she tried to deny it, the attraction was still there.

"That's more like it," he said, caressing her arm, his fingers nibbling at the curve of her breasts. "More like the words I seem to recall." His tone became softly seductive. "Words like, *please . . . more . . . forever . . . oh, forever.*"

"*Stop*. That's enough. I don't want to hear any more." She had heard enough, enough to make her remember her passionate moans, her breathless pleas, her sighs of satisfaction. Leaving had been the farthest thing from her mind. She would have stayed with Marc forever, only he hadn't wanted her forever. That was the problem, and she wasn't going to give him a second chance to hurt her. Breaking free, she started running down the hall toward the open French doors.

"Not so fast," he said softly, moving in front of her and blocking her escape. "We have a lot of catching up to do. I said you're more beautiful than ever, but the beauty I once knew went more than skin deep, much, much deeper, too deep to judge by sight alone, so I've yet to see if that's still there." Smiling confidently, he closed the distance between them and pressed her back against the wall. "Show me, Meggie," he said, feathering her lips with his. "Show me, tell me, let me feel."

"No," Megan protested, turning her face away so that his lips missed hers and caressed the curve of her neck. *"I said no, Marc."* Her hands went to his chest as she tried to push him away. How dare he touch her so intimately? Had he forgotten how they had parted, how he had hurt her?

A humid August breeze wafted through the open doors, and as she inhaled deeply, the scented sweetness of the rose garden tantalized her nostrils with the same flowery fragrance that had drifted toward the bayou that summer, the summer she had spent with Marc.

"Mmm," Marc murmured, his arms tightening to draw her closer. "Now that's a word I don't remember." He nibbled at her earlobe and traced it with his tongue. "You never used to say no."

"An unfortunate omission on my part, but I was young and foolish, wasn't I? I'm not the same anymore, believe me, I'm not the same."

A taunting smile curved one corner of Marc's mouth. "I don't believe you." His hands moved slowly up her back, rested momentarily on her shoulders, then stroked lightly over the silken fabric of her bodice. His eyes darkened while his fingers flexed, tantalizing her once again as they had so often in the past. "You still have the eyes of a tigress; why should your body be any different?"

"My eyes and my body are no concern of yours," Megan said tartly.

"Of course not," Marc said, straightening away from her. "They stopped being my concern the day you got your paycheck."

Her paycheck. As if any amount of money could make up for the pain and misery she had endured. Without thinking about what she was doing, she raised her hand and struck it across Marc's cheek.

Marc's cruel smile blended with the imprint of her fingers. "Now that's going to cost you," he said, grabbing her wrist, pulling her arm behind her back and bringing her body up against his. "The polite games are over. I never did feel that I got full value for my money, but I'm willing to let you make up for it right now." His mouth ground against hers, violating, possessing, dominating her with the fierce power of his enraged masculinity.

This was a Marc she didn't recognize, a frightening Marc without the tiniest shred of the gentleness she had known and loved. She struggled to free herself, but arms of steel bound her to him until at last the tears came and she whimpered helplessly beneath his strength.

His lips softened, releasing her from his rage, but still holding her tightly against him. "That doesn't work for us, does it?" he rasped, his voice ragged with emotion. "I want to hate you, have every reason to hate you, but I can't, I just can't." He caught her face between his hands, lifted it to his and studied her tear-streaked cheeks as if waiting for a response. "Why can't I hate you, Meggie?"

She shook her head silently. What could she say? His words were the echo of her thoughts.

The small combo on the terrace introduced the leisurely strains of "My Love Is Forever," and Marc's lips brushed over her ear while he hummed in time to the music. "I'll never forget you." His hands moved higher, thumbs teasing just below her breasts. "I never have, you know." His warm breath teased the inner curve of her ear, tugging at erotic strings deep within the core of her body. "I don't think I ever will."

Gasping at the force of her reaction, Megan pulled away and flattened herself against the wall, but not before Marc had felt her flesh peaking beneath his touch.

"Tell me again," he whispered softly. "Convince me that you really mean no when every sensuous fiber of your body is reaching out to me . . . shouting yes."

"Let me go, Marc," she said firmly, as sanity returned and she refused to be intimidated by his strength or the erotic memories his raw masculinity could evoke. "Let me go or you'll regret it."

"Really?" he taunted. "Why would I regret holding you? I never have before." He cupped her breasts and drew small circles around their tips. "And you still feel soft, desirable . . . exceedingly touchable."

Too touchable, Megan thought, much too touchable. Once, Marc's touch had meant more to her than anything in the world. . . . She had longed for it, begged for it, but now . . . "I mean it, Marc," she said, trying to disengage his fingers from her waist. "Think about it. This isn't the bayou; there's a terrace full of people just outside that door. If you don't let me go, I'll cry out and you'll have to explain what you were doing."

"To all the guests? Every one of them? Well, I wouldn't want that. I much prefer being alone with you. I always have . . . especially when you cry out. . . . I've always considered that pleasure very privately mine." Releasing her, he leaned forward and rested one hand on the wall. "Where do you suggest we go? To the bayou, our old meeting place?"

"Marc, don't make things any harder for us by bringing up the past." She turned away, trying to avoid his touch. "I'm a different person now. You are too. We're both older and wiser, too wise to get involved again." The band on the terrace had shifted from a fox-trot to the "Blue Danube Waltz." Megan's nerves tensed, throbbing in time to the music. She couldn't make a scene, couldn't ruin her grandmother's wedding.

"Since when did age have anything to do with

wisdom?" he asked, his tone hard and cynical. "Eight years ago I thought I knew everything, but I was sadly mistaken. I didn't know the first thing about you, did I?" He gripped her shoulders and pressed her head against the wall. "How did you ever have the nerve to come back? Tell me, Meggie, how can you face me?"

How could she face him? What he really meant was how dare she show up and flaunt her success in his face. What had he expected her to do, curl up and die? "I haven't done anything I'm ashamed of," she said, "so don't try to lay your guilt trip on me."

Shrugging free once again, she walked rapidly toward the open French doors, her auburn hair glowing softly beneath the shimmering crystals of the Baccarat chandeliers that had hung at Fremont Oaks for more than a hundred years. Fremont Oaks reeked of tradition, money, breeding. It always had and it always would, which was why she would never fit in, never, not ever. She had been a fool to return.

The hall seemed to be getting longer, the door farther away. Fremont Oaks was huge, endless halls, countless rooms, all dusted and polished by an army of obsequious servants. But she wasn't one of them, not anymore. She increased her pace, eager to escape from the hidden thoughts and feelings she didn't want to consider, but Marc caught up with her and gripped her shoulder.

"My guilt trip," he chuckled bitterly, the words vibrating in her ears. "That's a joke. We both know what really happened. You took my money, ran to New York and stayed there for eight full years," he said, his voice lowering in disbelief. "Now you're back, all fancy and sophisticated, and I paid for it. A stiff price, even for a body as beautiful as yours."

"Prices, money, buying your way through life; that's all you can think of, isn't it? Well, you're wrong." His accusation hurt her, made her feel as cheap as if she had . . . Trying to disprove him, she blurted out the words, the words she had never meant to say, not ever again. "I loved you, Marc."

"You love me?" he demanded, pressing the length of his body against her back. "You certainly have a strange way of showing it."

Her flesh tensed as he molded it to his. She hadn't gotten over him. She'd never get over him, but she couldn't let him know, she'd never let him know. "Loved, Marc, I said loved, past tense." Reaching up, she tried to pull his hands off her shoulders. "Who said anything about me loving you *now?* Did I? Never. Forget it, Marc. Whatever we felt for each other died a long time ago." Died with our baby, she finished silently, unable to voice the painful words as she finally wrenched herself free. She had to get away from him—fast.

"Our love didn't die, Meggie," Marc said, his voice ruthlessly smooth. "It was murdered. You killed it with your greed."

"I killed it." Without realizing what she was doing, she lashed out, slapping her hand sharply across Marc's right cheek and leaving a bright red imprint. "How dare you? How dare *you* say that to me?" The stream of defensive, accusing words racing through her mind remained choked in her throat. She couldn't say any more, not now. With tear-filled eyes she ran down the hall toward the open French doors, away from the past, away from Marc.

The gray-blue sky still held back its ever-present threat of rain and an intermittent hint of sun peeked between the clouds as Megan's high heels left the plush beige carpeting and clattered onto the red brick terrace, which characterized the handcrafted elegance of Fremont Oaks. The house itself, surrounded by acres of land and narrow bayous, was an antebellum mansion with a white-columned exterior, a huge portico and a seemingly endless supply of rooms, half of which were no longer used.

Ancient magnolia trees dotted the lawns and shaded the terrace where the refreshments were being served. A linen-covered buffet table holding silver trays of tea sandwiches and small cakes stood to the right of the door, and a large silver punch bowl adorned a round table near the steps leading to the garden. Clusters of elderly men in sports coats and women wearing flowered polyester dresses gathered around the white wrought-iron furniture, but Megan couldn't join them, not with the tears running so freely down her cheeks; tears of anger, tears of regret, streaking her carefully applied makeup, releasing the anguish that had been locked in her heart for eight long years.

Walking to the end of the balcony, she grasped the granite balustrade and looked down at the sundial perched in the center of the neatly mown lawn. Once again her thoughts returned to the past, to that fateful August day when Marc didn't come riding. She had waited in her jeans and yellow tie-front T-shirt, but he had never come. Instead his father had summoned her to the library, told her that Marc had gone away for a few weeks and that he had arranged for her to attend Columbia University. He had handed her a check that had already been made out, and all her tearful entreaties to speak with Marc had done nothing to change his mind.

"It's all been settled," Louis Fremont had said. "These things are unfortunate, but they do happen. In any case, Marc's gone out of town and it would be better for everyone concerned if he doesn't see you again. To be honest about it, he doesn't want to."

"That's not true. He couldn't have left me." Leaning forward in the maroon leather chair, she had gripped the edge of the mahogany desk. "He loves me."

"I'm sorry. Marc should have known better. You're

just a child." Louis Fremont had toyed with a paper-weight, making snow drift in his hand.

"I'm not a child. I'm eighteen years old. I love Marc and he loves me. I'm not going anywhere until I see him," she had said, pounding on the desk.

"He doesn't want to see you, Meggie," Fremont had stated emphatically. "It's too embarrassing for him. That's why he asked me to speak to you. You have to understand, he's getting married soon. To Deirdre Collins, our friends' daughter, last year's Mardi Gras queen." Muted sunlight had glinted through the mullioned windows at his back. "Breeding matters to us. That's just the way things are."

Breeding. Did he mean that just because her mother . . . Well, maybe Louis Fremont believed those things, but not Marc, never Marc. Hadn't he told her that she was beautiful, fragile? "No." Marc wouldn't do this to her. He was much too kind and gentle ever to hurt her like this. "He told me he loved me." The leather chair had felt damp and sticky beneath her denim jeans.

"Sometimes men say things they don't mean," Louis Fremont had said, placing the paperweight back on the desk. "Your grandmother should have told you that." He had tapped his fingers against the mahogany patina and seemed to be uncomfortable with the situation, but the cruelty had remained in his icy-blue eyes.

"My grandmother doesn't talk about these things . . . ever since my mother . . ." Why was she explaining? Louis Fremont knew how shattered Nora had been when she had learned of her unmarried daughter's way of life, her pregnancy. She herself had heard the whispered comments often enough.

"We both know what this would do to Nora. For her sake, take the money and go to New York."

"I'm not running away. I love Marc and I'm not ashamed of what I've done. I'll tell Nora what happened. She'll understand." She had glanced around, seeking some sort of confirmation, but every object in the book-lined room was as coldly dispassionate as the man behind the desk. She felt her hopes dwindling, her fears mounting.

Louis Fremont shook his head. "No she wouldn't. She sent your mother away . . . never spoke to her again. Learning that you're no better would kill Nora. It's not fair to her, not after all she's done for you." Fremont had leaned back; the sun created silver highlights in his hair. "Besides, if you insist on staying and making a fuss, we'd have to let Nora go. The situation would be too uncomfortable to let her keep working for us. You'll have to face up to the truth, Meggie. You have no choice. You did wrong and you're no longer welcome at Fremont Oaks."

A sickening weakness paralyzed her. Marc's father was right; her grandmother would never understand how she felt about Marc. Although unspoken, Nora's message had always been the same as Louis Fremont's. "Prove yourself, don't be like your mother; good girls don't." But with Marc, it wasn't good or bad, it was love. Yet he . . . "But what about Marc?" Megan asked angrily. "I didn't do this alone." Fair was fair. Why should she be the only one to suffer? Why should Marc get off scot-free?

"Fremont Oaks is Marc's home. His and his children's to come."

His and his children's to come. Louis Fremont's words reverberated in Megan's mind as clearly as if he were standing before her. *Marc's children, but with another woman, not with her.* Of course, she wasn't good enough, not for marriage, just for the bayou. There was no such thing as fairness or equality, not at Fremont Oaks.

The humiliation of a lifetime flooded her face and she knew she had to fight back or die. All right, she had decided angrily, why shouldn't she make Marc pay for using her, for hurting her like this? Why did the Fremonts always have to win? It was about time she got something out of life. Why shouldn't she take this chance to leave Louisiana and make something of herself?

She had felt a shell closing around her heart as she glared at Louis, her eyes as narrow and cold as his own. "You're right. Marc never meant anything more to me than that check you're holding. I knew that sooner or later he'd pay off." They think I'm no good anyway; what do I have to lose by proving them right? This is probably the only chance I'm ever going to get to escape from this horrible place; why shouldn't I take it? "Thanks, this is my ticket out of here." She had reached for the check, then stood and left the room.

That was her last memory of Fremont Oaks, her last contact with Marc and his family until today. And now, after all these years, everything was coming back. Had she been foolish to return, even for her grandmother's wedding, even for her job?

Chapter Two

The wedding's music and laughter drifted over Megan, breaking into the privacy of her thoughts. You could cloak the past, she decided, conceal it even from yourself, but sooner or later it emerged, floating to the surface and reminding you that it remained with you, still a very important part of your life. Now, as her memories became poignantly real, her greatest desire was to leave Fremont Oaks and return to New York— to forget about Marc, the Fremonts and every hateful thing they represented.

She could have left as soon as the wedding was over if she hadn't accepted an assignment to write a feature article on Fremont Industries. She had made good use of the check Louis had given her by moving to New York and enrolling in Columbia University's School of Journalism. Accustomed to a life of loneliness and books, she had studied diligently and managed to maintain an A-minus average. In her junior year she had been selected for the apprenticeship program at *Commerce World* magazine, one of New York's most prestigious financial publications. Now, five years later, after being a research editor, reviewing books, writing fillers and charting market trends, she was one of *Commerce World*'s most respected feature writers.

When she had told Jerry Butler, the editor in chief, that she needed time off to attend her grandmother's wedding at Fremont Oaks, his scowling features had flexed into one of his rare smiles. "Great," he had said, "you know Nessac Petroleum is trying to take control of Fremont Industries. We did an article on *Nessac* last month and now *Fremont* wants equal time. Since you'll be down there anyway, the job is yours."

So, despite her personal animosities, she was stuck there, at least until she had completed her research. Well, she decided, brooding and crying isn't going to accomplish anything. You've shed enough tears over Marc to last you a lifetime. Sighing, she took out her compact, repaired her makeup, then turned and walked toward the rose garden where her grandmother and some friends were admiring Tim's handiwork.

Tim's wavy white hair contrasted with his leathery face, and he winced as he tugged uncomfortably at the starched collar of his new white shirt. "Now, this is a very special plant," he said, pointing to a small, thorny bush displaying one perfect pink rose. "I grew this hybrid in the greenhouse, then transplanted it to the garden knowing it would bloom today. I've named it the Pink Nora in honor of my beautiful wife." Carefully avoiding the thorns, he caught the rose between two fingers and hugged Nora close to his side.

Nora's cheeks blushed as rosy as the flower's petals. "Oh, Tim," she said, patting his suntanned hand. "It's absolutely lovely."

Why, Grandma's like a young girl, Megan thought, watching the short, slightly stout woman in amazement. I've always seen her as older, dependable, totally unsentimental, with hardly a romantic bone in her body, but now, with Tim, she's like a flirtatious teenager, entirely different from the seriously sensible grandmother I've always known. She's like—like—a woman in love.

A woman in love. Could being in love make a woman of any age feel young and carefree? Was love and not age responsible for the mindless ecstasy she had shared with Marc eight years before? Was that why she couldn't control the attraction she felt for him, even now? Megan rejected the suggestion. Love and Marc were two words she didn't want occupying the same brain wave.

"Ah, there she is," Tim said, smiling at his friends, releasing the rose and looking up at Megan as she approached. "Pretty little Meggie, only she's not so little anymore." He winked appreciatively. "I'm a lucky man, because when I married Nora, I brought two beautiful women into my family."

"Careful, Tim, Grandma has a temper; you wouldn't want to make her jealous."

"Why not?" Tim asked, winking at Megan conspiratorially. "A little jealousy is good for a woman . . . keeps her on her toes, and speaking of toes, are you willing to risk yours with a lead-footed old gardener?"

"I thought you'd never ask," Megan said, holding out her hand. "Now I know why I've always wanted a grandfather. Two beautiful women, indeed. Tim Gregory, you do wonders for a lady's ego."

The combo was playing a fox-trot, but Tim's feet created their own bobbing rhythm and Megan kept tripping over herself in an attempt to follow him. He hadn't lied about his lead feet.

"Getting tired?" Tim asked.

"Well, it's been quite a day." In more ways than one, she thought wryly. "Don't forget I had that early flight in from New York." She shifted her foot to avoid Tim's.

"I'm glad you could come; you've made Nora very happy. She told me you might not be here because you hated Louisiana, never wanted to come back, and you always insisted that she meet you in New York on her vacation."

Megan kissed Tim on the cheek and smiled. "It took a special occasion to get me back here. Like a wedding that got me a handsome new grandfather." Despite his sometimes brusque manner, Megan had always liked Tim, who'd been the gardener at Fremont Oaks for as long as she could remember.

"Ah," Tim said. "I can see New York has mended your manners. What happened to the wild young girl who used to feed my prize ferns to the rabbits?"

"I don't know what you're talking about. Besides, I was careful to take only a few leaves at a time. How did you find out?"

"I always had my suspicions. Then, when you went to New York, my emaciated ferns underwent a miraculous recovery . . . full and leafy, just like they always should have been."

"You'd better start watching them again," she chuckled. "I still can't resist a hungry rabbit." She pulled her foot back as Tim stepped on her toe.

"I know all about you and your weakness for lost creatures, Meggie. That's why I never stopped you. I remember the time I helped you put a splint on that mockingbird's wing, so I know just how softhearted you are about any helpless little animal."

Probably because I've always felt like one myself, Megan thought, helpless . . . rejected. "Well, you keep that information to yourself, Tim Gregory. I'm supposed to be a hard-nosed, brittle reporter." She forgot about following the music and concentrated on avoiding Tim's feet. Hard-nosed, cynical, elegant, that's the image I want. Please don't remind me about the skinny little girl who used to cry over rabbits and mockingbirds.

"Don't want anyone to know what a soft touch you are, hmm? Well, don't worry about me. I never said anything before, did I?"

"No, Tim, you're a good secret keeper and a good man too. I'm happy for Nora and proud to have you as my grandfather."

The music stopped and Tim turned toward the deserted rose garden. "All these compliments, my, my." He shook his head. "We'd better get back to Nora before my head grows too big for my old straw hat. Now, where is she?" He surveyed the parklike grounds. "Ah, over there," he said, motioning toward a white wrought-iron settee where Nora was seated.

Marc was resting on the balustrade beside her, one hand hooked over the branch of a magnolia tree. Even in that relaxed position, every aspect of his demeanor exuded aristocratic wealth. His impeccably tailored light gray suit fit smoothly over his lean muscular body, and gold cuff links glittered at his wrists. His complexion was tanned by sun-filled hours of tennis and horseback riding. He was every inch the well-bred southern gentleman, all egotistical six-feet-three of him.

Megan held back. She didn't want to see Marc, but she couldn't snub Tim and her grandmother. How would she explain? Reluctantly, she followed Tim's lead.

"He really likes your grandmother," Tim said as they approached the settee.

"Who?"

"Mr. Marc. He spends a lot of time in the kitchen just sitting there, talking to her, drinking coffee, asking questions. Nora likes him too. In fact, when she told him we were getting married, he insisted on giving us this party, said we were like family, made Nora very happy. He's a fine fellow."

"Really?" *Fine* was hardly the word Megan would use to describe Marc, and she couldn't believe that he was just being benevolent. "I wonder what he expects in return?" She scoffed silently at the possibility that Marc meant what he said about Tim and Nora being part of the family. They were his servants, his house-keeper and his gardener, and when they had outlived their usefulness, he would send them away just as he had sent her away.

"What he expects in return?" Tim repeated. "Why, nothing." He looked at her quizzically. "What could we ever do for him?" His eyes narrowed thoughtfully. "Meggie? You sound angry . . . bitter. He wouldn't be the reason you've been staying away?"

"What do you mean?" Megan drew back, wondering if Marc had told Tim about them.

"Nothing much. Only a gardener, being outside so much, gets to see a lot of different things, like people riding off together, then disappearing into the trees."

"Tim, you haven't mentioned this to my grandmother." Fear shot through Megan like jagged icicles. She clutched his arm. Nora would never understand her weakness, and she'd never be able to face the disappointment in her grandmother's eyes.

Tim shook his head. "Not a word. I told you I can keep a secret. Besides, you know Nora; she's a puritan. After what happened to your mother, hearing that you'd been sneaking around with Mr. Marc would break her heart. So be careful while you're here, will you? We don't want Nora getting upset." Tim walked around a long table with a silver punch bowl and trays of cookies and stepped in front of Nora. "Mind if we join you?" he asked, resting his hand on Nora's shoulder.

"Not at all," Marc said, lowering his arm. "I was keeping your wife company while you were off dancing."

"Ah, well," Tim said. "I never could resist a pretty redhead, and Meggie's a good dancer too."

"Is that so? Hmm, she does look rather irresistible," Marc said, holding his hand out to Megan. "Will you do me the honor?"

Honor? Marc wouldn't know the meaning of the word, and dancing with him was the last thing in the world Megan wanted to do. She had every reason to hate him, but still, when he looked at her . . . why court trouble? "Thanks, Marc, but I'm really tired. It's been a long day."

"They're playing a fox-trot," Marc said. "Nice quiet music. I promise that you'll find it relaxing."

"I don't know." Megan sought the right words, but they wouldn't come. How could she explain that, for her, being in his arms was anything but relaxing?

"If you don't dance with me, everyone will think you don't like me. Isn't that right, Nora?"

"Don't be silly. Of course she likes you. You heard her, she's just tired. It's that trip from New York. Still, one little dance . . . Go on, Meggie, dance with him. You can rest later. After all, my wedding is a special occasion. You wouldn't want Mr. Marc to think you don't like him."

Megan hesitated for another moment, still trying to get out of dancing with Marc, but at this point she couldn't think of any graceful way to refuse. "All right, just one dance." She put her hand on his arm and began walking toward the center of the terrace.

"You might at least smile."

"Why?" she snapped. "You know I don't want to dance with you."

"Ah, but I also believe I can change your mind." Pulling her back against him, he held her for a moment while he swayed in time to the languid music. His muscular flesh pressed sensuously against hers. "Very easily."

"Don't bet on it," Megan said, twisting free despite the melting sensation that liquified her bones and urged her to stay.

"I'm not a gambling man," Marc said, slipping his arm around her waist and starting down the steps, "but that's one bet I'll gladly take; I never could turn down a sure thing." He smiled confidently. "Let's go this way." He turned left at the foot of the steps. "The lower patio's less crowded."

"I don't mind the crowd."

"Ah, but *I* do," he said softly. "We never finished our little chat, remember? And I've been waiting for another chance to be alone with you all day."

"Our discussion is over, so there's no need for us to be alone, and from now on anything you have to tell me you can say in front of my grandmother." Nora, she reminded herself, think of Nora. Don't weaken, don't think about Marc. Her grandmother's face flickered in her mind. *Good girls don't.*

"In front of Nora?" Marc chuckled softly. "I don't think so." He led her off the brick path and onto the grass. "She may be your grandmother, but she doesn't know you, not the way I do." The music grew fainter, and a row of towering cypress trees separated them from the terrace.

"Marc, please, let's go back." The gaiety of the wedding was fading and Marc's presence was becoming too dominant. She had to return to the safety of other people. Being alone with Marc was a danger she couldn't afford to risk. "I can't walk here," she said as her high heels sank into the moist soil and she fell against him. His arm tightened around her, molding her body to the lean masculinity of his. Megan felt herself warming, expanding, reaching out to him; Nora's admonishing image faded into oblivion.

"Then I'll have to carry you." He swept her into his arms and she could feel his heart beating against her breasts. "I've always enjoyed holding you in my arms, feeling your body against mine, writhing, arching, yearning." His husky whispers warmed the shell of her ear and sent erotic memories flaming through her veins.

"No, you don't have to carry me." She kicked and tried to twist free. "Marc, put me down." Her fists pounded against his chest, but he was too strong and he only held her closer.

"I will, but not now, not just yet." He increased his pace, swiftly moving across the lawn, away from the house and down to the clump of wild cypress trees at the edge of the bayou. His footsteps crunched when they hit the clamshell ridge. "Stop fighting me, Meggie. I've been waiting a long time to hold you in my arms again, and this is one battle I don't intend to lose."

"Of course not; you've never lost at anything, have you? Well, sorry to break your lifelong streak by hitting you with your first one, but then again, it might be a very interesting change of pace for you to not get your way for once," Megan said emphatically as Marc lifted the curtain of Spanish moss and entered the leafy arbor behind it. "Not there. I don't want to go there." Defiance fled and her heart raced as the rapture of her memories blended with a powerful trepidation of the present.

Marc's lips curved in a cynical smile as his thumb tilted her chin, turning it toward him. "I told you that you owed me something." His softly confident voice and taut masculinity told her that he was prepared to receive his payment now.

"I don't owe you a thing. Stop talking like that. You can't force me." She tried to twist free. How could she have forgotten that Fremont Oaks wasn't a democracy? That the Fremonts ruled the place with an iron hand?

"Force you? Hmm, I never even thought about that, never considered the possibility that I'd have to. Still, the idea does have some merit; it just might be that interesting change of pace you were talking about."

"Please, Marc, I don't want any change of pace. I don't want this. I don't want to be here." She was begging now, aware that she could fight neither his superior strength nor her own desire.

"Really? And you used to be so eager."

"Please," she whispered, "don't remind me. I don't want to remember."

"You don't? Then why did you come back?" He set her down beside a gnarled old cypress and pressed her back against the trunk. "After all this time, why did you finally come back?"

Why had she come back? That was what was disturbing him. He really thought that he had frightened her away forever, so now he was angry with her for returning and flaunting her new image, her independence. Well, aristocratic Fremont or not, she'd soon tell him what he could do about that. If he thought that he could resurrect the weak-kneed, fawning teenager of the past just to bolster his sagging ego, he was sadly mistaken. "I didn't come back for this," she said. "That's for sure. I should have known better than to trust you. You never intended to dance with me, did you? Public appearances were never your big thing." Scorn laced her words as she remembered all too well his constant desire for secrecy. "This is what you had in mind all along, isn't it? Well, forget it, because it's not going to work. I'm leaving." She took a step, then fell back when her heel caught on a clamshell.

Marc stepped in front of her, blocking her path. "You don't really believe that, do you? You don't really believe I'd let you leave now that you're finally here, now that we're alone in our own special place." Strong, cruelly possessive hands gripped her shoulders.

"You can't stop me." Her voice rose above the croaking of the frogs, a cacophony of useless chatter.

"Do I have to? Knuckled fingers stroked slowly up the side of her neck and beneath her auburn hair. "I never did before. In fact, if I remember correctly, you were the one who always asked me, even begged me to stay."

"I was too young to know what I was doing." Her breath quickened in response to his touch; his fingers were stroking, kneading, caressing, starting a fire deep within her that she didn't know how to extinguish, not without his help. Dear God, she didn't want to give in, didn't want to ask for it, didn't want to beg for the joyful release that only he could bring. Closing her eyes, she pressed her legs together as if tautening her muscles could contain the passion simmering in her veins. "Oh, Marc, I was so young."

"That's what I kept telling myself, what kept eating away at me each time I held you in my arms." His hand opened, fingers teasing through her hair, curving it over her cheek. "But you're not too young anymore. So answer my question. Why did you come back? You knew you'd see me, that I'd be here waiting for you, that I'd always be waiting."

"Always?" she asked with barely concealed skepticism. "Why would you be waiting for me?" She slapped his hand off her face, remembering how he had told his father to send her away. "You were the one who paid my way out of here. How could you ever think I'd come back to you, that I'd even want to see you again?" Reaching up, she broke a piece of moss off a branch and wound it around her fingers. She wasn't going to let him intimidate her, not this time.

Marc's arm slipped around her waist, pulling her toward him, making her aware of the firm strength of his body, the delicacy of her own. "How indeed? After all this time? After you'd gotten what you wanted?" His lips caressed her temples, then brushed her lowered eyelids. "After all those nights I've lain awake, remembering but trying to forget the warmth of your body, the softness of your skin, the clean fragrant smell that was you. I never have, you know." His tongue traced the inner curve of her ear.

Desire warmed and weakened her body. "Don't do this, Marc." She wanted to move away, to put some distance between herself and Marc, but she couldn't; her legs refused to obey the dictates of her mind.

"Don't do what? Don't touch you? Don't talk about making love to you? Why waste time asking for the impossible? Surely you remember that I could never see you without wanting to hold you in my arms. That was your weapon against me, the one thing I couldn't resist. You've always been my weakness, the forbidden pleasure that tortured my soul. Yet still you came back, didn't you? And no matter what you say, no matter how you've changed, at Fremont Oaks, in this bayou, you'll always belong to me." He framed her face, slowly drawing it closer until his lips brushed against hers.

Forbidden pleasure. Always belong to him. How true, how helplessly true. She closed her eyes, not wanting to see the face she had once loved so much, unable to view Marc's strong, masculine features without reaching out to touch them. This was the gentle, sensitive Marc she could never forget, the dark-haired prince of her dreams.

"Meggie." He murmured her name against her mouth. "Sweet Meggie, don't you remember the moss? Don't you remember how soft it felt against your back?" His hands went to her shoulders, urging her down. "I've never forgotten how soft your skin felt against mine."

Megan trembled, her limbs weak with an unwelcome longing. This was madness, complete insanity, the road to despair. She didn't want to respond, yet she felt herself weakening. Opening her hand, she released the moss she had been stroking, the concrete reminder of the memories evoked by Marc's impassioned questions. "Don't do this, Marc. Stop it."

"No," he said softly, his hands trailing down her back, curving over her hips, caressing, lingering. "I won't stop. I can't and neither can you. I knew that the minute I saw you and so did you. Tell me the truth; admit that nothing has changed, that we still can't keep our hands off each other." He cupped her breast, tenderly kneading until he sensed the tautening response. "I want to see you looking up at me again, your lips parted, your eyes moist with desire, joy, contentment."

"Marc," she sighed. "Oh, Marc." The frogs had stopped croaking—a hush, silence, just Marc.

"Shh." His finger brushed across her lips, traced the center line, tenderly prodded them apart. "Kiss me, Meggie. Let me see the hunger that I yearn to satisfy."

Gasping, Megan drew back her tongue as Marc stroked lightly over her teeth. Unable to control herself, she trembled when she felt that hunger gnawing deep within her.

"You're trembling," he said, "just as you've always trembled, just as I knew you would." Tenderly he kissed her shining hair. "Nothing has really changed, not between us. You've always wanted me as much as I've wanted you, so why are you fighting me now?"

"I'm not fighting you, Marc; I just don't want to have anything to do with you." She pressed her palms against his chest, but she didn't really try to push him away; she couldn't. "I'd have to be a fool to get involved with you again, to fall into your arms, let you use me, make love to me, then quietly disappear when you no longer wanted me around."

"I used you?" Loathing contorted his features as his muscles hardened, transforming him into a contemptuous person she didn't recognize. "Why, you mercenary little witch." He grabbed her arms and drew her to him, crushing her breasts against his chest. "I wasn't even here when you took off for New York, when you demanded a paycheck for something I considered priceless. How dare you twist things and blame me for something you did, something you had obviously been planning for a very long time?"

"Something you considered priceless? Then how come the check was all made out?" She lifted her head, meeting his gaze, daring him to contradict her. "I'm not twisting anything. I had no choice in the matter, not once your father told me I couldn't stay here. What was I supposed to do? Where was I supposed to go? I'd never known any other home."

"My father what?"

"Oh, come off it, Marc. Don't play games with me. You know what happened as well as I. You told him what to say. He was merely your spokesman because you didn't even have the decency to tell me yourself." Then, her anger rising to a pitch she couldn't control, she blurted out everything that had happened in his father's library, every humiliating word, every hostile scream of reprisal that had been simmering within her for the past eight years. Having started, she couldn't stop herself as, once again, the images of that hot August day appeared in her mind as clearly as if they were happening right before her eyes.

Marc listened quietly, his face growing paler by the minute. "I don't believe you," he said when she was drained, finished at last. "And I'll prove that you're lying, prove that you're every bit as deceitful as you ever were." Holding her hand tightly, he strode toward the house, forcing her to run to keep up with him. "Imagine, inventing a story like that and expecting me to believe it."

His parents were in the drawing room with Frank Dunston, the family attorney, and his wife, Elaine. Austrian crystal chandeliers and sconces illuminated a marble fireplace with a gold rococo-framed mirror above its mantel, while fresh cut flowers sprouted from a silver bowl on a bombé marquetry chest as well as every other table in the room. Floral arrangements were among the few pleasant memories Megan had of Fremont Oaks.

Denise Fremont and Elaine Dunston were seated on one of the gray velvet sofas flanking the fireplace. Frank Dunston sat in a tapestry-covered Louis XV chair between the two sofas and Louis Fremont rested his elbow against the fireplace mantel. Both men wore navy-blue blazers; Elaine Dunston wore a beige linen suit and Marc's silver-blond mother's jewel-necked silk dress accentuated the slate-blue of her eyes.

The foursome had been drinking and chatting quietly when Marc burst into the room with a protesting Megan at his side. As if they were one person, the four turned in shock toward the intruders.

"Marc, what's the meaning of this?" his father demanded.

"That's what I'd like to know, Dad. I think we have to talk . . . alone."

Louis Fremont narrowed his eyes at Megan, hesitated for a moment, then said, "All right, in the library. Frank, you come along too. I have a feeling we may need you."

Silently, they left the drawing room and crossed the hall to the library. Frank sat in a burgundy leather wing chair, Megan sat on the tan sofa and Marc stood behind her.

"Now," Louis said, closing the door and settling himself at the desk, "tell me what this is all about."

Without hesitation, Marc recounted the story Megan had just told him.

"Well, what's the problem?" Louis asked. "I offered her the check and she took it practically before the ink had a chance to dry. You were her ticket to New York. Oh, sure, she protested a little, but once she saw that the check was all there was and she couldn't get any more, she stopped her little act and made no bones about it. She was only after your money and I can prove it." Louis reached into his jacket and took out a thin gold cigarette case. "She's nothing but a conniving little blackmailer."

"Act?" Megan said, rising to her feet. "Little blackmailer. How dare you? You're the one who's lying. You know you gave me no choice. I had to take that check. What was I supposed to do? Collapse? Let my whole life fall apart?"

"The money to get to New York was bad enough," Louis continued, puffing on his cigarette and acting as if Megan were nonexistent. "But it's the blackmail I'm talking about—I'm thinking of the letters we got afterward. You remember, Frank." He looked at Dunston, who nodded knowingly. "Marc, you were busy with that Food and Drug Administration case, so we never showed them to you. No sense in it since we knew they were a scam." He reached for the crystal ashtray on his desk and flicked the ashes off his cigarette.

"Scam?" Megan and Marc repeated the word simultaneously.

"When you told me you were breaking your engagement to Deirdre because of her," Louis said, pointing to Megan, "I asked if you had to marry her, and you told me that wasn't a possibility." He chuckled derisively. "She had other ideas. Tried to hit us with a paternity suit. Obviously, the child wasn't yours. I

knew she was lying, so I had Frank answer her letters."
His lips twisted in anger as he stubbed out his cigarette.
"Cheap little tramp, what's she after now?"

"You never knew," Megan said, looking up at Marc
as she realized the implication of Louis's statement.
"You never knew I was pregnant." All the energy
drained from her body as she suddenly understood
what had happened eight years before. Marc had never
received her letters.

A stunned look froze Marc's features. "Pregnant?
You?" His fingers slipped beneath her chin, tilting her
head back toward him. "Meggie, what are you talking
about?" Unconcealed pain lurked in the depths of his
darkening blue eyes.

"When I went to New York I didn't know I was
pregnant," Megan said, blinking back the tears. "I
found out later."

"What are you telling me, Meggie? We have a
child?" Marc moved to the front of the sofa, knelt
before her and clasped her hands in his. "We have a
child?"

Mutely, she clutched his hands and shook her head.

"Dammit, Marc," Louis said. "I asked you. Don't
you remember what you told me? It wasn't yours." His
hand trembled as he pulled another cigarette from his
thin gold case. "The girl's an uncontrollable liar.
Worthless trash, that's all she is."

"Shut up!" Marc snapped. "The baby, Meggie, what
happened to the baby?"

"He warned me not to bother you," Megan murmured, so caught up in the misery of her own memories
that she didn't even hear Marc. "Said I was harassing
you, that you didn't want any contact with me, advised
me to take the steps necessary to correct my unfortunate condition." Her voice broke and she couldn't
continue.

"You didn't. Oh, Meggie, how could you?" Marc

dropped her hands and straightened away from her. "How could you hate me that much?"

"But, Marc," she protested, realizing his mistaken belief, "you don't understand."

"Oh, I understand all right. I understand all too well. You were young and ambitious. All you cared about was getting to New York, at any price. I knew all that; you told me, remember?" He combed his fingers through his hair, then cupped his nape. "But the baby, Meggie, it was mine too. Did you ever stop to think that I might have wanted it even if you didn't?" He slammed the flat of his palm against the sofa and paced nervously to the bar. His hands shook as he poured some liquor into a glass and downed it in one unthinking swallow.

"It was an accident," she said. "I was running for a bus . . . there was an icy patch and I slipped."

Marc crossed to the fireplace, tossed his empty glass into the flameless hearth and stared blindly at the shards of broken glass, broken lives. "I can't believe what I'm hearing. I just can't believe it."

Frank Dunston cleared his throat and fingered his dark, pencil-thin mustache. "That's all in the past," he said. "Something that happened eight years ago, and one thing my experience as an attorney has taught me is that some incidents are best forgotten. I'd say this is one of them. Take my advice and put it behind you. It's too late to do anything about it now." He turned to Megan. "I assume you'll be returning to New York after the wedding?"

Megan shook her head. "I'm afraid it's not that simple. I work for *Commerce World* magazine and my editor has assigned me to do a feature article on Fremont Industries . . . to help combat Nessac's take-over attempt. . . . I'll be staying on until my research is completed."

"*Commerce World* magazine," Marc said. "I knew

they were sending down a reporter, but I never dreamed it would be you."

"Well, it is," Megan said, straightening her back and crossing her arms over her breasts. "I'm one of the senior feature writers, and when my editor learned I was coming here for the wedding and that I knew your family, he gave me the assignment. In his opinion I was the most qualified writer for the job." She might be boasting, but she was proud of her position, proud of what she had made of herself, and she wanted them to know it.

"Under the circumstances—" Louis said.

"Under the circumstances, nothing," Megan interrupted, realizing Louis was going to tell her that she was too biased to write the article. Well, this was one time he wasn't going to ship her out of Louisiana just because her presence made him uncomfortable. She wasn't going to lose an assignment because of him. He didn't have enough money in his checkbook to pay for that. "I'm a professional, and once I've accepted an assignment, I'll never back off, no matter how uncomfortable the situation may be for me personally. Now stop me if I'm wrong, but I believe this publicity is extremely important to you because Nessac Petroleum is breathing down your corporate neck and, unless I'm mistaken, I don't think you want them to take a bite out of it. So I guess we'll all have to put our private feelings aside, at least until I've written the article . . . for the sake of our work."

"I guess we will," Marc said, leaning an elbow against the fireplace, his taut features struggling to conceal his simmering emotions. "We definitely will. You didn't walk out on me, Meggie," he whispered. "You weren't interested in me only for my money." He looked at her as if he were seeing her for the first time, his eyes filled with disappointment and regret. "And now you're here on an assignment, writing an article.

I'm happy for your success, but saddened by its cost."
His brow furrowed mournfully. "I'll help you, Meggie.
I'll help you all I can. Things will be just fine."

"You're right," Megan said, walking to the door.
Keep things businesslike, she told herself. Don't let
Marc think he's doing you any favors. Favors have to be
repaid. "Of course things will be just fine. Why
shouldn't they? We're both too professional to let
anything interfere with our business obligations, aren't
we?"

"That's what I'm counting on," Marc said. "No
matter how hostile you are toward me as an individual,
I know you won't let that influence your article on my
corporation. You're a pro and you value your reputation. That's what really matters to you now, isn't it?"

"Right. This time we'll both be getting what we
want; I'll be advancing my career and you'll be getting
the publicity you need."

"And then?" Marc asked softly, as if they were alone
in the room, as if his father and Dunston didn't exist.

"And then I'll complete my research and return to
New York, to my career, to the people I enjoy being
with." Her gaze moved quietly over the three men in
the library. "And once I'm gone, I'll never come back
again, not ever." She left the room, closing the door
behind her.

Just before the door clicked shut, she heard Marc's
whispered words. "Never is a long time."

Chapter Three

$\mathcal{M}$egan avoided Marc for the rest of the afternoon and slept that night in the small bedroom off the kitchen where she had spent her entire childhood. All these years she had believed Louis and thought that Marc hadn't wanted anything to do with her because she wasn't good enough for him. Now, although she tried not to dwell on Louis's confession, she found herself unable to avoid it. How could Marc's father have hated her so much that he'd tell her to destroy his own grandchild?

And Marc—true, he had been upset by what his father had done, even more upset when he had learned about their child, but upset as he had been, he hadn't really defended her against his father's accusations. Obviously, to some extent, he agreed with his father and, although her feelings toward him might now be stronger than ever, she'd have to be a complete fool to give in to them. No matter what happened from this point on, one thing was certain: She couldn't afford to become involved with Marc again.

At eight the next morning when she and Marc drove to New Orleans, his attitude, as well as hers, was one of pure business. The atmosphere between them was like a balloon about to break, and they both sensed that the slightest pinprick of a personal remark would make it explode, and their flimsy truce would be over; so neither of them could risk the questions that were gnawing at their hearts.

Megan's luggage had been stowed in the trunk of Marc's black Porsche because he had indicated that they wouldn't be returning to Baton Rouge for at least a week. She had made hotel reservations in the French Quarter not far from Marc's office so that she'd be able to concentrate on the business operation and get her research completed as quickly as possible.

Louisiana had changed in the eight years since Megan had gone to New York, and now New Orleans, besides being the home of jazz and jambalaya, was one of the South's fastest growing commercial centers. Fremont Industries' corporate headquarters occupied a concrete and glass skyscraper near Lafayette Square, and despite the other tall buildings nearby, it seemed to dominate the area.

"Very impressive," Megan said, looking up at the glistening rectangular building with steel lettering above the top-floor windows.

"It's meant to be," Marc said, leading her through the automatically opening bronze doors. "Good morning, Edna." He waved to the blond receptionist seated in the center of the high-ceilinged, marble-floored lobby.

"FREMONT INDUSTRIES—A HERITAGE OF LIFE." Megan read the words above the large mural on the opposite wall. The mural started with fur-hatted trappers in canoes and ended with a skyscraper depicting a different Fremont product at each of its windows. A heritage of arrogance, she thought.

"That's a history of Louisiana," Marc explained, "in Fremont terms. It began when the first Marc Louis Fremont arrived in 1750 and it's up to me to see that it continues." He studied the mural for another moment, then tightened his jaw and guided her toward the elevator. "Come on, I've got to get upstairs." The words he hadn't spoken hung between them, more meaningful than any he had voiced; his heritage had continued through her, but only briefly, incompletely.

"It's very colorful," Megan said quickly, trying to relieve the tension.

"It's supposed to be intimidating, to set the mood the minute you walk into the building. That's how my father planned it, so that by the time you get upstairs, you're thoroughly in awe of both Fremont Industries and him." The elevator's bronze doors opened and Marc tapped the penthouse button.

"Does it work?" Megan couldn't be sure if the reporter or the woman in her was asking the question, but she felt a need to probe, to determine if she had actually detected a cynical note in Marc's voice.

"You tell me. Are you in awe of my father?"

"Awe isn't the word," Megan said, now certain of the sarcasm coloring Marc's statement.

"And I'm not foolish enough to ask you what the word is." Marc closed his eyes and tilted his head back on the elevator wall. "What he did to us was unforgivable, but, Meggie, he's an old man. Don't hold it against him; I'm trying not to."

Don't say anything, Megan ordered herself, nothing at all. Remember that until that article is written you have to work with the Fremonts. Don't make your job any harder than it already is by arguing over the past. What had Frank Dunston said? Forget it, forget it right now. Looking up silently, she watched the lighted numbers flick on and off as the elevator rose toward the penthouse. She could stop herself from thinking about the past, but she still had to contend with the present.

The lobby had obviously been planned to be coldly intimidating, but the executive suite exuded a welcoming elegance. Warm oak paneling covered the walls, and thick maroon carpeting muffled their footsteps as they left the elevator and crossed the floor to the double glass doors stating OFFICE OF THE PRESIDENT in blocked gold lettering.

At their approach, the doors slid open and a gray-haired woman in a tailored brown suit came forward to greet them.

"Megan Mahlar," Marc said, "meet my secretary, Mrs. Lorna Jamison. She's like my right arm. I couldn't function without her."

"Oh, Mr. Fremont." Mrs. Jamison's cheeks glowed vividly above her white blouse. She smiled and opened the heavy oak door with Marc's name on it.

He definitely has the gift of charm, Megan decided; no woman between the ages of nine and ninety is immune. No wonder I feel the way I do about him. She stepped inside, her eyes scanning the inner office, making mental notes that might be useful for her article. Oriental rugs, huge mahogany desk and credenza in front of a window wall, tan leather sofa, two brown chairs, small glass and chrome tables, floor-to-ceiling bookcases.

A walnut-framed photo of an attractive blond woman and a dark-haired child sat on the credenza. Marc's sister, Jacqui; Megan recognized her immediately, and the boy must be her son. Nora had mentioned him in her letters. Louis's grandson, the one he wanted, the one to whom he was so devoted, of whom he was so proud.

Megan turned away; the photo was too painful a

reminder of how mercilessly he had rejected both her and her child—Marc's child.

"I wasn't trying to embarrass you, Mrs. Jamison. It's just that Miss Mahlar is writing an article on Fremont Industries, so I wanted her to know just how valuable you are both to me and the company," Marc said, placing his tan leather attaché case on his desk.

"Thank you, Mr. Fremont. I'm glad you're pleased with my work, but I'm only doing my job. Now, what about a security badge? Shall I order one for Miss Mahlar? She'll need it if she's going to be here for any length of time."

"Good idea," Marc said, turning to Megan. "Do you see what I mean by efficiency? She knows exactly what has to be done. Why don't you go with her and get your picture taken? Can you do it now, Mrs. Jamison?"

"Of course, Mr. Fremont. I'll take care of it immediately." She smiled at Megan. "Miss Mahlar, will you please come with me?"

Megan got the impression that Marc was relieved to be rid of her, that her presence somehow disturbed him, but she didn't mind; in fact, she welcomed the opportunity to speak privately with his secretary. "How long have you been working for Fremont Industries?" she asked while she and Mrs. Jamison rode the elevator down to the first floor.

"I've been with the company for fifteen years and Mr. Fremont's secretary for six."

"That's a long time. I take it you like working here. Are most of the other employees happy with their jobs?" A contented staff indicated good management and stability, two factors which could be very important to a company's growth. Valuable information for *Commerce World* readers.

"I can't speak for anyone else, Miss Mahlar, but as far as I'm concerned, if you do your job, the company treats you right." The elevator stopped, and Mrs. Jamison motioned Megan to a door marked SECURITY.

Inside the office, a slender woman in a gray uniform sat behind a brown Formica counter watching a row of overhead TV monitors that ran the length of the room. Behind her was a door marked PRIVATE—NO ADMITTANCE. "Good morning, Mrs. Jamison," she said. "What can I do for you?"

"Miss Mahlar will be working with Mr. Fremont for a while so she'll need a temporary badge."

The guard pulled a pad from beneath the counter. "For how long?"

Mrs. Jamison looked at Megan.

"About a week, perhaps a few days longer."

"Okay. Please stand on that arrow and look directly at that large black X on the wall behind me." She pressed a button on the counter. "Good, now please fill out this form, then I'll prepare your badge." She handed Megan a pen and paper.

Megan had just written down her name and address when the door flew open with such force that the knob slammed into the wall. An attractive young brunet wearing high-heeled white sandals, a flowered silk blouse and a slim red skirt with a slit up the side stormed into the office.

"It's not fair; it's just not fair," she said to the middle-aged woman behind her.

"You know company policy," the older woman said, "and I don't make it. Now, just sign for your severance pay and hand in your badge. I'm only following orders." She nodded to the uniformed woman behind the counter. "This is June Clayson. I called about her a few minutes ago."

"Yes, of course. Excuse me, I'll be back in a minute." The security guard opened the door marked PRIVATE.

"You know why I'm being fired, don't you?" the

brunet said. "Because Jack Adams grew tired of me. He has his new secretary all picked out—that curvy blonde in the steno pool."

Megan blocked out Mrs. Jamison and concentrated on what June was saying. The reporter in her sensed a story; why not pay attention? One never knew. And it wasn't as if she was snooping where she wasn't welcome; after all, June Clayson was connected to Fremont Industries, the company she was writing about.

"I don't know anything about that," the older woman said, obviously uncomfortable. "I'm only doing my job."

"He told me he loved me," June said. "That he was going to divorce his wife and marry me; a loveless marriage, he called it." She shook her head. "Boy, was I ever a fool. I never meant anything more to him than a few hours on his office couch. Now he's tossing me aside with two weeks' severance pay."

"Have you been with the company long?" Megan asked.

"I've been Jack's secretary for nearly ten months."

"Jack? Is he an executive with Fremont Industries?"

"Financial VP and grade-A heel."

"So you think you're being treated unfairly?" Megan's adrenaline was racing. Wouldn't the stockholders find this tidbit interesting? Not that they'd care about Jack's morality, but a top executive who played around on company time was wasting corporate funds and lowering profits, which affected dividends. Every investor cared about money, and one hundred percent of *Commerce World*'s readers were investors. June Clayson's tale was definitely worth pursuing.

"You're a woman, what do you think? Why should I suffer just because I fell in love with the wrong man? You don't see anyone firing Jack, do you? Of course not. Two days from now he'll be making it again with that little blonde from the steno pool. On the same damned couch. That's why he's getting rid of me. So I ask you, have I been treated fairly?"

There's no such thing as fair where the Fremonts are concerned, Megan thought as her mind echoed the conclusion she had reached eight years before in Louis's library.

"Calm down, Miss Clayson," Mrs. Jamison said. "This is a business office; a little decorum, please."

"Decorum, oh, yes, indeed," June said, smiling bitterly. "By all means, let's have some decorum."

The security guard returned carrying a white sheet of paper and a brown envelope. "Accounting sent up your severance pay, Miss Clayson. Please sign here for it and let me have your badge."

"Oh, take it." She tossed it on the counter. "What do I care about a stupid badge? It's my paycheck I'll be missing." She signed her name, grabbed the envelope and headed for the door. "Good jobs aren't that easy to find . . . any more than good men."

Megan followed her. "Look, Miss Clayson, I'm Megan Mahlar, a reporter for *Commerce World* magazine, and I'm really interested in what you have to say. May I buy you a cup of coffee?"

"Sure. Why not?" June shrugged, her hand resting on the brass doorknob. "I'm not going anywhere. I've got all the time in the world." She opened the door and strode into the hall, her high heels clattering against the marble.

"Miss Mahlar," Mrs. Jamison said, coming up behind Megan and handing her her badge, "I really don't think that would be such a good idea. Mr. Fremont will be expecting you to return with me."

"Just tell him I'm doing research. I'm sure he'll understand." She fell into step beside June Clayson. "Is there a coffee shop nearby?"

Five minutes later, Megan and June were sitting at a little round table in a patisserie half a block away from

Fremont Industries. Red-checked gingham covered the windows, and ceiling fans revolved overhead. A jungle of healthy ferns lined window boxes built along the far side of the large, rectangular room.

After they had ordered, Megan moved a white milk-glass vase aside and set her tape recorder on the table, adjusting it so the microphone would record June's voice and not the piped-in music. "Now, tell me exactly what happened."

"Do you have to use that?" June asked, pointing to the tape recorder. "I don't mind telling you what happened, but I'm not sure I want it recorded."

"I won't use it if it makes you uncomfortable, but for my own protection, I'd prefer to have a tape to refer back to when I sit down to write the article."

"Well . . . okay, if you really think so. I don't know much about this sort of thing. I've never been interviewed before."

"Just try to forget about it and tell me what happened."

"I had been working in the steno pool for six months when Jack's secretary quit and he requested me." June stopped speaking while the waitress served café au lait and beignets, the square, sugar-coated doughnuts for which New Orleans is famous. "Private secretary to the financial VP. Quite a coup for a kid just out of high school. Then after I'd been there for a few weeks, we started working late. One thing led to another and, well, you can figure out the rest."

Unfortunately I can, Megan thought wryly. The story was all too common. "How old are you, June?" She watched as June's face crumpled and the defiant woman became a tearful young girl.

"Nineteen, and I feel as if my life is over. Like I've been used and thrown away. Do you know what I mean?" Her voice started to crack and she dabbed at her eyes with a paper napkin. "It's funny, you hear about these things all the time, but you never think it's going to happen to you."

Megan put down her beignet and wiped the powdered sugar off her hands. "I know exactly what you mean. . . . It happened to me when I was eighteen," she said quietly, sharing something she had never told anyone else before. And even before that, before she was born, hadn't her father deserted her pregnant, unmarried mother? Oh, yes, Megan thought, I know all about those things. It hurt her to talk about it, but June was suffering and Megan could never bear to see anyone else in pain. Hungry rabbits and mockingbird wings, she thought. Little Meggie breaking through Megan's tough shield.

"It did? I mean, well, you seem so much older, so sure of yourself. I didn't think anything like this could happen to someone like you." June shook her head despondently. "Tell me," she asked softly, "does it ever stop hurting?"

"If you're smart, you'll put it behind you and make sure it doesn't happen again." Megan couldn't answer June's question because she knew that she would hurt for the rest of her life. Hadn't meeting Marc at her grandmother's wedding shown her that?

"I hear what you're saying, but it's so hard to do. If you could have heard the things he told me. He doesn't love his wife, he only stays with her because of the children. That's why . . . Oh, what's the use? It's funny, I may be young, but I always considered myself sophisticated, mature for my age, too mature for the boys I used to date. Jack was so different. I really loved him . . . had my whole life planned around him. . . . So how do I go on living?"

If you could have heard the things he told me. Megan sighed as she remembered Louis Fremont's statement about men sometimes saying things they don't mean.

She clicked off her tape recorder. June's words were too personal to use in any article. As competent as she was, she didn't have ink in her blood, like Jerry and many of *Commerce World*'s other writers. Her Achilles' heel as a reporter was her belief that some stories were best left unwritten. "You have to go on living. Believe me, no man is worth crying over, especially a creep who would treat you like Adams did. You meant about as much to him as a good steak, maybe less." Megan smiled bitterly, realizing she was giving June the same pep talk she had been giving herself for the past eight years.

"And I cost a lot less too," June said cynically. "Fremont Industries picked up the tab for my services, but the way I feel about Jack . . . Well, money just doesn't enter into it."

"The way you *feel* about Jack? Don't you mean the way you *felt* about him?"

"I should say that, shouldn't I? The truth is that I'm not really sure what I would do if he walked in here and told me he wanted me back." She fingered the red carnation in the milk-glass vase. "If you could see him, you'd know what I mean. He's so mature, sophisticated . . . I still can't believe he did this to me. He told me he loved me. I guess I should be ashamed to admit it, but I still love him." She made a fist and crumpled her napkin.

"I wish there was something I could say to make this easier, but there really isn't," Megan said, toying with a black plastic ashtray. "Maybe it's part of growing up, part of being a woman. Just imagine what his wife must be going through. It doesn't sound as if you're his first affair, the only woman he's handed this line. Think of what it must be like to be married to a man like Jack."

"You're right. I've never thought of that. If *I'm* desperate because he's dumping me for that little blonde, how must his wife feel? They've been married twenty-five years, you know. If he lied to me . . . why, he must be lying to her." June pressed her lips together and thought for a moment. "That creep deserves to be punished." She patted the recorder. "You've got it all down on tape? You'll smear his name all over your magazine? Tell everyone what a heel he is?"

"You'd want that? I thought you still loved him."

"I do, that's the crazy part of it. I mean, I love him if he loves me, but if he doesn't love me, then I hate him. He's hurt me so much that I want to hurt him back, make him suffer the way he's made me suffer." She pressed her fingers against her temples as if she were trying to reach into her mind. "I'm not making any sense, am I?"

"It's not crazy at all," Megan said, remembering how helpless she had felt, how she had yearned for revenge. Even a short while before, when Jerry had assigned her the feature on Fremont Industries, she had gleefully seized it as an opportunity to get back at Marc, realizing that with just a few carefully chosen innuendos she could make her readers doubt his managerial capabilities and sway Fremont's stockholders toward Nessac. But, almost immediately, she had discarded that idea as being unworthy of the professional standards she had set for herself. "I just wish there was some way I could make this easier for you, but there's no simple cure. It's got to take time." Unfortunately, Megan thought, feeding hungry rabbits is a lot simpler than healing a broken heart. "I'm sorry I can't be more helpful."

"You have helped. I needed someone to talk to and I'm too ashamed to tell my parents. Besides, my father would shoot Jack if he ever found out about this." June thought for a moment, then clapped her hand over her mouth. "Good grief. What have I been saying? You can't print this in a magazine. I'd die if my parents saw it . . . and all their friends." June was on the verge of tears. "Oh, what have I done?"

"Don't worry. This is not for the magazine. I promise not to print anything you've told me." Megan patted June's hand. More than anyone, she understood the importance of having someone to talk to when your world was falling apart. Unfortunately, she had had no one. A naive eighteen-year-old girl—alone, pregnant—in a strange city. "Look," she said, "I'll be in town for a while and here's my address in New York. Sometimes it helps to get away." She scribbled her home phone number on the back of her business card and handed it to June.

"Thanks, and if I can ever help you with anything while you're in New Orleans, just give me a call." June wrote her address and phone number on a napkin and handed it to Megan.

When Megan returned to Marc's office, Mrs. Jamison looked up from her desk, frowned and pressed the intercom. "Mr. Fremont said for you to go right in." She motioned to the door marked PRIVATE.

Megan took a deep breath as she turned the knob. She was certain that June's story wasn't the sort of publicity that Marc had had in mind when he had consented to the article, but his attitude didn't bother her in the least. Her allegiance was to her readers, and if they weren't going to get the truth about Fremont Industries, she'd just as soon not write the story.

"Where the devil have you been?" Marc snapped from behind his desk, his anger emphasized by the graying sky beyond his window.

"Doing research." Megan closed the door and leaned against it. "Didn't Mrs. Jamison tell you?"

"She said that you'd run off with some girl we'd just fired. I'm surprised at you, Meggie, going after a cheap shot like that."

"Cheap shot? I don't know," she said, crossing the

room and perching herself on the corner of his desk. "Disgruntled employees are often a very reliable source of information, and speaking with June gave me some insight into the caliber of executives working for Fremont Industries."

"Just what is that supposed to mean?" He tossed his pen on the desk and pushed back his chair. His white shirt and dark gray suit accentuated his rigidly set, tanned features and bestowed upon him a commanding aura of power.

"Listen for yourself." Megan put the tape recorder on his desk and, as she switched it on, June began telling her story.

Marc's features hardened when the tape played Megan's whispered account of her first experience with love, but he walked to the window and said nothing until the tape was finished. Then he turned and faced Megan angrily. "She's making it up."

"Don't be ridiculous, Marc. Why would she do that?"

"To cover up her own incompetence. Nobody enjoys being fired."

"Of course," Megan said dryly. How had she expected Marc to react? Hadn't he believed the worst of her, the story his father had concocted about her demanding money? What was the cliché about birds of a feather?

"That sort of thing doesn't go on around here."

"Sure," Megan said, slipping the recorder back in to her canvas satchel. It was pointless to argue with Marc about the veracity of June's story because she'd already decided that this information was too personal to use in her article.

"You don't believe me, do you?" he said.

"What difference does that make? Believing you was the worst mistake of my life, but that doesn't matter anymore. I'm a competent reporter now, totally impartial, interested only in the truth." She went to the side of the room and studied the bookshelves. Mostly legal tomes with a smattering of business books and scientific magazines. Louis Fremont's library shelves had contained leather-bound classics. "What is the truth, Marc?"

Chapter Four

An expectant silence hung over Marc's office as he quietly considered his response. "The truth? Well, you'd better want to know, because I intend to get to the bottom of this." He slammed his fist against the wall and crossed to his desk. "This company bears my name and I value the reputation of both far too much to tolerate this sort of rumor. I'll prove that June Clayson is lying." Marc pressed his intercom button. "Mrs. Jamison, please call Jack Adams and tell him I want to see him in my office."

"What's that going to prove?" Megan asked, turning to face him. "He's probably going to lie."

"He's going to lie, but June Clayson is telling the truth? I wouldn't be so sure. Let's just wait and see. I know Jack. He's older than me, with a wife and three kids. Why would he want to bother with a cheap—"

"Go ahead, you can say it. Cheap little tramp, that's what you mean, isn't it? That's what you think of June and that's what you thought of me. Just like your father. You . . ."

"What I thought of *you*? A *tramp*? What the devil are you talking about?" Standing up, he closed the distance between them and gripped her arm. "Just what is that snide crack supposed to mean? I thought this arrangement was going to be strictly business, no personal discussions, no references to the past."

Two sharp raps on the door stopped Megan's answer mid-breath.

"Later," Marc said, releasing her.

"Mr. Adams is here." Mrs. Jamison ushered a tall, gray-haired man with a toothy smile and football-player shoulders into the room.

"Thank you, Mrs. Jamison," Marc said, offering his hand to Jack Adams.

"Something about the board meeting?" Adams asked, checking his calendar watch.

"No, this is a more personal matter. I'd like you to meet Miss Megan Mahlar."

"I'm very pleased to meet you." Jack's smile broadened as he caught Megan's slender hand between both of his and patted it warmly.

Megan nodded silently, pulled her hand free and wiped it on her skirt. No wonder June had fallen for him. The man had somehow managed to combine a gray-haired fatherly image with the suave sensuality of a movie hero.

"She's going to be doing an article about Fremont Industries," Marc said.

"And she wants my input? I'd be delighted."

"I'll bet," Megan murmured.

"Excuse me?" Jack said.

"Forget it, Jack. At times Miss Mahlar has a warped sense of humor." He frowned directly at Megan, making no attempt to disguise his irritation. "Actually, we're hoping she finds your input totally useless. It's not the sort of thing we'd want in any article. Sit down, Jack." Marc motioned Adams to the leather sofa. Then he and Megan sat in the brown chairs. "Okay, Meggie, let's hear that tape."

Megan put the recorder on the glass coffee table and switched it on.

"Lies," Adams said after he had listened to it. "She's making it all up, trying to get back at me because I fired her."

"Why did you fire her?" Marc asked.

"How many reasons do you want?" Adams lighted a cigarette and tossed the match into the onyx ashtray. "Her typing was lousy. She didn't know shorthand. She was getting my phone messages garbled. Is that enough or shall I continue? Ah, what's the point, Marc, you know how these young kids are."

"She said she worked for you for ten months." Marc leaned forward in his chair and meshed his hands over his knees. "That's a long time to tolerate an inferior performance."

"Well, you know how it is, she's a cute kid. I didn't want to fire her."

"What changed your mind?" Marc asked.

"I don't know; I guess it finally got to me." Adams tapped the ash off his cigarette.

"It had nothing to do with the blonde in the steno pool?" Megan asked, waving the smoke away from her face.

"Of course not. Listen, what's this to you anyway? Say, you're not going to let her publish this drivel, are you, Marc? I've got my reputation to think of. . . . I'm a married man."

"What about the blonde, Jack?" Marc answered Jack's question with one of his own. "Is she in line for the job?"

Marc's blue eyes turned to steel, cutting into Jack the

way Louis Fremont's had cut into Megan. Breeding, she thought. Marc's just like his father. He can be as cruel and heartless as Louis. How could I ever have loved him? And why do I still remember, still yearn for the gentleness that could never have been?

"Well, yes. I have spoken to her about it. But not because of what you think. She's a very good secretary."

"How would you know, Jack?" Marc's lips were taut with anger. "Have you been availing yourself of her services?"

"Listen, Marc, can we talk privately? Man to man?"

"I'd like to oblige, but if we do that, Miss Mahlar will accuse me of a cover-up. Why don't you tell me what's on your mind? I'm sure we can count on Miss Mahlar's discretion."

"I've been with this company for twenty-five years," Adams said. "I'm a good worker and a good family man, but you know how these kids are. They don't wear anything under their clothes. I'm only normal. I mean, what's a man to do? Speak to your father, Marc. He'll understand."

"Don't insult my father. He'd never tolerate something like this. June Clayson was telling the truth, wasn't she, Adams?" Marc's voice rose angrily as he kept pressuring Jack, pursuing the truth.

Megan watched him in surprise. He was really tearing into Jack, not allowing him any excuses, any lying avenue of escape. She found herself smiling silently, liking Marc more than ever. He wasn't at all like his father, he really wasn't.

"Well, yes, sort of, but what kind of fool was she to think I'd ever marry her?" Adams stubbed out his cigarette and reached for another. "I mean, well, you know my wife. I'm a happily married man."

"That's right, Jack, I do know your wife. Cara is a

wonderful woman, so how could you do something like this?" Marc asked. "The girl's nineteen. You've got kids older than she."

Adams stiffened. "There's kids and then there's kids. My daughters are different. And June, well, you'd know if you'd met her."

Yes, I've met her, Megan thought. She's a young woman in pain—no different from your daughters. Breeding—damn these people with their double and triple standards. All people hurt the same.

"You told her you loved her," Megan said, folding her moist hands on the skirt of her green silk shirtwaist in an effort to be calm. "She believed you."

"I don't remember what I said."

"Of course not. You were lying . . . just using her," she asserted. That's the problem, Megan thought, staring at Jack angrily but not trusting herself to say anything further. June fell in love with you and you can't even remember what you said. There's nothing wrong with two adults making love, but when one takes it seriously and the other doesn't—how do you stop the hurt?

"Okay, Jack," Marc said, "I get the picture and I don't like it. Not one bit. I won't even mention the governmental problems we could have if Miss Clayson chooses to take legal action . . . sexual harassment . . . Equal Employment Opportunity Commission. If you didn't have such an excellent work record and I wasn't concerned for your family, I'd have you out of here so fast you wouldn't know what hit you, but I guess that twenty-five years makes a difference."

"Fire me? For what? June's not Snow White. She didn't exactly fight me off." He tossed his unlighted cigarette into the ashtray and stood. "And who the hell are you to tell me what to do? You don't spend your nights knitting afghans."

Marc rose slowly to his feet, towering over the other

man. "My nights are my business and so is your company time," he said, his voice hushed with tautly controlled anger. "I'm going to forget what you said, Jack. I realize you're upset. You've been with the company a long time, and I owe you something. But this is it," he emphasized. "No more. If I ever hear of anything like this again, I'll expect your resignation. Now get out of here." He motioned toward the door. "You disgust me."

"Things were much better when your father was in charge," Adams said, storming out of the office.

"Damn," Marc said, slamming his fist against the back of the chair. "The man was using the steno pool as his own private harem. How could I not know about something like this? I'm sorry, Meggie. I owe you an apology and I'd like to ask you for a favor; don't print any of this. It could hurt us a lot. It's just the kind of publicity we don't need, not with Nessac's takeover attempt."

"Don't worry, I'm not going to use it. I told you, I'm a financial reporter, not a gossip columnist." She picked up her tape recorder and walked to the window. "This isn't the type of stuff I'm interested in, not for a feature article." Leaning against the window, she surveyed the scene before her.

The breathtaking penthouse view swept over the tops of lower buildings, and on to the muddy Mississippi River, where the past merged with the present as an old riverboat steamed between the modern tankers crowding the docks. Megan's thoughts were equally muddled. Either Marc was an accomplished actor or he was genuinely upset by what Jack Adams had done, upset as an individual as well as the company president. Which was the real Marc: the man in the bayou, the man who had just chastised Jack, or the man who echoed his father's opinions? At the moment, she was too confused to decide, and she turned away from the window when Marc opened the office door and asked Mrs. Jamison to come in.

"Yes, Mr. Fremont?" Mrs. Jamison's pencil was poised over her steno pad.

"There's a problem that I want corrected. A Miss June Clayson was mistakenly fired this morning. Will you please contact personnel and tell them that I'd like her rehired, but not for the same position. In fact, I'd like to promote her, have her work up here, under you. Can you find a place for her?"

"June Clayson?" Mrs. Jamison raised an eyebrow in surprise.

"Yes. Do you know her?"

"No, but I was downstairs . . ."

"Then you understand."

"Yes, of course, Mr. Fremont. I have just the spot for June. Delilah's. You know she's leaving. Her baby is due next month."

"Good. And one more thing. Mr. Adams needs a new secretary. He's been having quite a bit of trouble finding someone he likes, so let's get someone special this time. I don't want him choosing just anybody from the steno pool. I'd like you to make the selection. Someone mature, dependable, dignified, rather like yourself, I imagine."

Mrs. Jamison continued taking notes, but the hint of a smile curved the corner of her lips. "I'll take care of it immediately, Mr. Fremont. Is there anything else?"

"No. That should do it. What time am I due at the lake?"

"They're expecting you at twelve."

He checked his watch. "It's eleven now. That gives me about half an hour to dictate some letters."

Megan reached into her purse and pulled out the napkin with June's address and phone number. June would be relieved that she didn't have to find another job. Perhaps if she called her right now, she could reach her before she told her parents that she had been fired. "Is there a phone I can use?"

Marc motioned to the one on his desk.

"Is there another one? I don't want to be in your way."

"You're not in my way, but if you'd like more privacy, you can use Mrs. Jamison's phone. She's going to be working with me for a while."

Mrs. Jamison's large semicircular desk had a view of the elevators and the entire outer office. Two younger women, one noticeably pregnant, typed at smaller desks along the opposite wall on either side of oak double doors with BOARD ROOM written on them in blocked brass letters.

Megan dialed June's number and waited while the phone rang. Three rings and no answer—Megan tapped her fingers nervously. Five rings—still no answer. The typewriters continued their incessant chatter.

"Hello," June said breathlessly.

"June, this is Megan Mahlar. I'm so glad I reached you. Listen, you've got your job back."

"Jack changed his mind? Wait a minute . . . I just walked in. I can't believe this . . . let me sit down."

"Forget about Jack," Megan said, suddenly annoyed with June. "As you said, he's a grade-A heel. You're going to be working for the president of Fremont Industries."

"Marc Fremont?" she gasped.

"Yes, that's why I was so anxious to reach you before you said anything to your parents. Now, instead of telling them that you were fired, you can crow about your promotion. Jack Adams is small-time compared to Marc Fremont."

"Marc Fremont's office, I can't believe it. Boy, that is a break. Thanks, Megan, I really appreciate this."

"That's okay. I was glad to help. Just try to be more sensible about things from now on."

"Oh, I will, you can be sure of that. I've learned my lesson."

"I'm glad to hear that. Now I'd better get off the phone. I'm sure you'll be hearing from personnel soon." She said good-bye and hung up.

"Excuse me, Miss Mahlar," Mrs. Jamison said, "but have you finished your call?"

"Yes, I'm sorry. I didn't realize you were waiting for your desk." Megan pushed back her chair and stood.

"Are you ready, Meggie?" Marc walked out of his office with his attaché case in one hand and two thick books in the other. "Come on, let's go. I don't want to be late." He used his shoulder to push open the glass door.

"Mr. Fremont," Mrs. Jamison called as they were about to leave. "Remember you've an appointment in Washington tomorrow."

"I know. I have a flight out first thing in the morning. Thanks for reminding me."

Megan picked up the napkin with June's name on it, dropped it into her canvas bag and, squaring her shoulders, joined Marc at the elevator. "Where are we going, Marc?"

"To our beach house on Lake Pontchartrain."

"Whose beach house?"

"My family's."

"Just a minute, Marc. I'm here to write an article on Fremont Industries and I'm not about to go romping around some secluded beach house with you."

"Trust me," Marc said, guiding her onto the elevator and pressing the lobby button.

"You've got to be kidding."

"I thought we had a business truce. You're not making things any easier."

Megan nodded silently. Marc was right. By making that snide innuendo she was violating her own rule about not letting the differences of their past sabotage the efficacy of her article.

"Now, if our personal animosities are out of the way, I'll explain the situation. As a matter of fact, the beach house is anything but a secluded lovers' nest and it's a very important part of Fremont Industries that I want featured in your article."

"A beach house an important part of Fremont Industries? Won't that sort of thing make a bad impression on your stockholders?" Despite her attempt to be impartial, she couldn't keep her hostility from seeping into her question. What was it June had said about wanting to hurt the people who had hurt you? "That their money's supporting your family's vacation retreat?"

"Stop it, Meggie, stop it right now," he said. "I can read you like a book. Despite all your declarations of professional impartiality, you're still searching for that little touch of scandal, aren't you?" They left the elevator and walked across the lobby.

"If I were, I wouldn't have to search very far, would I?" Looking at the mural, she decided that the wording should read: A HERITAGE OF LIES. The bronze doors slid apart, releasing them from Louis Fremont's imposing monument.

"Okay, so we've discovered a rotten apple," Marc agreed as he opened the Porsche's trunk and dropped in his attaché case and books. "But if this Adams thing has been going on for years, why was June Clayson the first secretary to complain?" He took off his tie, folded it into his jacket pocket, then tossed the jacket over his seat.

"She probably wasn't. Don't forget that you heard her story only because I happened to record it."

"Don't remind me," Marc said as he unbuttoned his collar and moved into the stream of traffic. "I'm not overjoyed to learn that I don't know what's happening in my own company. How could I be so close to someone, trust him to do what I'd expect . . ." He shook his head. "Not that I'm completely convinced it was entirely Jack's fault. You heard what he said about her clothes, her appearance, coming on to him; I've seen some of these young secretaries, and typing isn't their strong point. That's why I'm transferring the girl to my office, where I can judge her competency for myself."

Megan glanced out the window as they passed the futuristic-looking Superdome. Judge June's competency indeed. She didn't for one minute believe this indignant act Marc was putting on. In view of his own life-style, he probably condoned Jack Adams' behavior; that scene in his office was undoubtedly an attempt to avoid some nasty publicity. And even though he had rehired June, wasn't he still accusing her of lying? Keeping her in his office because he wasn't really sure if she was telling the truth, waiting for her to prove her reliability.

"In any case, I'm not going to apologize to anyone for taking some time off this afternoon," Marc went on. "As a matter of fact, I really want this particular little project highlighted in your article. That's why I'm taking you to see it. I believe it's an accomplishment of which Fremont Industries can be proud."

And there probably aren't many of those, Megan added silently as she pulled out a yellow pad and began writing a description of the Fremont Building, Marc's office and the security arrangements, noting which facilities were suitable for photographs. She wanted to get her ideas down while they were fresh in her mind, and even more important, she wanted to avoid arguing with Marc. It wasn't worth the risk; she had her job to think of.

Marc drove quietly, caught up in the privacy of his

thoughts as he left the expressway, paid the toll and entered the Lake Pontchartrain Causeway.

When he exited the causeway, he drove through a labyrinth of streets lined with towering oak trees, then turned onto a narrow shell lane. Flowering wisteria and oleander shrubs filled the sunny sites between the oaks and trailed over the Porsche's fenders.

"We're here," Marc said, pressing a button that activated a wide wrought-iron gate. "You remember our beach house, don't you?" The gate closed behind the car.

"I've never been here," Megan said. "Your parents always hired part-time help when they went to the beach."

"Well, we don't come here too often anymore either." The vista of shrubbery cleared, revealing an old white frame house with bright blue shutters, two Victorian turrets and a wide jasmine-covered veranda. "So I've donated it to the hospital. We still keep the guest cottage for our own use." He indicated a small house near the edge of the lawn just before it sloped down to a sandy beach.

When he stopped the car in the driveway, the front door flew open and five small children wearing bathing suits ran across the lawn. Megan watched in astonishment while Marc squatted, ruffled the wispy blond hair of two little girls and scooped a boy of about four into his arms. Marc was right, his beach house certainly wasn't any secluded lovers' nest. But what was it, then? What were these children doing here?

"My friends," Marc explained, getting to his feet and lifting the boy onto his shoulders. "This is Miss Mahlar, and this"—he tugged at the boy's foot—"is Craig." Marc's entire body seemed to be smiling. His fondness for the child was obvious and he seemed pleasantly relaxed, more at ease than Megan had ever seen him . . . except for that summer in the bayou.

He'd make a wonderful father, she thought. Then, forcing the painful conjecture from her mind, she held her hand out to Craig. "I'm very pleased to meet you." She did the same when Marc introduced her to the other children.

A short plump woman carrying a diaper-clad toddler came out of the house and headed across the lawn. "They were waiting for you, Mr. Fremont. I tried to keep them in the house, but you promised to bring the beach toys and . . ." She shrugged helplessly.

"No problem, Mrs. Lawson," Marc said after introducing Megan. "Where's Lonnie? Is his mother out of the hospital? Has he gone home?" He set Craig down, walked around the car, opened up the trunk and began handing the children small boats, kickboards, snorkeling sets, plastic tubes and various other water toys.

"She picked him up yesterday," Mrs. Lawson said. "They were both anxious to get home."

"Good," Marc said. "I'm always happy when the kids get to go home."

A small, striped kitten padded across the lawn and rubbed his neck against Megan's leg. "Hi there, what's your name?" she asked, bending to pick him up.

"Ribbons," one little girl said, "because his stripes look like little ribbons."

"Well," Megan said, "I have a striped cat named Tiger and I'll bet he'd like to meet Ribbons." She stroked Ribbons' neck. Until now, she hadn't realized just how much she had missed Tiger. Still, Billy, the young boy who lived in the apartment next door, was taking good care of him, and he was better off at home.

"Are we going swimming?" Craig asked.

"In a minute." Marc handed a pail-and-shovel set to one of the girls, then shut the trunk. "Come on." His hand closed over Megan's. "Let's go change." Circling a white stone fountain, he headed for the cottage.

Megan set Ribbons on the grass. "What do you

mean, you gave this house to the hospital?" she asked as she trotted across the lawn, avoiding several long wooden picnic tables while trying to keep up with Marc's swift pace. "These kids don't look sick." She was confused by the change in him, confused by the return of the sensitive and caring man she had known in the bayou, the man she had loved, the man who had never really existed.

"They're not, at least not physically, and what I'm trying to do is lessen any emotional problems." He paused. "Little kids are so easily hurt by a world beyond their control," he said thoughtfully. "Look, let me explain; when I assumed the presidency of Fremont Industries, I was nominated to the board of directors of Doctor's Memorial Hospital. It's mainly a figurehead position. I'm just supposed to sign a fat yearly check, make my donation and put in an appearance at some fund-raisers. That's all we Fremonts have ever done, but one of the nurses happened to mention that some patients, mostly single parents, were putting off treatment requiring hospitalization because they didn't have any place to leave their children." He unlocked the cottage door and motioned Megan into a small entryway.

Hand-hooked blue and white rugs covered waxed oak floors, and blue toile paper brightened the walls. A bronze gas lantern hung from the ceiling. To the left of the narrow hall was a small sitting room with a bay window overlooking the beach.

"This small house is perfect for my family's needs," Marc said as he led her down the hall, "so I donated the main building to the hospital and set up Fremont House, a temporary place where patients can leave their children for as long as they need. The time varies depending on the severity of the illness. Craig's mother is receiving extensive chemotherapy. He's been here for five weeks; others have to stay less than a week. It doesn't matter to us. If the hospital refers them, we take them. We have three paid employees, two house-mothers and a handyman-gardener, and since we're connected with the hospital, we have no shortage of volunteer help from doctors, nurses and psychologists."

Megan couldn't help noticing how Marc kept saying "we." Obviously, Fremont House was something he was proud of. *A heritage of life?*

"You need a swimsuit. I'm sure Jacqui has a spare one somewhere," Marc said, entering a small bedroom at the end of the hall and opening the doors of a tall oak armoire. "Ah, here's what we're looking for." He held up a skimpy black bikini.

"I'm not going swimming, Marc. If you'll just tell me more about this project . . ."

"You heard Craig, didn't you? The kids are waiting out on the beach. Now if you really want to find out what Fremont House is all about, you'll come along with me." He tossed the bikini on the bed. "You can change in here. I'll meet you outside. It's faster if you go through the utility room back that way." He pointed down the hall, then left the room, closing the door behind him.

Megan sat on the edge of the mattress and fingered the bikini. Jacqui, a petite but shapely brunet, was smaller than she, but this wouldn't be the first time Megan had shared her clothes, although in the past they had been discards that Nora had lengthened by adding trim to the hem. That was why Megan had spent most of her time running around in washed-out jeans. At least they'd been her own.

Still, it hardly made any sense for her to play the martyr by sitting around in a hot silk dress while everyone else was cooling off in the lake. Besides, she wanted to learn more about this place. A human-interest angle was never out of place, not even in a business journal.

She changed into the swimsuit and checked herself in the mirror. She'd never worn a bikini. Sleek tank suits were the preferred attire at the health club where she swam two evenings a week. In comparison, the bikini seemed more comfortable—just two pieces of stretch fabric that clung to her body's most intimate parts and revealed all the rest.

The result wasn't at all unappealing. Gently curving hips that flowed into long, lean legs—flat abdomen—firm breasts that rounded out the shapeless bikini top. Without being smug about it, she acknowledged that maturity had made her figure much more lushly feminine than it had been in the past.

Still, as attractive as the bikini looked, it wasn't enough to go out in. Since she had borrowed the swimsuit, she might as well look for a cover-up. Rummaging through the closet, she found an old white terrycloth jacket with lace pockets and inserts, which Jacqui probably hadn't worn in years. Megan slid her arms through the sleeves, buttoned the large pearlized buttons and went outside.

Chapter Five

$\mathcal{M}$arc had changed into trim white bathing trunks and was down on the sand throwing a light multicolored beach ball to the children. For a minute, Megan remained on the grassy ridge, observing the movements of his body, his rippling shoulder muscles, the taut sinews of his thighs, his large hands curving easily around the beach ball. The tip of her tongue flicked between her lips as, without wanting to, she remembered the touch of those hands and the explosive joy the strength of his body had brought to hers. Despite her determination not to become personally involved with him again, she couldn't deny the immutable desire engendered by the simplest of Marc's gestures.

Suddenly, as if sensing her presence, Marc turned to catch a wild throw from Craig and saw Megan looking down at him. Releasing the ball, he let it fall to the sand, and his gaze enveloped her, moving quickly over her face, the robe, the bare beauty of her long, slender legs.

The pressure of his eyes bored into her, his unwavering stare making her feel as if he were piercing the folds and fibers of her mind as well as those of her body. Crossing her arms in front of her, she tried to shield herself from the intense scrutiny that insisted they were the only two people in the world, existing solely for each other.

Cut it out, she told herself. Stop acting like a starry-eyed teenager. You're an attractive woman, you know that; Marc's not the only man who's found you physically desirable. Control yourself; you can't afford to get involved with him again. Breaking eye contact, she surveyed the beach as if she were trying to choose the best place to swim. Although the public beaches might be crowded, this area of the lake was deserted except for the gray and white gulls, swooping low and skimming across the top of the water. After a few moments, she walked slowly down the slope.

Marc waited at the bottom of the slope and reached out to help her. "How long have you been standing there?" His hands slid up her arms, caressing her shoulders, ruffling the terrycloth fabric, probing the hidden flesh.

His warmly welcoming touch ignited a hungry ache deep within her—not good or bad—only Marc. "I just came out." Lowering her gaze from his, she saw the dark curling hair on his chest and suppressed an urge to nuzzle against it as she had so often in the past. Stop it, she warned herself again. He means nothing to you and you mean even less to him.

"You were watching me. Why? What were you thinking?" he asked, his hands slipping to her waist and pulling her closer.

Warm sand sifted between her toes as she tried to

maintain her position. "I wasn't thinking anything, nothing really important." She backed away, intending to create a barrier between them, but her palms resting on his bare chest sensed the swift intake of his breath and her startled gaze met his. She closed her eyes, remembering how she had loved to stroke and tease him, to revel in the reactions her small hands could unleash in his powerfully masculine body.

Marc's head dipped, his forehead resting against her hair. "Stop fighting me, Meggie," he whispered raggedly, "pretending that we've never known each other. Can't you tell that just seeing you—you make my heart beat faster than any other woman ever could." He clasped her hand tightly against his chest, making her aware of his rapidly beating heart. "Feel me, Meggie; feel what you do to me. You've been driving me wild from the first moment I saw you. How long do you expect me to continue this little charade? How long do you think I can last?" His suntanned features were carved teak, motionless except for the pulsing muscle in his firmly set jaw. "How long can you last?"

She didn't know what she could expect of him, but her own quivering body made no secret of the burgeoning desire that kept her from moving away. Taking a deep breath, she opened her eyes and her gaze traveled lower, following his matted chest hair as it tapered to a V and disappeared beneath his waistband. His magnetism lured her—more than anything she wanted to reach out and touch him, pretend that all the ugly accusations they had hurled at each other had never really been voiced. Pretend, she told herself, just pretend.

"Mr. Fremont? Aren't you going to play with us?" Craig squeezed between them, holding the beach ball and tugging at the hem of Marc's swim trunks.

"Sorry, Craig. I got sidetracked." Marc released Megan and, taking the ball from Craig, returned to the group. "Come on, Meggie. You haven't forgotten how to toss a ball."

Megan joined the circle; but after a few minutes of playing catch in the sunless humidity, her light terry-cloth robe felt like a fur coat. Odd how a damp, gloomy day like this could still be so hot and sticky. If she didn't shed the robe, she'd swelter. She fingered the top button, then glanced at Marc and changed her mind. What on earth was wrong with her? Why was she so embarrassed in front of Marc, with whom she had once been so intimate, Marc who in that first intimacy had taught her the passionate sensuality of her own youthful body? She began unbuttoning the coat.

"Lunch," Mrs. Lawson called from a bright blue picnic table at the edge of the lawn. "You kids can wash in the fountain."

The children ran up the slope and Marc caught Megan's hand. "Are you especially fond of peanut butter and jelly or would you rather cool off with a swim?" He smiled and held his stomach as if the mere thought of eating peanut butter and jelly was too ludicrous to even consider.

Megan brushed the hair off her forehead and wiped away the perspiration. "Peanut butter and jelly?" she laughed. "As delicious as that sounds, I'll go for the swim, definitely a swim." Quickly, she shrugged off her robe and let it slip to the sand.

Marc whistled softly. "I've never seen you in a bathing suit." His eyes ran a caressing inventory of her feminine attributes. "I should have invited you to the lake long before this."

Should have invited her to the lake. Just like that. As if it had been an oversight, something that had simply slipped his mind. Well, she wasn't going to play along with his polite little game. She didn't believe in fairy tales, not anymore. "Yes, you should have," Megan agreed. "I would have really enjoyed coming here, but you never took me anywhere . . . in public, that is. I was good enough only for the bayou, where there was no chance of anyone seeing us."

Relief washed over her as once again she released some of the resentment that she had been holding in check for eight long years, and without waiting for Marc's response, not wanting to hear it, she ran into the lake.

Cooling swim, she thought as the tepid water lapped at her ankles, scarcely rising with each step she took; it was like walking into a bathtub. When the water finally swirled above her waist, she raised her arms and began swimming.

The water rose in a swell as Marc cut through the surface and swam toward her with swift, knifelike strokes. "Good enough only for the bayou, what's that supposed to mean?" he asked, coming up behind her, grabbing her ankle and pulling her toward him. "Are you complaining about the bayou? Implying that I *forced* you to meet me there?"

"Let me go—I can't swim with you holding on to my foot," she sputtered as she lost her balance and her face dipped beneath the glassy surface.

Gripping her under her arms, Marc lifted her above the water. "I'm not letting you go until you explain just what that snide remark was supposed to mean. Where did you expect me to take you? To Antoine's? In those damned jeans? Sure, you're quite the lady now, but eight years ago, I didn't even know if you owned a dress."

"That wasn't what stopped you. Admit the truth, Marc. You made love to me, but you were ashamed to be seen with me, ashamed of what your fancy friends would think. In your eyes, I was a tramp, just like you think June Clayson is a tramp, just like your father said;

and you didn't care one bit about my feelings, did you?"

"So that's what you meant in my office." An expression of pain flickered across Marc's face. "Well, you're wrong, very wrong. After we started meeting, I never thought of you as anything except Meggie, my Meggie . . . and I cared," he said, drawing her to him until their nearly bare flesh met beneath the water. "I cared more than you'll ever know." His legs slipped between hers, the strength of his body keeping her afloat. "I still care."

The lake surrounded them, a warm, lubricous cocoon; and as Marc tread water, his torso tempted a response she didn't want to give.

"I still want you, Meggie." His mouth closed over hers, tasting lightly, seductively demanding a response. "I knew that the first moment I saw you back at Fremont Oaks, and despite everything that's happened, despite all the changes that have occurred, this wanting has remained constant; it hasn't changed at all."

Tasting the salt on his lips, Megan felt herself weakening, her body shifting closer to his even as her mind chided her for being a fool. What was it June had said about hating Jack while still loving him, about going back to him if only he would ask her? Was it true for her as well? Did she feel that way about Marc? If only she could forget, give in, open herself to the joy that only Marc could give, just this once. No, she told herself, you're not June, not a gullible teenager, and you're through letting Marc treat you as an object to serve his needs, an object devoid of human emotions.

Pushing him away, she swam to the raft, levered herself onto the smooth, sun-bleached boards and combed her fingers through her hair. Water trickled down her back as she squeezed the ends, then fluffed them out until they curled around her face. Crossing her ankle over her thigh, she began rubbing it.

Marc cut through the water and the raft tilted as he joined her. "Did I do that?" he asked, sitting beside her, shifting her leg over his and probing the darkening bruise at her ankle. "I'm sorry. I didn't mean to hurt you." Bending his head, he pressed his lips lightly over the bruise.

Megan shivered despite the warm humidity. "It's nothing. Just a spasm." Their hands touched for a moment and she jerked hers away. Dangerous, so dangerous. Her emotional ties to Marc were so tenacious that the slightest contact could ignite an explosion of erotic memories.

"I *never* meant to hurt you." His fingers teased her calf, stroking lightly over her skin. "Not at the bayou and not now. You have to believe me, Meggie. I don't care what you say, we can't continue like this. We have to talk."

"No." She rejected her own needs as well as Marc's as, frightened by her own vulnerability, she scooted back away from him. The raft pitched and water lapped over its side, puddling onto the surface. "I'm not a fool, Marc. If you didn't want to hurt me, you wouldn't have. Even if you didn't know what your father had done, you could have come after me; Nora knew where I was. But you didn't, did you? You believed your father because you wanted to, because deep in your heart that's what you thought too. You didn't trust me any more than you trust June, and you never will trust me, not really. That's why I don't want you touching me, why I don't want to get involved with you again."

"Not get involved? Ah, Meggie," he said, smiling wryly, "have we ever been uninvolved? In fact, knowing what we now know, can't you see that we're more involved than ever? Have any two people shared more than we?" Refusing to release her, he continued caressing her calf, her knee, the flaring curve of her thigh. "You keep telling me not to touch you, but, Meggie, sweetheart"—his voice grew hoarse as he leaned over her—"if you don't let me touch you . . ." His voice broke and, groaning unevenly, he urged her down against the smooth, damp boards.

She straightened her leg as he provocatively circled her thigh, edging closer to the core yearning for his touch. "Marc, please." She struggled for time, for an excuse to reject him even as she hungered for him. "The children. Someone will see us."

"We're too far out. In our own little world, just as we always were . . . as we were always meant to be." Their lips were nearly touching and his body shifted, his legs urging hers apart. The water undulated beneath the raft, rocking them gently over its billowing surface.

"Oh, Marc," she murmured, caught between the love that wouldn't release her and the humiliation she couldn't forget.

"I couldn't sleep last night, knowing you were right downstairs . . . not being able to go to you . . . hold you . . . lose myself in the soft, welcoming warmth of your body." He rested on one elbow as his free hand played over her abdomen, then slipped under her bikini top. "Oh, Meggie, my own sweet Meggie."

Pride needled at her thoughts, urging her to stop him, but her unvoiced protests faded beneath his tender caresses and she felt herself sinking into that mindless abyss where nothing mattered except having him continue the magic he was weaving through her body. She turned and shifted closer as her flesh burgeoned and peaked beneath his gentle fondling. She knew that she was being foolish, that the barriers between them were too sturdy to be shattered. Yet, how could anything that felt so wonderful possibly be wicked? How could she reject this pleasure that every fiber of her being urged her to accept? She'd stop him in a few minutes, but for now . . .

"Mr. Fremont, Mr. Fremont." Mrs. Lawson's voice was barely audible as she shouted to him from the shallow water.

Marc sat up and shielded his eyes. "Damn." He made no attempt to conceal his annoyance.

"It's Craig," Megan said, pointing to the small boy clutching a green dragon tube and bobbing midway between the raft and the shore. While she watched, the tube slipped out of his hands and he flailed in the water trying to reach it. "Oh, no." A small eddy swirled around him as he went under, then surfaced again and struggled to turn onto his back. *He can't swim.* The realization flashed into Megan's mind. *He's going to drown.* Forgetting about her ankle, she dived off the raft and swam toward him.

The water surged wildly when Marc quickly followed her into the lake. His strokes were faster, more powerful, and he reached Craig before she did.

"You promised we'd go swimming," Craig said tearfully when Marc lifted him out of the water. "So I was swimming out to the raft." He sniffed, swallowing a sob. "Then the tube slipped and I couldn't stand and I nearly almost didn't catch it." He clutched Marc's neck and began sobbing against it. "Then I remembered what the swimming lady told us about turning on our backs and staying on top of the water."

"It was smart of you to remember," Marc said, patting Craig's back. "You're fine now. Just hold on. We're not that far out; you'll be able to stand in a minute. But you could have been hurt. Don't you remember the rule about not going in the water by yourself?"

Megan marveled at Marc's calmness until she noticed the throbbing muscle in his jaw. Obviously he was controlling his own inner tension, trying to comfort and caution Craig without sending him into a tearful panic. He'd make a wonderful father, she thought once again, a wonderful father.

"I wasn't by myself. I had the dragon. I was swimming to you. I wanted to surprise you."

Megan's breathing slowed to its normal pace as she held the tube and followed Marc in. Seeing any swimmer in trouble was a frightening experience, but a helpless child—it made her sick inside. "These things aren't really safe," she said, holding up the tube. "They give a false sense of security. You shouldn't be letting the children use them."

"You're right," Marc agreed, setting Craig down. "To tell the truth, I didn't pay much attention to what I was buying. I just had Mrs. Jamison call a store on Canal Street and order some beach toys. I suppose I should have been more specific."

Mrs. Lawson was waiting on the beach. "Thank heavens you got to him in time. I was cleaning off the table and he asked if he could go to you. I thought you were sitting on the sand, so I said yes without thinking. I had no idea you were out on the raft."

"Fortunately he wasn't hurt, just a bit shaken, but I think we'd better review the rules again. And I'll get rid of this." Marc took the tube from Megan. He seemed agitated, more nervous than Megan had ever seen him. "Throw them all out."

"Right away, Mr. Fremont, and I'll talk to the children about going into the lake by themselves," Mrs. Lawson said, taking Craig's hand. "Right now, as a matter of fact. Just before they take their naps. I was so sure they understood the rules, but I guess I was mistaken. I'm so sorry. I should have been watching him. You can't take anything for granted where children are concerned." She bent to speak to Craig, who nodded fervently as they headed up the slope.

"That's one experience I wouldn't want to relive," Marc said, shaking his head and pressing his fingers into the back of his neck. "Maybe this place is too close to the lake. I thought of it as a great play area for children, but I didn't consider the dangers. I never remember any problems when I was young." He spoke without looking at Megan. "Let's go back to the cottage and change. Swimming seems to have lost its appeal."

Picking up her beach robe, Megan tugged at the damp bikini which now felt wet and sticky against her skin. She agreed with Marc—the frightening episode with Craig had definitely made the lake uninviting. And yet, if Craig hadn't been in trouble, if Mrs. Lawson hadn't called out to them . . . She despised herself for still wanting Marc, for still responding to his touch. What had Marc asked? "Have we ever been uninvolved?" Had there ever been a complete day when she hadn't thought about him, a night when he hadn't invaded her dreams? Were the fibers of their lives too closely interwoven ever to be unraveled?

A breeze skimmed over the lake, but instead of cooling her it enveloped her in its sweltering blast. The high humidity that kept everything from drying intensified her discomfort. She felt too hot to move and too tense to stand still. Right now, she'd trade the entire Lake Pontchartrain waterfront for one air-conditioned room.

"Are you coming?" Marc called to her impatiently from the edge of the sand, his curt tone making his question more of a demand than a request.

"You go on in. I'll be along in a few minutes." She needed to be alone, to consider what she was doing and devise a method of control. Unfortunately, there wasn't any logical answer, because she could always think clearly when she was alone, but when Marc touched her—how could she ever convince herself that something that felt so good could be so wrong?

She stayed on the beach a while longer to give Marc a decent start on getting changed, then she returned to the cottage. Her feet were all sandy and she didn't want to track the grit into the house. Why should she? Someone like her grandmother would probably have to clean it.

Remembering the shower in the utility room, she went around to the side door. The ideal place to clean off, she thought. She locked the door connecting the utility room to the rest of the house, turned on the shower and stripped off her bathing suit.

The shower's needlelike spray was much cooler than the lake's tepid water and Megan felt refreshed when she toweled herself dry. She rolled her suit in the towel, put on the beach jacket and unlocked the door. She walked out into the hall and the thick blue and white rug runners muffled her footsteps, but the floorboards separated and shifted under her weight, groaning once as she proceeded toward the bedroom. The house seemed uninhabited, almost eerie, silent except for some sentimental music streaming through the living room arch.

After depositing the suit and towel in her bedroom, she followed the music to the brown and white living room with its oak and mahogany furniture. Marc, holding an ice-filled glass, was standing by the bay window overlooking the lake. Still wearing his snug-fitting white swim trunks, he seemed so immersed in his own thoughts that she hesitated to intrude on his privacy.

"Lovers all alone, sweet lovers all alone . . ." A throaty female singer purred emotionally from the tape deck built into one of the oak bookcases flanking the fieldstone fireplace.

Silently, Megan turned and started back toward her bedroom, but the floorboards creaked beneath her feet and Marc turned to her, his face pale and gaunt, his eyes almost lifeless. He looked so wretchedly miserable to Megan that she was moved, without considering her actions, to cross the room and put her hand on his arm. Had he swallowed some lake water, overexerted himself? "Marc, are you all right?"

He combed his fingers through his hair and patted her hand. "I'm fine . . . It's just . . . How could I have been so stupid? This idea seemed so great. I thought I was doing something concrete, something better than just making a contribution and never knowing how it was being spent. I wanted to help the parents by putting their minds at ease. Hmmph, what a laugh. Me organizing a home for children. I didn't know the first thing about what I was doing, did I? What do I know about caring for other people's children? I couldn't even take care of my own. I should stick to signing checks. That's all we Fremonts seem capable of doing."

Leaning forward, he closed his eyes and pressed his forehead against the windowpane. "He could have drowned, Meggie. If we hadn't been there, if we hadn't reached him in time, he could have drowned. How could I ever have lived with something like that on my conscience? Don't I have enough to make amends for? My own child . . . your baby?"

Megan stroked his bare back, caressing his shoulder. Could this really be Marc Fremont, who was usually so arrogant, so sure of himself? She had never seen him this upset, never realized that this man whom she had always envisioned as indestructible could ever doubt himself. "You remember what Frank said, Marc; some things are best forgotten."

"If only I could," Marc said, slamming his fist against the window ledge. "If only I could."

"Craig *didn't* drown, Marc. Everything's okay. And Fremont House is a wonderful idea," Megan said, trying to rescue Marc from the tragedies of the past. "A wonderful place. It is something concrete, something really worthwhile," she continued, remembering her own ever-present childhood fear that if her grandmother became ill, there would be no one to take care of her. Selfish, perhaps, but it was how she had seen the world. Wouldn't a child with a sick parent feel the same? Wouldn't this place help ease the trauma of being alone?

"Needing you more than I can say." The singer crooned on, her voice a deep silky-smooth velvet.

"I just keep seeing Craig struggling in the water . . . thinking about what could have happened . . . thinking about what happened eight years ago." Marc's voice broke, as if completing his thought were too agonizing a chore to consider.

The images wrought by Marc's words flashed into Megan's mind and she remembered what he had said about wanting their child even if she didn't. Of course he'd be upset about a child in danger. He cared about children, didn't he? That was why he was so proud of Fremont House. Why he had brought her here.

Now, seeing the self-inflicted misery that was gnawing at his confidence, she couldn't stop herself from reaching out to him. "No," she said, placing both hands on his shoulders, resting her face against his back and trying to comfort him. "Don't even think about it." Tears welled up in her eyes. She couldn't bear to see Marc in pain; she loved him too much. "Nothing could have prevented what happened to me; it was an accident. And Craig, well, Craig's just fine."

Turning, he circled her with his arms and pressed his lips into the hollow of her neck. "Ah, Meggie, I've never been so frightened, so afraid that I wouldn't get there in time, that once again when a child needed me I wouldn't be there."

"But you *did* help Craig, Marc. That's what really counts, doesn't it? This time you *were* there in time. You saved him." She blinked back the tears forming in her eyes, her long lashes teasing the matted curls on his chest. Could this torn-apart Marc be the same man who just a few hours before had been so coldly unemotional with Jack Adams? "I was frightened too, Marc, but nothing happened. It's okay, Craig's fine." Her hands moved slowly down his back, reassuring fingers stroking against his firmly muscled skin. "And Fremont House is a wonderful place, a wonderful idea."

Silently, they clung together, mourning their unborn child, comforting each other while reaffirming another small boy's survival. Megan never knew exactly when those calm, soothing movements intensified and became more demanding, but suddenly Marc's hands curved over her hips and began caressing her with an explosive urgency.

"You're my own special person." The singer's voice was husky with love.

"Meggie, don't say no. Please, darling, I need you so much. Don't . . ."

An irrepressible yearning flared within her, a desire to comfort, to love—words were unnecessary. Mindlessly, she pressed closer and let her body sense the rising need of his.

"Sweetheart." He urged her back until her knees touched the edge of the brown cotton sofa. His hands on her shoulders, he coaxed her down to the soft cushions. "Let me," he said, kneeling before her as his thumbs traced the curve of her chin and his fingertips stroked her delicately arching neck. "Ah, Meggie, I need you so." He fumbled with the top button on her robe, released it, then went on to the next. "You're beautiful, so very beautiful." He opened the last button and slowly pulled the robe back over her shoulders.

"The special lover in my life." The singer's voice was breathlessly seductive, luring the man she loved into the warming depths of her arms.

Megan's eyes grew moist as she watched Marc. She

was wearing only the robe. No one else had ever been able to make her feel so truly beautiful just by looking at her. Suddenly she understood what Marc had meant when he said that he needed to touch her, and catching one of his hands in hers, she brought it to her lips.

Lifting her legs onto the sofa, he sat down beside her. His free hand went to her breasts, cupping them tenderly, tantalizing their sensitive tips. "I've dreamed about this for so long," he said. "All those years when you were away . . . waiting for you . . . hoping you'd return."

Sighing, he kissed her breasts, tracing their voluptuous curves and burying his face in the velvety valley between them. "So lovely, so very lovely," he murmured, his lips gliding lower.

His sensitive tongue created a provocative tension deep within her body and she wanted him to continue, wanted him to complete the magic that his fingers and lips had begun. Her hips arched, pressing into his, physically communicating a need too elemental for words.

"My feeling for you grows with each passing day."

Marc stretched out beside her, urging her deeper into the cushions while continuing the tormenting pleasure of his hands and lips. His caresses consumed her, arousing her until she writhed feverishly in his arms, her mind a kaleidoscope of flesh and fabric, his nylon swimsuit silky against the satin texture of her skin, his muscular legs sliding sensuously across hers.

"Take this off," he said, tugging at the terrycloth robe that still covered her arms.

She raised herself slightly and her breasts grazed his muscular chest. "Oh, Marc."

He slipped the robe off her arms and pressed her to him. His body felt warm and firmly masculine against the softness of hers.

Clasping him closer, she matched her movements to

the sensuous torment of his, and the comfort she'd intended for Marc expanded to envelop them both.

"Ah, Meggie, that feels so good. You feel so good." Pressing her back against the cushions, he lifted himself, slipped out of his swimsuit and let it drop to the floor.

So good. Marc's words echoed her thoughts. Their bodies were so wonderfully matched, each insatiably famished for the other. "Oh, Marc. Please . . . I . . ." She closed her eyes as he stroked her hips, her stomach —lower.

"Tell me," he urged. "Tell me you want me." His lips nuzzled her breasts, his tongue tracing the pattern of their tautening peaks. "You know how much I want you."

Marc wanted her now. Yet, no matter what he said, eight years ago he had rejected her. He hadn't come after her, had he? Wouldn't he have come to New York if she had really meant something to him? Revenge, a small voice urged. This is your chance. Push him away. Reject him just as he rejected you. "No, Marc, please, no." Her plea was so weak that even she didn't believe it.

"Shh, stop fighting me. Just let yourself go. Let it happen." His legs shifted, slipping between hers, urging them apart.

"Oh, Marc. I . . ." All thoughts of revenge faded as Marc's fingers traced circles on her thighs and her need for his love overwhelmed any idea of vengeance.

"I know, sweetheart," Marc said, slipping his hands beneath her hips and lifting her toward him. "I know."

"Oh . . . please." Megan's breath was raggedly harsh and gasping. She closed her eyes and arched her body toward his.

Groaning deep in his throat, he pressed intimately against her, his hands curving over her hips, stroking, coaxing, until at last their bodies met—the ultimate unity.

"Marc," she moaned, shuddering and gripping his shoulders. "Oh, Marc." She was spinning, whirling so fast, so high—she could no longer breathe. Desperately, she clasped him closer.

Marc's jagged breathing matched her own. They moved in unison, hungrily seeking the same elusive destination. For Megan, time ceased to exist; all that mattered was the mutual journey of joy she and Marc were pursuing.

Opening her eyes, she saw Marc's features, tense with desire, soft with wonder. The road before her widened and surged violently as she realized she was home; Marc was home. Crying out, she tightened her grip as they both began the slow descent from the heights they had scaled together.

They lay still, nestled in each other's arms, bodies entwined, unable and unwilling to move. After a few moments, when their breathing had quieted, Marc rolled to his side, taking Megan with him and pressing her head against his chest. Twining a strand of auburn hair around his finger, he lifted it to his lips and kissed it tenderly. "Sweet," he said, "so very sweet."

Megan didn't say anything; she didn't want to talk, didn't want to think, didn't want to move. She just wanted to stay there in the security of Marc's arms, the only place she had ever felt truly wanted, truly loved.

Marc's hands stroked smoothly over her body, soothing, calming, telling her they were still together. Curving her hair behind her ear, he kissed her cheek, her earlobe, her arching neck.

Say it, Megan begged silently. Please say you love me. I need to hear it so much. Say it even if you don't mean it; make me feel special once again. Make this feeling last.

Marc cupped her chin, tilting her face toward his. "We have to talk, Meggie." His voice was ragged and breathlessly uneven. "There are things I have to know, things I have to say, painful secrets we've both kept bottled up for much too long."

"No," she protested, burying her face in the damp warmth of his chest. "No." She didn't want to talk and she didn't want to listen to any more painful secrets; the revealing confrontation with his father the day before had been distressing enough. All she now wanted was to hear Marc say that he loved her. That was what she needed right now, love and acceptance. She shook her head, nuzzling her cheeks against his curling chest hairs, inhaling the musky scent that could arouse her even when she had been so very thoroughly loved, when she should be sated.

"Yes," Marc insisted, shifting to a sitting position and carrying her up with him. "I have things to say and questions that need answers." He reached for his trunks and handed her the robe.

She moved away from him when he stood to adjust his trunks around his waist. The robe hung limply between her fingers and, suddenly conscious of her nakedness, she pulled it over her shoulders. What was there to talk about? Nothing she wanted to face; she wasn't proud of her behavior. Once again her passion for Marc had overcome all her other sensibilities and now, as she reflected on it, she felt a shroud of guilt and humiliation swirling over her.

Intellectually, she was liberated enough to acknowledge that what had just happened between Marc and herself wasn't anything to be ashamed of, no more for her than for him. Women had the same needs as men, didn't they? That was an accepted fact nowadays, wasn't it? Still, the childhood whispers about her mother; Louis Fremont's chilling voice, saying, "Breeding—tramp"; her grandmother's warning,

"Good girls don't," were embedded so deeply in her soul that they couldn't be swept away by the strength of normal reasoning.

Marc knelt by the sofa, pushed the robe aside and buried his face in the valley between her breasts. "Don't look like that," he whispered, "so unhappy, as if you regret what's happened, what we've done."

Megan combed her fingers through his hair, clasping him closer, loving his touch, wanting more than anything to be in his arms once again. She might be shamed by the helpless love she felt for him, but she couldn't regret what had happened between them; it was too beautiful, too filled with boundless joy. And she was too honest to play the martyr and let him take the blame for something that had been so mutual. "I wanted you to make love to me, Marc; I wanted it very much. I don't regret what happened, not really. I'm just confused, unsure of who I am, of what I feel."

"I told you before," Marc said, looking up at her and bringing her hands to his lips. "You're Meggie, my Meggie . . . always were, and always will be."

"No," Megan said, "not anymore. You don't know the woman I am now, you really don't." She hesitated, picturing her new image, the impression Jerry and the other staff at *Commerce World* had of her, the opinion of all her New York friends and professional associates. They knew nothing about little Meggie and would be shocked if they did. "I have changed, Marc. I'm really different."

"How different? Not different enough to change what we felt just now. Surely that was the same, stronger if anything."

Megan closed her eyes. How true. In the silence of her mind she admitted that she wasn't different enough to change her feelings for Marc, but she was wise enough to question them—question whether those feelings still had the power to negate her other needs.

And she was wary enough to doubt whether she could ever again trust Marc as completely as she had all those years before on the bayou. She needed to think, and she couldn't think sensibly when Marc was holding her, touching her like this. She opened her eyes and pulled her hands free. "I want to get dressed," she said, buttoning her robe and stepping away from the sofa. "I think we'd better return to the city and get back to work, back to something impersonal, something I know how to do, something I can handle without all those painful questions and recriminations."

Marc rose to his feet and looked at her for several long moments. He seemed to be considering what she had said, pondering his response. Finally, he took a deep breath and nodded. "All right," he said. "I won't press you. I'll give you the time you need. I really don't have any choice, do I?"

Megan met his gaze and shook her head. "Neither of us does, Marc; neither of us does." Sighing, she turned and left the room.

Chapter Six

N o choice at all. The words echoed in Megan's mind as she strode down the hall to Jacqui's room and closed the door. It was an all too accurate description of her reactions toward Marc. When she was with him and he reached out to her, touched her, she wanted nothing more than to go into his arms and stay there forever, but when she was alone and could think clearly, she realized that the woman he was making love to was the girl from the bayou, someone who no longer existed, someone she had spent eight long years trying to eradicate.

She tossed Jacqui's beach robe on the bed and began changing into her own clothes—lace panties and bra, panty hose, beige satin teddy; she slipped her arms through the sleeves of her green silk dress and studied her reflection in the gold-framed cheval mirror. Expensive fabric, hand-tailored shirtwaist collar, slim, side-

slit skirt, fitted but not tight—conservatively feminine
—exactly the image she wanted.

She adjusted her collar, then stepped closer to the
mirror and examined her face. Her makeup had washed
away to reveal a sun-pinkened complexion which highlighted her freckles. Frowning, she carefully reapplied
her makeup until the light sprinkling across her nose
was hidden once again. Now, for my hair, she thought
as, wincing, she brushed it back and tried to unsnarl the
tangled mass. Hopeless, absolutely hopeless. The curls
were so tightly coiled that she looked like a clone of
Little Orphan Annie; she'd never be able to restore
that natural, softly tousled look without using the blow
dryer that was packed in her overnight case. She put
the brush back in her purse. She'd have to wait until
she got to her hotel room and unpacked, because she
wasn't about to start rummaging in her luggage now.

"Meggie," Marc said, tapping lightly at the door, "I
have some things to discuss with Mrs. Lawson; just
close the front door and meet me at the car when you're
ready."

"Okay, I'll only be a minute." Still frowning into the
mirror, she caught the ends of her hair and pulled them
tightly over her ears; they bounced back into frizzy
little curls as soon as she let them go. Instant perm, she
thought; great for some people, but not for her, not for
the image she wanted. She took a white silk kerchief
from her canvas carryall and covered her hair. What
couldn't be corrected had to be covered, she decided as
she left the room and went into the hall.

Outside, the sky had darkened and gray clouds were
sprinkling a mist that seemed too slight to be called
rain. When Megan reached the car, Marc was leaning
against the front fender speaking with Mrs. Lawson; no
children were anywhere in sight.

"The kids are sleeping," Marc said as if he could read
her thoughts. "I was just telling Mrs. Lawson that I

intend to speak to a contractor about fencing off the lawn. It won't be perfect, but it will still be somewhat of a deterrent."

"Would it be possible for me to come back?" Megan asked Mrs. Lawson. "Go through the place and speak to some of the children?"

Mrs. Lawson looked at Marc.

"Sure," he said. "Maybe on the weekend. That way you'll get to meet some of our volunteer staff. Just don't ask any upsetting questions. You know why the kids are here." A gust of wind puffed through the branches of a gnarled oak tree, rustling the leaves and sending some blackbirds into flight. Marc's gaze followed them. "We'd better get going," he said. "I think we're in for a summer storm."

Megan leaned back and stared out the windshield as they drove through the winding streets and onto the Lake Pontchartrain Causeway. Marc had been right about the weather. The filmy mist had become a heavy rain drumming on the roof and streaming down the windows. The wipers clicking across the windshield had a hypnotic effect and she felt her eyelids drooping.

"Tired?" Marc asked, putting his arm around her shoulder and drawing her closer.

"It's the weather," Megan explained. "Every time it rained when I was little, my grandmother would give me some milk and cookies and I'd take the book I was reading and curl up in that big blue velvet chair she kept in her bedroom; I wonder if she still has it, I mean now that she's moved into Tim's cottage."

"Nora's been busy redecorating the place," Marc said. "They moved some things over last week. My parents offered them some bedroom furniture. Nora chose a rosewood set from one of the back bedrooms."

"If she didn't take the blue chair, maybe I could have it for my apartment," Megan said, remembering how big and comfortable the overstuffed chair had been.

"A reminder from the past, from Fremont Oaks? Funny, I was under the impression that that was exactly the sort of thing you didn't want."

Megan stiffened, shifted out of his reach and stared at him for a minute. "I guess it wasn't all bad," she admitted, to herself as well as him. "It's just that even in the comfort of the blue chair, I was still alone." She grew silent, remembering the many times she had snuggled in the chair, trying to lose herself in the pages of a fantasy while the music and laughter from one of Jacqui's numerous cotillion dances drifted through the house.

"I'm sorry," Marc said, his fingers tightening around the wheel, "sorry for all those years of loneliness, sorry I couldn't do anything about it."

"You did, Marc. You helped a lot. You were the first friend I ever had."

Marc looked away from the road for a minute and turned to her. "And now?"

"Now I have lots of friends."

"I was more than a friend."

Megan turned away and studied her reflection in the window, unwilling to admit how special he had been, not wanting to tell him that she had never been able to feel as close to anyone else.

"I'm sorry. I shouldn't have asked. I had no right."

Megan said nothing. She wished she could love another, more suitable, more attainable man, but her heart had a mind of its own, and that quirky twist it gave whenever she saw Marc was reserved for him and him alone.

She pressed closer to the door and concentrated on the view. They had reached the middle of the causeway with no land visible in any direction, just water, endless water, as brown and muddled as her future.

"Will you be coming back to the office with me?" Marc asked.

"I don't think so," Megan replied. She wasn't going anywhere with her hair looking like a ball of tangled orange yarn. "I have some ideas I want to jot down, questions I don't want to forget. Please drop me at the hotel."

"You don't have to stay at the hotel. We have a townhouse in the city. It's very comfortable; you could stay there."

Stay at Marc's townhouse, with him? Visions of Louis's smirking features made her reject the invitation before she had even considered it. "There's no need for me to impose," she said. "I can stay at the hotel. *Commerce World* will foot the bill."

"Don't make up excuses about imposing on me when what you really mean is that you don't need me anymore, not so long as you have *Commerce World* magazine, your job, your independence." His voice was a dry monotone as he left the causeway and drove onto the expressway.

Without thinking, she reached out and touched his arm. His body tensed and his muscles throbbed beneath his white silk sleeve. "I can't stay at your house, Marc. Surely you can understand that."

"I don't understand. I'm asking you to stay with me, talk to me . . ."

Sleep with me. Her mind completed the unspoken words, the most important ones, not merely as a sexual union, but because the emotional commitment she felt for him during their lovemaking diminished all other considerations. Each time he held her she forgot about New York, her job, everything, and that was one risk she couldn't afford to take.

"I said I'd give you time, wait for you, but you're shutting me out, not even giving me a chance." He left the expressway, drove toward the French Quarter and pointed out the red brick hospital with which Fremont House was associated.

"How much talking do you think we'd do if I stayed with you? How much did we do this afternoon?" She shook her head. "I need time to think, Marc, and I can't think clearly when you're around."

Marc turned onto St. Charles Avenue and parked in front of the small French Quarter hotel where she had made reservations. He shut off the ignition, slid one arm over the back of her seat and edged closer. "Did you ever consider that maybe you are thinking clearly and just don't want to accept the conclusions of those thoughts?" He smiled enigmatically and, without giving her a chance to answer, left the car and stepped around to open the trunk and take out her gray tapestry luggage.

A short wiry man with a thick white mustache and beard hurried out of the hotel wheeling a chrome luggage cart. "I'll take that in for you," he said, lifting Megan's valise and overnight case onto the cart.

"I have a hearing in Washington tomorrow," Marc said while the bellman took Megan's luggage into the hotel. "A new drug with the FDA. Will you come with me?"

"Well, I don't know." Being at Fremont headquarters with Marc was one thing, but going to Washington after what had happened at the beach house was quite another. If she really wanted to think the situation out, then the best thing to do would be to put as much distance between Marc and herself as possible. But she had never been to an FDA hearing and it might provide an interesting new aspect for her article. Oh, why not chance it? "Yes, of course," Megan said. "I'd be happy to go."

"I'll pick you up at eight. Take some things with you. We may have to stay over." Two fingers stroked lightly across her cheek as Marc looked down at her. For a moment she thought he was going to kiss her, but he didn't. "I'll see you tomorrow," he said, dropping his hand and turning back to his car.

Megan remained on the sidewalk until he had driven away, then she went into the lobby and signed the register. The hotel was a converted white brick mansion with black wrought-iron balconies and a marble-fountained atrium. Kirman carpets covered the lobby's oak parquet floors and overstuffed maroon and gray chairs circled low fruitwood tables.

Her room was painted a sunny yellow and had a mahogany four-poster bed and an elaborately carved walnut armoire. A white-tiled bathroom with a claw-footed tub cut into the wall at the right of the door. Megan tipped the bellman, closed the door and began unbuttoning her dress. Except for the steady hum of the window's air conditioner, the room was silent—an ideal place to think.

What Marc had said about shutting him out was true; he frightened her because he alone could make her want to be little Meggie again, the girl he held in his arms, the girl she wanted to forget. She unzipped her suitcase and pulled out a maroon silk caftan with huge orange and pink flowers; not the recommended colors for a redhead, but somehow this outfit enhanced rather than clashed with her hair.

Still, she thought, as she stepped out of her undergarments and into her caftan, she couldn't keep running away forever; and if she had really matured into a professionally successful woman, there was no reason why she shouldn't be able to establish a mature, unemotional relationship with Marc.

She sat down at the organdy-skirted dressing table, sprayed some conditioner on her hair, combed it through and began blowing it dry. That was what she'd do, she decided as she ran a brush through her hair and tugged at the kinks until they had been transformed into a soft billow of fiery curls; insist upon a business relationship, just as she'd do if Marc were any other corporate president about whose company she was writing.

And if he were, she'd want to find out everything she could, spend as much time with him as possible, invite him out to dinner and let *Commerce World* pick up the tab. She smiled to herself; the thought of paying for Marc's dinner was an indulgence she couldn't resist.

She set down the dryer, gave her hair one last fluff with the brush, nodded approvingly, then went to the telephone and dialed Marc's office. Mrs. Jamison put her right through.

"What's on your mind?" Marc said.

"Well, I was just sitting here, making myself comfortable, and I thought—" She hesitated a moment, leaned back against the headboard of the four-poster and stretched her legs. Somehow this wasn't quite as easy as she had expected it to be. "I thought perhaps you'd like to have dinner with me." She toyed with the coiled telephone wire and waited for him to answer. Try as she might, she couldn't think of Marc as just another business contact.

Now it was Marc's turn to hesitate. "I'd love to Meggie, but tonight . . ." He paused again, seemed to be considering, evaluating, deciding. "I promised my mother. It's for the hospital; I just can't."

Megan swallowed and forced herself to speak lightly. Even now, with all her success, she found rejection difficult to accept, especially from Marc. Cover it up in your usual way—with a spate of light banter, she told herself, so he doesn't know how crushed you really feel. "Well, that's all right; it doesn't matter," she said. "I have things to do too. It's only that I thought, since I am doing the story . . ."

"I do want to see you, Meggie," Marc said, his voice

low and serious. "It's just that tonight's the hospital ball, our big fund-raiser. We're making our annual donation. I have to show up."

"Of course," she said in that same uninterested, light tone. "No problem, Marc. I'll see you in the morning." She hung up the phone, then sat forward, drew her knees up to her chest and curved her arms around them. She'd been a fool to call Marc, to think that he'd be sitting around just waiting for her to invite him out to dinner. Good grief, wouldn't she ever learn?

A clanging bell below her window broke into her haze of self-recrimination and, leaving the bed, she drew the sheer white underdrape aside to look down at St. Charles Avenue, where the last streetcars in New Orleans still chugged over the grassy median. Quaint, old-fashioned vehicles, she thought, much more pleasant than the siren-shrieking cars that raced past her Lexington Avenue apartment. *Sirens.* She pressed her forehead against the window. Now that was one memory she'd like to forget.

She jumped when the phone rang, but she welcomed the interruption. Ever since the day she had slipped on the ice, the shriek of a siren had started a silent, unremitting wail within her.

"Hello," she said, picking up the receiver.

Marc was on the other end. "I was thinking," he said, "you could come with me. It's formal, white tie; I don't know if you have anything suitable."

Megan thought about the halter-necked black jersey gown in her suitcase; she never went anywhere without it because it took up so little space, was uncrushable and entirely appropriate for most formal occasions. She could wear it tonight, but still, the way Marc had said, "If you have anything suitable," made her think that he was concerned about *her* suitability as well as that of her clothes. Well, he didn't have to concern himself about how she'd fit in with the socialites at the charity ball because she had no intention of going.

"Thanks, Marc, but I really hadn't planned on something like this, so I don't have anything appropriate."

"There are some boutiques in the Garden District. If any of them are still open, you might find something there."

"That's all right, Marc. I'm not in the mood for anything fancy. It's really not worth the effort; I'll be fine."

"I can leave early and meet you for a nightcap."

"Don't bother, Marc. I think I'll turn in early. Have a good time. I'll see you in the morning." She hung up, stared at the phone for a moment, then started walking restlessly around the room.

She felt as tense as a caged tigress; she had to get out, but where? The hospital, she thought; Marc had pointed it out. Perhaps she could interview the administrator and get his opinion on the efficacy of Fremont House. She picked up the phone and got connected with his secretary, who suggested an appointment for later that week. When Megan explained that she'd be out of town for the next day or two, she agreed to a four-thirty appointment.

Later that afternoon, when Megan arrived at the administrator's office, his bespectacled blond secretary, Lila Saunders, was profusely apologetic. "I'm sorry," she said. "There've been some last-minute problems with the hospital ball. Mr. Channing had to leave early, but perhaps I can help."

Why not give it a try? Megan thought. She often found that secretaries knew more about what was going on than their bosses did. "I'm interested in a new program the hospital has for dependent children."

"Oh, you mean Fremont House. I can tell you about

that; I do volunteer work there on Wednesday afternoons." She motioned Megan toward a seat by her desk. "Make yourself comfortable and fire away."

Megan spoke with Lila for almost two hours and found that Fremont House was one of the hospital's most innovative and successful programs.

"The staff's really hot on it," Lila said. "It was Marc Fremont's idea; rumor has it that his father was opposed, didn't think his company should become involved with the patients on such a personal basis."

Of course, Megan agreed, Louis always was more comfortable when he could settle problems with a check. The human element would only cloud the issue as far as he was concerned. "But Marc got it through despite his objections, and it's working out well?" Megan asked, adjusting her tape recorder so she'd hear Lila clearly.

"Well, we've had some failures, some kids who couldn't adjust, but for the most part the results have been great. You'd be surprised at the number of mothers who'd put off treatment because they had no place to leave their kids. Now they're coming in, and if we treat something in the early stages, well, you know how much better the recovery rate is. Anyway, staff psychologists screen all the volunteers, tell them what to say, not to get the kids nervous, to put them at ease with the situation. It's a very well run program." She checked her watch. "Is there anything else?"

Megan looked at her watch. "Six-thirty. I had no idea. I didn't mean to keep you so late."

"It's all right. I had to hang around anyway, just in case there were any other problem calls from the ball committee."

Megan's stomach growled, reminding her that since she'd rejected Mrs. Lawson's peanut butter and jelly sandwich, she hadn't had any lunch. Lila was probably ready for dinner too and, despite her independent streak, Megan hated eating in restaurants alone. "May I take you to dinner, if you've no other plans?"

"Thanks, I'd love it." Lila suggested making reservations at a Canal Street hotel near the French Quarter.

"This place doesn't favor unescorted women," Lila explained when they were seated at a small table near the back of the restaurant. "We're lucky they didn't put us near the kitchen."

Then why did you suggest coming here? Megan wanted to ask. The doorman had been indifferent, and she'd thought the maître d' was going to faint when he saw her canvas carryall. She'd never have chosen to eat at a place like this, never have spent her money anywhere they treated her like a second-class citizen, but the choice hadn't been hers, it had been Lila's. "Would you like to leave and go somewhere else?" she asked, half hoping that Lila would say yes.

"No," Lila said, accepting her menu from a tuxedoed waiter whose regal bearing made Megan feel that she should be serving him. "The reason I came here"—Lila waited for the pompous penguin to leave, then leaned across the table—"is that the hospital ball is right upstairs and I always like to take a peek . . . just to see how the other half lives, if you know what I mean."

Megan knew exactly what she meant, but as far as she was concerned, her childhood backstairs view of the upper crust's life-style had provided her with enough insights to last her a lifetime. Besides, Marc was going to the ball and he was the last one she wanted to see tonight. But why tell Lila of her relationship with Marc? The blue-eyed secretary would only start the rumor mills spinning. Instead Megan studied the menu's prices and said, "I hope the food is good."

"Excellent," Lila replied. "Even for women." Her eyes smiled over the top of her menu.

Despite their haughty waiter, dinner was surprisingly

pleasant, and by the time they were enjoying coffee and an almond torte, Megan had to agree that the food was excellent; her onion soup and Creole crab were the tastiest she had ever eaten, and Lila's barbecued shrimp looked equally appetizing.

"I think I'll go back to my hotel," Megan said after she had paid the bill with her corporate credit card. "It's not far from here."

"You're sure you don't want to peek in at the ball?" Lila asked as they walked through the lobby. "Some of the gowns and jewels are absolutely beautiful."

"No, thanks, I'm really tired. The most beautiful thing I can think of seeing right now is the canopy above my bed." Thank God my ball-peeking days are over, Megan thought, shivering at the unpleasant memories of Jacqui's cotillion parties. "You don't mind staying alone?"

"Not at all. I do this every year, and I'm sure some of the other secretaries will be along soon." She settled herself in one of the plush red velvet chairs scattered around the oak-paneled lobby and waved Megan off. "I hope I've helped with your article. Be sure to send me a copy when it comes out."

Megan promised she would, then said good-bye and walked across the scrolled red carpeting toward the exit. Outside the gold-framed glass doors several limousines had just pulled to the curb, and hotel valets were helping some of the beautiful people Lila was waiting for out of their cars. Megan watched a porcelain-faced blonde in a jewel-studded green gown clasp her tuxedoed escort's arm as they stepped under the marquee. Lila was right: The gowns were exquisite, the jewels beyond description.

When Megan's gaze shifted to the diamond tiara and black taffeta gown of the woman behind them, her heart quavered. Denise Fremont. Louis stood beside her. Then the man with the porcelain doll must be

Marc. Dear God, she didn't want him seeing her here, not when the woman he was with was dressed to the teeth and she was so—unsuitable. But she couldn't avoid it, not now; the doorman was holding the door open, waiting for her to leave so Marc and his party could enter.

Think independence and success, she ordered herself as she thanked the doorman, nodded to a startled trio of Fremonts and Marc's date, then strode quickly away. She hadn't the nerve to look back, so she couldn't be sure, but she was almost certain that they had all stopped mid-stride and were watching her disappear around the corner. You're a crowd-stopper, she told herself, but somehow the joke didn't make her laugh.

Her heart kept pace with her feet and it was still beating rapidly when she closed the door of her hotel room and collapsed on the yellow-striped satin slipper chair. Visions of the beautiful blonde beside Marc flashed through her mind. She was the sort of woman his parents respected, someone from their background, with a similar heritage and life-style. Wasn't that what Louis had said when he banished her to New York and told her that Marc would be marrying Deirdre?

He hadn't married Deirdre; she'd learned that years ago, from her grandmother's letters. But any woman he did marry would certainly have to be a Deirdre clone, a beautiful, wealthy debutante, with all the right credentials, credentials no amount of professional success would ever bring her because they couldn't be earned. They were the sort you had to be born with.

Realizing that nothing permanent could ever come of her relationship with Marc and at the same time accepting that she'd never stop loving him, Megan threw herself on the canopied bed and cried herself to sleep.

When she awoke the next morning, her pillow was

damp, but her mind was determined. Louisiana would always be poison for her. No matter how successful she became, she'd always feel inferior whenever she met the Fremonts. The answer was to avoid them, to complete the article and return to New York where people respected her achievements and didn't look down their noses at her lineage.

She was waiting in the hotel lobby when the Fremont limousine pulled to the curb and the chauffeur opened the door for her.

"Good morning," she said, straightening the skirt on her white linen Chanel-type suit and slipping in beside Marc.

"What were you doing there last night?" he demanded, dispensing with the amenities.

"What was I doing where?" she responded, playing for time.

"You know damned well where I mean, at the hotel. I thought you weren't in the mood for anything fancy, that you were turning in early."

"Oh, the hotel," she said nonchalantly. "Someone took me to dinner." For some perverse reason she wanted to make Marc jealous, so she didn't mention that her dinner date was a woman and that she had picked up the tab. Let him draw his own conclusions, a green-eyed monster whispered in her ear. Make him think that you didn't have to sit home just because he turned you down.

"I see," Marc said brusquely. "I wasn't aware you knew anyone in New Orleans."

"I have my contacts." She smiled sweetly, enjoying his obvious discomfort. It was only fair, wasn't it? After all, she had cried her eyes out over his little blond beauty, hadn't she?

"I see," Marc repeated, opening the portfolio on his lap while obviously fighting his curiosity and trying to keep himself from asking about her dinner date. "Please excuse me, there are some papers I want to review before the hearing."

Marc's silent treatment continued all during the flight to Washington, and any ideas Megan had of making him jealous were quashed by the solicitous treatment he received from the stewardesses. As for her, so far as they were concerned she might not have even been there; in fact, she was sure they would have preferred it that way.

Marc's silence did not extend to the FDA hearing, where he and his Washington attorney skillfully presented the case for approving their new drug.

"It's an orphan drug," he explained after the hearing had adjourned and a private limousine was taking them to their hotel. "For a rare disease. We'll lose money on it, so the stockholders won't be too happy, but some Canadian physicians have had such astounding success with it that we have to take it on."

Nodding silently, Megan flipped through the notes she had taken at the hearing. The before and after photos and films Marc had shown spoke for themselves, and if this new drug could halt the frightening disease's nerve deterioration in even one patient, then as far as she was concerned, the expense was well worth it.

"We're here," Marc said when the limousine pulled into the circular driveway of a well-known Washington hotel. "I'll check in, then we'll freshen up and have a drink before dinner. Is that okay with you?"

Megan waited near the desk while Marc registered. The lobby had an aura of sedate elegance, with thick Oriental carpets, dark wood paneling, burnished maroon leather. Not surprising, she thought; surely she hadn't expected Marc to stay at some inexpensive motel.

"Let's go," Marc said. "We're on the tenth floor." He followed the bellman into the elevator.

The tenth-floor hallway with its rich gray carpeting and striped gold wallpaper repeated the lobby's elegance. The bellman opened a door midway down the hall and motioned them into a sitting room furnished in country French with bombé fruitwood chests, blue and white damask sofas, crystal lamps, plush beige carpeting and apricot satin drapes. On either side of the sitting room was a door that led to two adjoining bedrooms.

Very cozy, Megan thought, but not at all what I had in mind. Yet, despite her annoyance, she wasn't about to make a scene in front of the bellman, so she waited until he had thanked Marc for the tip and left.

"I thought this would be more comfortable," Marc said, reading her mind and silencing her protests before she could voice them. "You've got your own bedroom with a lock and its own separate entrance to the hall, but if you should want to relax in the sitting room, it's here. However, if you'd rather have something else, I'll check with the desk." His indifferent tone indicated that where she stayed didn't matter to him.

Truthfully, Megan didn't feel comfortable sharing the suite with Marc, but she didn't think she could insist on a change without sounding like a distrustful prude. After all, they did have separate bedrooms, so what difference did the sitting room make? She didn't even have to use it.

"No need to change," she said. "This will be fine."

"Great. Why don't you freshen up. I have a few calls to make. No sense in your waiting around; I'll make dinner reservations and meet you upstairs in the bar." He watched while Megan crossed the sitting room and locked her bedroom's adjoining door.

Chapter Seven

*T*he color scheme in the adjoining bedroom, dominated by a huge bed with a padded, apricot headboard, matched that of the sitting room. Megan kicked off her shoes, shrugged out of her jacket and, while unbuttoning her blouse, walked into the mirrored dressing room. Her skirt was creased, just as she'd known it would be, from sitting in the airplane and then in the hearing room. She phoned for valet service and hung her outfit in the door's clothing compartment; it would be cleaned and pressed by morning. This hotel catered to the needs of hurried businesspeople.

After showering and reapplying her makeup, she noted some pertinent facts about the hearing into her tape recorder, then changed into a black silk dress with a narrow, back-slit skirt, a straight-across, spaghetti-strapped bodice and a fitted jacket with a high ruffled neck and ruffles at the wrists. Sling-back high-heeled sandals and a matching black silk envelope purse completed her outfit.

She'd taken nearly an hour to get ready, so she was sure Marc had gone, but she knocked on his door as she passed it on her way to the elevator. No answer. He must have left. Well, he did say he'd meet her in the upstairs bar. She entered the elevator and pressed the button for the rooftop lounge.

Less than a minute later the elevator doors opened onto a small foyer with dark green carpeting and several gilded chairs with tapestry-covered seats and backs. Paintings of English country scenes hung from the oak-paneled walls. To the left was the restaurant entrance guarded by an officious maître d', and to the right was the darker, unguarded lounge. Megan walked into the lounge, checked quickly along the crowded bar, saw several business-suited men, a few women, no Marc.

If he wasn't in his room and he wasn't there . . . Well, he had told her they'd meet in the upstairs bar, so unless there was another one . . . She checked with the cocktail waitress, who assured her that except for the coffee shop and banquet halls all the food facilities were up there. Megan thanked her, ordered mineral water with a twist of lime and settled herself at a small table near the entrance, where she'd be sure to see Marc as soon as he approached.

"Megan? Megan Mahlar?"

At the sound of her name, Megan turned toward the bar. The voice sounded familiar, but for the moment, she couldn't place it.

"Megan, what the devil are you doing here?" A tall, sandy-haired man with a thick mustache picked up his drink, patted his companion's sport-jacketed shoulder and began walking toward her. "Why didn't you tell me you were going to be in Washington?"

"Larry, Larry Briggs," Megan said, standing as he approached her table. Larry was *Commerce World*'s Washington correspondent; ordinarily she would have called him, but this had all happened so fast. Until yesterday she hadn't even known she was coming. "An unexpected trip," she explained, shaking his hand and motioning him into the seat next to hers. "And meeting you here is an unexpected pleasure."

"Oh? Is there something I don't know about?" He jiggled the ice in his glass and stared at Megan. "Washington is my baby, or is Jerry contemplating a change? Level with me, Megan."

Good grief, Larry thought she was after his job. "Don't be ridiculous, Larry. I couldn't fill one toe of your shoe." She went on to explain about her feature on Fremont Industries and the FDA hearing.

"Well, I didn't think Jerry or you would pull a stunt like that, but in this business you never know." He signaled to the waitress and ordered another round of drinks. Two men Larry knew from the SEC came in and he invited them to their table.

Now four people were crowded around a table for two, but they were all so engrossed in a conversation about interest rates and the economy that no one seemed to notice. Neither did Megan notice Marc until he had walked past her table, stood at the bar and begun questioning the cocktail waitress. When Megan finally saw him, she rose from her chair and waved to him.

"Sit down, Marc," she said, after introducing him to the other men at the table. "The most amazing stroke of luck; I was waiting for you when I ran into Larry."

"Amazing," Marc agreed dryly, taking a chair from an adjacent table and frowning as everyone shifted to make room for him. "A real stroke of luck."

As soon as he had settled himself and ordered a bourbon on the rocks, the others resumed their interrupted conversation and Megan forgot about him. These were her sort of people, people who spoke the same language, respected her opinions and didn't care a jot about who her parents were.

Marc interjected a question or comment now and then, but mostly he sat quietly and listened. Finally, he checked his watch and reminded Megan that he'd made dinner reservations.

"Perhaps you'd like to join us," Megan said, inviting the others.

"Yes, of course," Marc said, his tone polite, but not at all welcoming.

"Not tonight," Larry said, shaking hands with Marc. "But thanks for asking; we'll take a rain check." He turned to Megan and grasped both her hands between his. "See you later."

Marc put his arm around Megan's waist and guided her across the foyer to the restaurant. "What did Larry mean, he'd see you later?" Marc asked after the maître d' had seated them at a center window table with a view of the Capitol. "Did you tell him you'd meet him later tonight?"

Megan shrugged indifferently. Her mind was still on the conversation she'd been having with Larry and the SEC men, mentally reviewing questions she might have asked, points she could have made. "It's just an expression; I didn't tell him I'd meet him, but what if I had, what difference would it have made to you?"

A tuxedoed waiter came by, handed them their menus and gave Marc a wine list. "I never would have told you to meet me in the bar if I'd known you'd be surrounded by a horde of men," Marc said after the waiter had gone. "It looked like a mass-market pickup. I'm surprised at you, Meggie."

Why he's jealous, Megan thought, amazed to find that his response annoyed rather than pleased her. "They're business associates, Marc. I enjoyed talking with them. In New York I meet with men like them all the time. If anyone was out of line, it was you. You might have tried being a bit more cordial."

"I didn't feel like being cordial," Marc said. "If you want to know the truth, I was more than a little upset to see you like that; for the first time you were someone different, someone I didn't recognize."

"An educated career woman with a personality and life you hadn't known existed?"

Marc looked at her for a moment, a cold, penetrating stare. "Let's order," he said, shifting his gaze to his menu without answering her question.

The food was perfect—shrimp cocktail, Caesar salad, duck à l'orange, poached pears and demitasse—but the conversation left a lot to be desired. Marc seemed intent on learning more about Megan's relationship with Larry, and Megan, although she had nothing to hide, was equally determined not to tell him. An important part of her independence, she realized, was living her life as she pleased and not having to answer to anyone, especially not Marc.

Marc was sipping a brandy and she was enjoying a coffee liqueur when a tall man whose rigid military posture was negated by a ruddy complexion and weak chin passed by the table, then stopped and retraced his steps.

"Megan Mahlar." Revulsion coated his words. "What an unpleasant surprise." His ruddy complexion deepened. "Who's your little hatchet going to cut to ribbons now? The President?"

"Regis," Megan said softly, "this isn't the place. Why don't you just forget it and leave me alone."

"Gladly," Regis said, "I thought the air in this vicinity had a decidedly foul odor, but until now I didn't know why." Smiling insidiously, he started for the door.

Springing like a panther, Marc grabbed Regis's arm and spun him around. "Would you care to explain that remark?" His tone was clearly more demanding than questioning. Conversation around them ceased and the recorded piano music vibrated through the room as if it were being played in an echo chamber.

"With pleasure," Regis said. "That bitch sitting across from you nearly put me out of business."

"What the . . ." The vein in Marc's jaw throbbed as the blood drained from his face and the back of his hand shot across Regis's cheek, then tightened into a fist. "Apologize, apologize right now."

Megan pushed back her chair and clutched Marc's arm. She'd never seen him this angry, this out of control. "Marc, please, stop it. I can handle it."

"He can't talk to you like that. I won't let him." Marc ignored Megan as his fingers tightened around Regis's arm.

The maître d' and three waiters approached the table. Two men grabbed Marc's arm and the others pulled Regis away. "Please, Mr. Fremont," the maître d' said.

"He insulted this lady. I can't let him get away with it. I'll pulverize him." He strained to free himself so he could get to Regis.

"Please stop," Megan pleaded. "For my sake, stop. This little lady is perfectly capable of taking care of herself."

Marc looked at Regis's retreating back and then at Megan. "Okay." He shrugged himself free. "Sorry for the scene," he told the maître d'. "But I'm not used to hearing a man insult a lady like that. He deserves a lot more than just a slap across his face, and he'll get it if I ever see him again."

The maître d' apologized, saying that Mr. Winthrop had dined there several times without any problem. A steady hum of conversation buzzed through the restaurant; the unexpected floor show was over and dull normalcy reigned once more. The waiters held out the chairs and waited for Megan and Marc to sit.

Marc waved them away. "We're leaving," he said. "Bill me for the usual charges." His arm circled Megan's shoulder protectively as he led her to the elevator.

"You didn't have to come charging in like that," Megan said when they returned to their suite. "I'm used to that sort of thing. It happens all the time." The emnity of people like Regis Winthrop didn't bother her because he was an immoral leach who preyed on the innocence of others.

"Oh, really?" Marc tossed his charcoal-gray jacket on the blue damask sofa and loosened his tie. "It was a first for me, perhaps you'd better explain it." He walked to the refrigerated bar next to the stereo and poured some brandy into a snifter.

"It's nothing important, not really. Regis Winthrop was running four-hundred-dollar seminars promising everyone who attended that he'd show them how to make millions. It sounded like a scam, so I signed up for one, did a little research and reported my findings in an article. Naturally Mr. Winthrop wasn't too pleased."

"But the way he spoke to you." Marc shook his head.

"It happens all the time," Megan said. "The investment industry is full of con men and it's my job to expose them. But I'm a big girl now and I can handle it; I didn't need you to defend me. Truthfully, I found your behavior more embarrassing than his."

"Oh, you did, did you? Well, maybe I'm just not used to women who hang around men, talk politics and finances and calmly accept insults that would curl my mother's hair."

"I'm not your mother, Marc, not some simpering deb, and not little Meggie. That's what I've been trying to tell you. I can take care of myself, stand on my own two feet; I don't need you to fight my battles and it bothers me when you do."

"Well, then maybe I'd just better leave you alone, because there's no way I'm ever going to be able to accept what you're asking of me."

"I know that, Marc, and I'm not asking, not anymore. Too much has happened to both of us, and we can't recapture the past, so there's just no point in trying." The plush beige carpet muted her steps as she walked swiftly into her bedroom and locked the door behind her.

As she sat down on the apricot velvet bedspread and began unbuttoning her jacket, she heard a door slam in the sitting room. Marc had left, but she couldn't be sure whether he had gone into his bedroom or left the suite completely.

She changed into her caftan and was brushing her hair at the marble vanity in the mirrored dressing area when someone rapped lightly on the door. Marc, she thought, her heart jumping despite her determination to remain indifferent. She opened the door without asking and found, to her chagrin, not Marc but a hotel chambermaid who'd come to turn down her bed. Megan continued brushing her hair while the maid turned back the velvet bedspread and fluffed the pillows.

"Will there be anything else?" the maid asked before she left the room.

"No thanks, that's just fine," Megan replied, self-consciously handing the maid a tip. Here was yet another difference between Marc and her; she was miserably uncomfortable with the obsequious service that he and his family took for granted. Her independent streak worked both ways; she didn't want to be anyone else's servant, but neither did she want others waiting on her.

There was so much about his life-style that made her resentful and ill at ease. Why, even when he came to her defense, he made her feel inferior, as if she couldn't care for herself. Despite what Marc had said about their working things out slowly, she knew it couldn't be done, not even if they tried forever.

In any case, she still had her job; that was what mattered to her, what she had worked for, what was really important. Yet, she admitted, walking to the window and pulling the drape aside so she could see the lighted Capitol building, a certain part of her had rejoiced when Marc came to her rescue, the part of her that still perceived him as her hero, that still wanted him as her knighted protector.

But that was a weakness she didn't care to succumb to, not ever again. Now she was perfectly capable of solving her own problems, and she didn't want to become dependent on Marc, no matter how momentarily romantic and comfortable it felt. Her job, her life in New York, those were the things that really mattered, the things that had substance and permanency; and if she intended to keep them, she'd better start thinking about her article. Searching through her canvas bag, she pulled out her yellow pad and walked to the bed.

A small chocolate heart wrapped in red foil and surrounded by a white paper doily lay on her pillow. Cupids covered the doily, which had SWEET DREAMS written on it in a feathery red script.

The chambermaid must have left it, a service of the hotel. Megan put the chocolate on the night table and fingered the doily, then she crumpled it and tossed it to the floor. Sweet dreams indeed; she hadn't had a sweet dream since that day eight years before when Louis had told her that Marc didn't really love her. That was the only problem with opting for independence and a career; somehow they couldn't comfort you through the long, lonely nights, couldn't stop your dreams from turning into nightmares.

And this night was no different from all the others; if anything, it was worse. Just knowing that Marc was so close, that she could open her door and, within moments, be at his, made her want to go to him. But she couldn't. Much as she yearned to feel his arms around her, she knew it was pointless. Why expose herself to a few hours of bliss when the final result would be endless years of misery? Clutching the pillow close to her body, she vainly courted sleep.

At eight the next morning, just after she had taken her neatly pressed white suit from the valet cabinet in her door, Marc rapped at the sitting-room door and called to her. Running her fingers through her hair to smooth out the sleepy knots, she opened the door and let him in.

"I've been thinking," he said, avoiding her eyes and walking to the window. "You probably have all the information you need about the FDA hearing. My attorney wants me to stay on for a few more days. I've other matters to attend to, but your time could probably be more profitably spent back in New Orleans."

"But . . ." For some inexplicable reason, she didn't want to be parted from Marc, not just yet.

"No buts," he said, coming to her and catching her face between his hands. "You didn't sleep any better than I did." His thumbs circled her lower eyelids. "Your eyes are red, cheeks all tear-stained. There's no point in our ripping each other apart by staying together like this. I could never tolerate anyone speaking to you the way that Winthrop fellow did. Go back to New Orleans, Meggie, and get your research finished before I return." He kissed her lightly on the cheek. "I don't want to see you when I get back. It will be better that way. You were right. We've both changed too much to recapture the past." The door clicked shut behind him as he left the room.

Following Marc's instructions, Megan packed her things, took a taxi to the airport and, by midafternoon, was back at her hotel in New Orleans' French Quarter. Too late to start working, but too early to stay in her room. Leaving the hotel, she reacquainted herself with the quaint charm of the *Vieux Carré*, the narrow streets, graceful iron grillwork and flower-filled patios —so refreshingly different from the concrete caverns of New York.

After a dinner of French bread and gumbo, she strolled along the Moon Walk and watched the barges make their way through the muddy Mississippi; so sure of where they were going, of the job they had to do; if only she could be half as certain. Still, this morning, in Washington, Marc hadn't given her any choice. Be gone before I get back, he had said, finally acknowledging what his father had said eight years ago, that he was just as ill-suited for her life-style as she was for his.

At ten o'clock the next morning, after another sleepless night, Megan took a taxi to the Fremont Building. Louis's mural glared at her, smugly insisting that he had been right all along. If her canvas carryall had had a stock of tomatoes, she would have thrown them all. Instead, she smiled and said good-morning to Edna. The receptionist glanced briefly at her badge, then returned her smile as she waited by the executive elevator. Megan breathed deeply when the elevator began its ascent. She hoped she'd be able to finish her research before Marc returned. It would suit her needs as well as his.

Marc's outer office was as sedately busy as it had been the day before, but Mrs. Jamison wasn't around. One of the younger secretaries was typing at a desk near the opposite wall and June Clayson and Delilah were bent over the middle drawer of a black-enamel file cabinet. The door to Marc's private office was open. Was someone else using it? Not Louis, she hoped. Hardly likely, she decided; he'd be sure to have his own office.

The phone buzzed and Delilah went to answer it.

"How are you?" Megan whispered to June.

"Fine," June replied, smiling. "Oh, I've had a few problems. Mrs. Jamison hinted that I might have to dress a bit differently. You know, bras, nylons, no sweaters . . . this is the president's office. But I don't mind. Everything else is great. It's so quiet here. Everyone's so nice and if there's safety in numbers . . ." She indicated the other women in the office.

"Safety in numbers? Have you had any problems?" Megan looked at the open door marked PRIVATE. She couldn't have; Marc wasn't even around.

"With Mr. Fremont?" June giggled. "Oh, no, I haven't even seen him. He's going to be in Washington for the rest of the week."

Megan sighed silently. *The rest of the week*. Thank God. If she didn't waste any time, she could get all her research done before he returned. "Is Mrs. Jamison here?"

"In there," June said, motioning to Marc's private office.

"I have to see her. I'll talk to you later."

"Okay, and thanks again, for helping me, I mean."

Megan said good-bye to June and walked toward Marc's office. "Mrs. Jamison?" She tapped lightly on the open office door.

"Oh, Miss Mahlar." Mrs. Jamison straightened a sheaf of letters and placed them at the center of Marc's desk. "Mr. Fremont mentioned that you'd be in today."

"Yes, he said he'd make arrangements for me to complete my research while he was in Washington." Before he returned, she added silently.

"What type of information would you like? Then I can set up your appointments accordingly."

"I'd like to know about the new products the company is introducing. Future plans. Projected earnings. The effect of government regulations." The words spilled out of Megan as her mind catalogued her research needs. Once she plunged into her work, all other considerations became meaningless.

Mrs. Jamison was silent for a moment. "I believe the man you'd find most helpful would be Mr. Bennett in our New Products Division. Excuse me." She picked up the telephone and began dialing.

The New Products Division was located on the second floor, a shouting mass of chrome, glass and artwork which made Megan feel immediately at home because the brightly attractive decor reminded her of the ad copies for *Commerce World* magazine. Xylon 3, one poster blared, the outdoor pest control that's safe around pets; Dapsam, the one glue that sticks to its job; Piny Forest, the room deodorizer you can live with. The stark white walls, decorated with insistent *buy me* messages, were like the colorful pages of a slick magazine, totally different from the lobby's pretentious mural.

Mrs. Jamison left Megan in the care of Steve Bennett, a tall, partially bald man with friendly brown eyes and a freckled complexion.

"Call me Steve," he said, clasping Megan's hand between his two broad ones. "So Marc finally arranged for the *Commerce World* interview. I kept telling him it would be a good idea to let the public in on what we're doing, especially now that Nessac's breathing down our neck. We're going to need all the stockholder support we can get." He pointed down the long, white-carpeted hall. "My office is that way. Now, exactly what would you like to know?"

"Everything. This is going to be a feature article. A ten-page spread. That's a lot of information."

"One of the best ways to learn about this company is to look at these walls," Steve said, indicating the colorful posters lining both sides of the corridor. "These are the products that made us the single largest chemical company in the South, and they're what still keep us growing."

"That's the area I'm really interested in," Megan said as they continued down the hall. "The growth of the company . . . plans for the future."

Steve showed her into his private office, sleekly modern with lean Danish teakwood furniture and a rectangular, glass-topped table surrounded by six white leather director's chairs.

"Our plans for the future are in our products," Steve said, motioning Megan to one of the director's chairs.

"These are your current products." Megan indicated the dark brown corkboard covered with magazine tear sheets. "What about the future? Mr. Fremont mentioned that the company was planning to introduce some exciting new items."

"We're always developing new products." Steve pressed his intercom button and asked his secretary to serve some coffee. "Exactly which one did you have in mind?"

"Mr. Fremont said that there were several about-to-be-released products that would interest our readers. Why don't you start with the ones you consider the most promising?" She put her tape recorder on the glass conference table and rummaged through her canvas satchel trying to find her yellow pad. Darn, it wasn't there. She remembered taking it from the cottage; she must have left it at the hotel. "May I borrow some writing paper?"

"Sure," Steve said. "I'll have my secretary bring it in with the coffee. Excuse me for a minute." He went to the outer office.

While Steve was gone, his secretary, a statuesque chignoned blonde with a flawless complexion and a toothpaste-commercial smile, brought Megan a cup of coffee and a yellow pad similar to the one she had lost.

"Mr. Bennett is on the phone," his secretary drawled. "He won't be but a minute. He thought you might be interested in this sales brochure." She handed Megan a shiny white folder with the words FREMONT SELLS FAST printed across the front. "Can I get you anything else? Do you take cream or sugar?"

"Thanks, this is fine." Opening the folder, Megan took some smaller leaflets out of the pockets. Each one extolled the virtue of a different product, consistently stating that Fremont on the label guaranteed quality in the box.

"Sorry for taking off like that." Steve returned, sat down opposite her and put his coffee cup on the table. "Some of our research is highly confidential and we don't usually like to discuss what we've been working on until we're ready to market. If the news gets out too soon, our competitors might jump the gun on us. I tried to check with Mr. Fremont, but I wasn't able to reach him. Anyway, Mrs. Jamison said you'd been cleared by him, so I guess I can start giving you a broad overview of our various product divisions."

"Fine," Megan said, grateful for Steve's prompt assistance, because she wanted to complete her research as quickly as possible. "Do you mind if I use this?" She pointed to the tape recorder.

"Not at all. I'm used to giving interviews. I know you people like those things." He leaned over the table, unfurled a corporate structure chart and began describing the duties and products of each division.

Since she was recording the entire interview, Megan

took very few notes, but she did jot down that Steve seemed extremely happy with his job and proud of the company for which he worked.

After a morning spent studying numerous graphs and sales brochures, they enjoyed a leisurely barbecued shrimp luncheon in the executive dining room, then returned to Steve's office.

"This is all very useful," Megan said, "but Mr. Fremont did mention that corporate earnings were being plowed back into research. That's the sort of thing I'm really interested in. If I can mention some promising new product that you're planning to introduce, then I'm sure Fremont Industries' stock would increase in value. That's what Mr. Fremont wants . . . why he agreed to the article."

Steve hesitated. "I don't know. You'd have to speak to Ty Carlson, our laboratory supervisor. That's more his line than mine."

"How can I reach him?"

"I'll put in a call. Excuse me." He picked up the phone.

Megan switched off the tape recorder. Now she was getting to the core of Fremont Industries—the research center. She knew exactly the approach she'd use in her article, how she'd tie it in with the orphan drug hearing.

"It's all set," Steve said. "Ty's scheduling a VIP tour for tomorrow. We can't take you into the restricted areas without Mr. Fremont's permission, but you will get a general overview of the place. I'll pick you up at your hotel, nine o'clock tomorrow morning."

Fremont Industries' laboratory and production facilities were concentrated in fifteen acres of low gray buildings separated by grass, shrubbery and tall oak trees. It was a self-contained world, a small city of white-jacketed chemists, overall-clad factory workers, hushed laboratories and noisy assembly lines. Acrid medicinal scents and odors of fertilizer permeated the air—waxes, ammonias, deodorants.

Before starting the tour Megan and Steve zipped into white coveralls and Ty showed them how to breathe through the visor-front masks.

"Some of our chemicals we work with in concentrated forms," he explained, "and these chemicals, concentrated, can harm the skin and the respiratory system. Marc Fremont insists on very strict safety standards. He doesn't believe in endangering our employees' health. At Fremont Industries, the people's welfare is the only thing that's more important than our product."

It was becoming more and more obvious to Megan that people mattered to Marc—his employees, the children at Fremont House. Certainly a different picture from the one she'd carried within her for the past eight years.

Forget about Marc, she told herself. Concentrate on the article. Your loyalty is to Jerry and the people at *Commerce World*. They're the ones who have faith in you. She wrote down what Ty had told her about Marc's attitude toward safety and also noted some of the warnings on the precautionary signs posted around the plant. Apparently Marc's staff was obeying his instructions and safety was an important aspect of Fremont Industries' research and manufacturing facilities.

After giving her a tour of the interior buildings, Ty and Steve showed Megan through the grounds. The last building Ty pointed out was the fertilizer manufacturing plant. "Can't go in there," he said. "Top secret right now." He drove through a hedge of oak trees behind the structure and stopped the Jeep at an eight-foot chain-link fence surrounding a deep ravine.

"We just sold that property to the local township for

landfill. The federal government has given us a contract to research waste management. If things work out, in a few years' time the town's trash should be producing enough methane to supply all their natural gas needs."

"That's an exciting venture," Megan said. "But a landfill, won't the people in the area object?"

"We're the only ones around here," Steve said, "and considering our own aromatic atmosphere, we could hardly issue any protests. No, this is the ideal spot for a trash dump. And it worked out well for us because we've been selling off a lot of property recently. Most of it's very valuable; but who'd want to buy this?"

During the drive back to New Orleans Megan questioned Steve about the property sales. "Is there any specific reason why Fremont Industries is selling off its land?" *Are you experiencing financial difficulties?* was what she really meant.

"The corporation owns a lot of property that came with the family's original land grants or was purchased over the years. The board has decided that it would be advantageous to unload some of our real property and increase our liquid assets." He turned to Megan and smiled. "We want the cash."

Well, at least Steve was up front about Fremont Industries' financial problems, Megan thought as she spent the next few days at the county recorder's office researching the land sales. But she was amazed to discover just how much cash those transactions had produced. Much more than Marc could possibly plow back into research, she noted on her pad. Now he'd be able to satisfy disgruntled stockholders by raising corporate dividends. And since, in accordance with Fremont Industries' fiscal year-end, their annual report wasn't due for another four months, her article could quite possibly be the first source of that information. A real coup. Jerry would be ecstatic.

Her last day in Louisiana was spent at Fremont

House, speaking with Mrs. Lawson and the children who idolized Marc and spoke about him in glowing terms. "He's a marvelous man," Mrs. Lawson said. "I can't begin to tell you the wonderful things he's done for these children."

Wonderful, wonderful, wonderful. Everywhere she went, that was all she ever heard about Marc. Well, he might be warm and considerate where the children and his employees were concerned, but when it came to her . . . She remembered what he'd told her in Washington—"Be gone before I get back." She blocked out his arrogant image—she didn't want to think about it.

Chapter Eight

Six days later, back in her New York apartment, Megan still thought of the research lab and manufacturing plant each time she wiped down her white Formica kitchen counter with an ammonia-saturated sponge. The odor was so similar to the chemical ones permeating Fremont Industries' research center that she couldn't avoid the comparison.

She was working at her apartment now because on her return to the city she had phoned Jerry to ask if she could write her rough draft at home. Fewer interruptions, she had explained. Also more comfortable, she thought as she looked down at her sleeveless black cotton cardigan and white designer jeans.

Her cat, Tiger, liked it too. Although he was a fairly self-sufficient striped-gray alley cat who spent most of his time curled up on one of her beige living-room chairs, he occasionally stirred himself long enough to come purring around her legs and hop into her lap.

Around five that evening, just as she had roughed out the last paragraph of her article, the telephone on her desk rang, rousing Tiger from his lazy solitude. Jumping off the sofa, he padded across the room and hopped into her lap. So much for fewer interruptions. Well, at least she had finished the first draft.

"Hello," she said, petting Tiger absently, her mind still engrossed in her article.

"Hi, there," Jerry said, "just checking up to see how things are going."

"Fine. I just dotted the last period on my first draft. What's up?"

"Nothing much. I wanted to see how you were coming along, to make sure you're not running into any snags, that you'll meet the deadline."

"No problems. In fact I'll be in tomorrow to show you what I've done and see what you think."

"Great. I'd like to get a look at it. Hold on a minute while I check my calendar." Megan heard Jerry shuffling papers and smiled to herself while she waited. Jerry's desk was probably in its usual unorganized state. He could never find anything without sifting through piles of paper. "Look," he said, returning to the phone, "I've got a ten o'clock meeting with a new advertiser, big bucks. Charlie Higgins is making the presentation and I promised I'd be there. We'll probably go to lunch and I'll be tied up for the rest of the day. But I really want to see your draft. Can you be in my office by eight? That'll give us two hours."

"I'll be there," Megan promised. "You know I've never been late for a conference."

"Okay, and don't forget to leave some space for that Las Vegas security analysts' convention next week. Marc Fremont's making a presentation. No doubt he'll try to fend off Nessac's sharks; should be an interesting session."

"No doubt. Don't worry, I'll be there with my faithful little recorder, and I'll see you bright and early tomorrow morning." She hung up the phone, then stroked Tiger's head, massaged his neck and nuzzled him against her cheek. "And so will Marc," she whispered into Tiger's ear. "I avoided him in New Orleans, but I'll have to see him in Las Vegas, even if he's on the podium and I'm in the audience. And seeing him is so painful; oh, Tiger, what am I going to do?" A pigeon flew by and perched on the window ledge. Tiger's back arched and he hissed as he leaped from her arms and ran stealthily to the window.

Staring at the papers spread across her desk, Megan decided that perhaps she wasn't the person best suited to write this story after all. Maybe she was too familiar with the Fremonts, knew the family too well, especially Marc. But it was too late now; she'd taken the assignment and she'd see it through to completion with the same meticulous detail she gave to all her articles.

She pulled the last sheet from her typewriter and stacked it neatly with the others she had finished. She was too tired now to read it and make revisions. Besides, she'd been so busy writing that she'd skipped lunch and it was practically dinner time. Her head throbbed and she sensed the beginnings of a queasy stomachache. She'd better get something to eat right away.

Switching on the TV, she swiveled it toward the kitchen and watched the news while she opened the refrigerator and poured some milk into Tiger's dish. Now for herself, she thought. She hadn't eaten in so long that her appetite had vanished, but she knew that lack of food was causing her throbbing headache. After all, she'd had nothing but coffee all day. Still, her stomach felt so jumpy that she decided on something bland. Scrambled eggs and toast were fast and easy.

She had beaten two eggs in a bowl, put a pat of butter in the skillet and set it on the stove when the doorbell rang.

Tiger stopped lapping his milk, padded across the room and scratched at the door. For a moment Megan wondered who it could be. Since she spent most of her time at work, she barely knew any of her neighbors, except for thirteen-year-old Billy and his parents, and she'd already paid him for cat-sitting Tiger. She put the spatula on the counter next to the stove and went to the door. "Who is it?"

"Marc." The voice was clear and impressive.

"Marc?" Megan asked incredulously. It couldn't be. He was in New Orleans staying away from her. Still, it certainly sounded like him. She squinted and peered through the small glass peephole. In New York one couldn't be too cautious.

"It's Marc, Meggie. Open the door, please."

Megan unlocked the two dead bolts and slid the door open on its chain. "What are you doing here?"

"I brought you a present." He indicated the big blue velvet chair beside him and the burly delivery man standing behind it. "But I can't give it to you unless you open the door," he said impatiently.

Megan was so stunned by the sight of her grandmother's chair that for a minute she did nothing, just held her hand on the chain and didn't move. Tiger crept through the open door, then sidled up against Marc's pant leg.

Marc picked him up and scratched behind his ears. "Well, fella, you must be Tiger." One hand stroked down Tiger's back while Tiger licked his other hand and purred contentedly.

"Get back in here, Tiger," Megan ordered. "Careful," she warned Marc, "he has a tendency to run away. Female companionship, if you know what I mean."

Eying her disdainfully, Tiger preened his fur on Marc's jacket.

"He's not going to run away," Marc said, stroking Tiger's neck. "He wouldn't do that to me. We're friends."

Traitorous cat, Megan thought, remembering how she had bought Tiger from a small boy whose mother was threatening to have the kitten destroyed. That's gratitude for you, making friends with a man I'm trying to put out of my life. Slipping the chain free of its socket, she opened the door.

Marc walked in with the delivery man carrying the chair behind him. He set Tiger down and the cat ambled back to his saucer of milk. Then Marc indicated the chair. "Where do you want this?" he asked.

Striding into the living room, he dropped his tan cowhide attaché case and a small flowered tin canister on the sofa.

"Put the chair over here," Megan said, patting the blank wall to the right of the window.

The delivery man placed the chair by the window and left. Tiger immediately leaped onto the new chair, preened himself for a moment or two, then, after meowing his approval, curled up and went to sleep.

"Thanks for the chair," Megan said. "I just hope I get a chance to use it. Tiger can be quite possessive." She sniffed. Something was burning. Quickly, she scanned the room. Typewriter, refinished rolltop desk, brown velvet sofa, two beige Queen Anne chairs, brass candlestick lamps, sofa, oak dining table—the kitchen archway was smoking. Tiger hissed and snarled, then fled to his basket in the bathroom.

The butter. She'd forgotten all about it. She dashed into the kitchen, shut off the burner and grabbed the smoking skillet. "Rats," she said as she dropped it in the sink. "I burned myself." She shook her hand, then brought it to her mouth.

"What's wrong with you? Why did you even touch it?" Marc grasped her hand and checked the reddening area. "The thing was smoking all over the place. Didn't you realize the handle would be hot?"

"I wasn't thinking about the handle, if you want to know the truth. I was too afraid this whole place might go up in flames." She glared at him even as the smoke clogged her nostrils and started her eyes tearing. Why did he have to find fault with everything she did? He made burning some butter sound like a capital offense.

Marc coughed and tried to clear his throat. "Let's get out of here before we choke to death. This smoke is impossible." Reaching up, he turned on the exhaust fan over the stove. "Come on." He grabbed her wrist and pulled her into the living room.

"Let me alone," Megan said, trying to twist free. "I can take care of it by myself."

"I know, you can take care of everything by yourself, can't you? The completely independent woman, that's you."

"That's exactly right."

"Well, independent women should be more careful; they shouldn't leave a pan on the stove without watching it." He checked the red mark on her palm. "That's going to blister. We'd better put it under cold water. Where's the bathroom?"

"I said I'd take care of it. I'm not a child," Megan said, pulling her hand free and starting down the small hallway that led to the bedroom and bath area. "I don't usually do things like this, and I wouldn't have forgotten about the skillet if you hadn't come to the door." She turned on the cold water and held her hand under it until the sting began to abate. "There, that should take care of it."

"You need some ointment," Marc said, calmly disregarding her protests while he checked over the contents of her medicine chest. Megan felt an immediate surge of resentment, as if Marc were invading her privacy, chipping away at the independence she had struggled to achieve.

Tiger slept in his basket, totally oblivious to their argument. Some protection, Megan thought wryly. The lazy tomcat would probably sleep through the night.

"Here," Marc said, holding up a small red and white plastic tube. "Sensatern, one of our products. It's got a local anesthetic." He shut off the cold water and gave her a towel.

"I know all about it. Sensatern cools the burn," Megan said, mimicking the slogan from the advertising brochure. "I've been all through your corporate headquarters and your lab, remember? While you were in Washington. I found out everything there is to know about your company, and I was gone before you returned. You did tell me you didn't want to see me, don't you remember?"

"How could I forget? Damn you, Meggie, every time I have anything to do with you I wind up feeling like a fool." He raked his fingers through his hair, rumpling its bluntly cut smoothness. "I told you to go away and then I found I couldn't stay away."

"That's just too bad, isn't it? Mean little Meggie bothering Marc, upsetting his life; and all the time I was only doing what you wanted. Oh, Marc, after all that happened, after all you said, why did you come here? Why did you have to open everything up again?" She ran into the bedroom and flung herself on the bed, no longer able to repress her tears.

"Meggie." Marc sat beside her on the bed. "Meggie, let me help you. That's going to blister." He tried to get her hand, but she had tucked it under her chin.

"Go away. Just go away. And stop calling me Meggie," she sniffed. "I'm Megan Mahlar, of New

York City and *Commerce World* magazine." She turned on her side, curling away from him. "Just leave me alone."

"Okay, Megan Mahlar, of New York City and *Commerce World* magazine; I'm not leaving until you calm down, so you'd better accept that and let me help you." A mocking grin tugged at the corner of his mouth as, gripping her shoulder, he turned her gently onto her back and began spreading the ointment lightly over her palm. "There, that'll take away the sting and keep the blistering under control."

Megan wanted to pull her hand away, but she didn't. The cooling sensation felt too pleasant to reject. The advertising copy was right: Sensatern dulled the prickling burn.

"Does that feel better?"

"It feels fine, good as new. Sensatern is a sensational discovery; I'll put that all into my article. Now, will you please follow your own advice and get out of my bedroom?"

"Sometimes self-given advice is the hardest to follow," Marc said. "I could say that I came merely to bring you the chair, but you know I'd be lying. The truth is that despite the differences in the way we think, I can't stay away from you."

"No." She tried to twist free.

Marc caught her wrist and pulled her arm over her head. "Yes," he insisted.

"Oh, Marc, don't do this. You know it's hopeless. Our attitudes are so different that we can't even talk about them."

"You're right. Sometimes talking is a waste of time." His head dipped and his lips brushed over hers in a feathery kiss. "A total waste of time." The kiss hardened, his lips ravaging hers, urging them to part.

"No, Marc, please. I don't want this."

"How can you be so sure?" Marc asked, his voice

low and husky. "I haven't even started." He stroked across her shoulder, down her arm; gently he cupped her breast.

"Stop it; please stop it," Megan said, trying to deny the treacherous warmth stealing through her body. Her mind raced, searching for a way to stop Marc while her thoughts were still her own. "Let me up. I haven't had dinner."

"Neither have I, but right now I'm more hungry for you than I am for any food." He traced the V neck of her cardigan, then slowly began releasing the buttons. "I have a breakfast appointment with my stockbroker tomorrow morning, but until then . . ." His whispered promises of joy warmed the curve of her ear.

Megan felt her resistance ebbing with each newly opened button and she acknowledged, to herself at least, that the hunger gnawing at the pit of her stomach couldn't be satisfied by food—she ached in her need for Marc.

Reaching behind her, Marc unhooked her bra and removed it along with her sweater. His hands teased lightly over her breasts, measuring their proud bounty and brushing the tips into a taut desire that quivered within the encircling warmth of his lips.

For a brief moment Megan thought about stopping him. Then his lips followed the path blazed by his hands—warm, moist, joyously sensuous. Her lips parted in a sigh and she closed her eyes as Marc's mouth caressed her breasts, tugging at the fragile chords that reached deep into her abdomen. She couldn't stop him now. She didn't want to because she'd shrivel and die if he didn't continue.

Shrugging out of his jacket and shirt, he tossed them both to the floor. The thud of his shoes followed as he lifted himself onto the bed and brushed Megan's hair off her heated face. "Back at Nora's wedding, you said that you once had loved me. Did you love me once,

Meggie? Did you ever really love me?" His palm flattened over her abdomen, still clad in the white denim of her jeans.

Marc's plaintive question melted her last shreds of resistance. "How can you even ask me that?" Stroking her fingers lightly across his lips to silence them, she remembered the boundless joy she always felt with him, remembered and wanted it again. "Didn't you know? When I kissed you in the bayou, couldn't you tell?" He was her entire world, the only man who could make her feel so truly beautiful, so truly loved.

"Oh, Meggie, sweetheart." He unzipped her jeans and, lifting her gently, peeled them down her legs. Ever so slowly, his hand retraced its path, grazing her ankle, her calf, circling her knee, the tender flesh of her thigh. His thumb hooked into her lacy panty and within seconds the flimsy bikini had joined her other clothing on the floor. A black and white montage against the carpeting.

Megan's torso arched with desire, and she had to touch him, feel him, know him as he was knowing her. Her knuckle bent across the jut of his jaw, then roamed over his chest, fingers combing through the mass of dark, matted hair. What was it about Marc that made her yearn for him as she had never yearned for any other man?

She sighed and tilted her head when he nuzzled her earlobe, the throbbing pulse in her neck, the delicate hollow above the valley of her breasts and then the breasts themselves. Her hands flattened against his muscular back as he lifted himself to slip out of his pants. "Don't leave me, Marc."

"Easy, sweet, I'm not going anywhere without you." He shifted closer, driving the thrusting urgency of his body into the welcoming softness of hers. "Oh, Meggie." Groaning, he brought his lips down on hers, his erotically demanding mouth echoing the passion of his body.

Their lovemaking was fiercer than it had ever been, as if by coming together with such wild abandon they could obliterate the problems that had kept them apart. In mindlessly rocketing movements they clung to each other, clung to each other, until at last the universe exploded and all their differences disappeared, making them one.

Megan's ragged breathing matched Marc's as he relaxed for a moment, then turned onto his back, taking her with him. His hands stroked over her, soothing her, calming her, returning her to reality. "So sweet, so delicate, so very fragile." He trailed kisses down the side of her throat, along her shoulder, the curve of her breast.

She rested her head on his chest, reveling in his musky, male scent, enjoying the feeling of being loved and protected. "Oh, Marc, I'm so . . ."

"I know, sweet. It's been a long time, but it's all over now. Just rest. I want to know the feel of you sleeping in my arms . . . waking to find you next to me."

"Marc, please, there's something . . ." She had to know if he shared his father's feelings about her, if he thought that her loving him like this made her something less than worthwhile.

"Shh." He pulled her closer. "Later . . . much later." His lips closed over hers, silencing her questions.

Sirens shrilled, their intensity increasing then diminishing as they sped down Lexington Avenue. Megan winced and shifted in the bed, her mind coming slowly awake, wandering, recreating an image from the past. Would she ever be able to hear a siren without remembering the day she had slipped on the ice? A twisted ankle, she'd thought. Nothing more. Until she'd tried to stand and had fainted from the searing pain in her abdomen. A short time later when she awoke, the ambulance was taking her to the hospital.

The memory remained a chilling nightmare. Reaching for the cover, she tried to pull it over her head and turn away from the noise. A strong, well-muscled arm drew her closer and her eyes sprang open. The past faded from her thoughts.

"Where do you think you're going?" Marc drawled, his voice drowsy with sleep. "It's not morning." Rolling over, he rested on one elbow and fanned her hair out on the pillow. "We have the night in front of us and I don't want to waste one minute, not one."

Megan traced the line at the curve of his neck where his suntan lightened and his dark chest hairs began. A few hours before Marc had been the same demanding yet gentle lover he had always been, caressing and kissing her until, unable to stand it any longer, she had cried out in her need, a need that he had teased and tantalized, then finally satisfied.

"Feeling shy?" he asked, nibbling gently at her finger.

"No." His tenderly erotic kisses were tugging at the strings of her desire, creating reactions that were anything but shy. When she was alone with Marc and he held her like this, all she felt was love and sweet contentment.

"I'm glad," he said, his eyes darkening as his breathing became rapid and uneven, "because I certainly don't feel shy." A self-assured smile curved his lips as his sensitive hands moved slowly over her body to show her exactly how he did feel.

If their previous lovemaking had been a violent obliteration of their differences, this time they made love slowly, searching, rediscovering and meeting each other's needs with an impassioned urgency that insured their mutual delight.

To Megan it seemed as if their relationship had achieved a new plateau of satisfaction and understanding that only maturity could grant. Sighing contentedly, she rested her head on Marc's chest, and for a while they lay together nestled in silence, holding and touching each other, totally relaxed until Megan clutched her stomach to still a whispered rumble which to her sounded like an amplified avalanche. Embarrassed, she tried to move away.

"Don't ever be ashamed of anything," Marc said, keeping her at his side. "Not with me. You're like a part of me and I'm intrigued by everything about your body, every texture, scent and sound." His hand closed over hers, gently stroking her stomach. "But eager as I am to continue this delightful voyage of discovery, I think we'd better get you some dinner." He glanced at the digital radio alarm on the skirted bedside table. "Ten o'clock. Is there someplace we can grab a quick bite?"

Nothing to be ashamed of. Intrigued by everything about her. A part of him. Wasn't that the way Marc had always made her feel? Ever since the first time she had pressed her lips to his on the bayou? Her heart swelled with emotion, and for a brief moment she yearned to kiss him and once again reaffirm their intimacy.

"Meggie? What about dinner?" Marc sat up against the headboard, his palm tenderly cupping her nape. "You know I'd like to keep you here forever, but . . ."

"I can wash the pan and scramble some eggs," she said, swinging her legs onto the floor and getting her robe out of the closet. Her insatiable hunger for Marc shamed her more than her growling stomach.

"Sounds good," Marc agreed, slipping into his trousers and following her into the kitchen.

A round pine table with a trailing philodendron centerpiece sat in the living room just outside the kitchen's bifold doors. The white Formica and stainless steel kitchen itself was as compact and efficiently organized as a ship's galley—opposing rows of top and bottom light oak cabinets, wall oven, range, dishwasher, stainless steel sink with a towel holder on the wall above it, toaster and coffee maker on the counters.

An odor of burned butter and stale smoke permeated the atmosphere, so Megan switched the exhaust fan to high, then poured the eggs that she had beaten earlier into the sink and scrubbed out the pan. "Take some eggs out of the refrigerator," she told Marc, "and there's a fork in that drawer."

"Where do you want these?" He held the egg basket in one hand and the fork in the other. The muscles on his bare chest flexed, and Megan thought that he'd be more comfortable wielding a tennis racket than a fork.

"Crack four eggs into this bowl and then mix them with the fork."

"How?" Marc held an egg in each hand.

"How do you crack an egg?" Megan rinsed out the pan and set it on the drainboard. "Good grief, you really are totally helpless. Haven't you ever . . ." Megan shook her head. Why was she asking? Didn't she know that he had never even had to boil water for himself? "You just crack them on the side of the bowl. Oh, never mind, I'll do it myself."

"On the side of the bowl, huh?" Marc smashed both eggs against the side of the bowl simultaneously. Shell and egg splattered over the bowl and his hands.

The shocked look of disbelief on Marc's face as he tried to shake the goo from his hands was absolutely hilarious, and Megan burst out laughing.

"You think it's funny?" Marc asked, flipping on the faucet with his elbow, then rinsing off his hands.

"No, it's just . . ." She tried to control herself, then

saw Marc's brooding bewilderment and began laughing again.

"Just what?" Ripping off a paper towel, Marc wiped his hands, then glared at her.

Megan shook her head and backed away. How could she explain the humor of the situation—a man who managed a billion-dollar corporation and was unable to crack an egg?

Marc stalked her, his dark eyebrows drawn together in a menacing Groucho Marx leer. "Exactly what do you find so humorous?"

"Marc, I was only . . . It's just that you looked so funny." She left the kitchen and circled the table, putting its width between them. Her green eyes sparkled as she clasped her hand over her mouth and tried to control her laughter. It was useless, absolutely useless, and an irrepressible series of throaty giggles exploded between her fingers.

"Aha, my fair beauty," Marc said, girdling her rib cage. "So you want to laugh, do you?" Twirling an imaginary mustache like the villain in a silent-movie melodrama, he prodded at her waist and teased her underarms until, convulsed by a fit of giggles, she fell back against the sofa. "I'll give you something to laugh about," he promised, following her down, sitting at the edge of the sofa and continuing his darting tickles.

"Stop it," she begged, trying futilely to catch her breath and strike back at him. "Oh, Marc, please stop it." Uncontrollable laughter was making her eyes tear.

"Promise not to laugh at me anymore," he said, now laughing as hard as she. "Come on, promise." Grabbing her wrists with one hand, he lifted them over her head.

"Yes, yes, I promise. Anything. Just stop tickling me." Curling over on her side, she tried to get away from him. She felt as if they were frolicking children, playing games, getting to know each other.

"Anything?" he repeated softly, the humorous tone abruptly disappearing from his voice and letting her know that the anything he had in mind definitely wasn't for children.

"Oh, Marc." Slowly, she turned back to him, her long lashes still glistening from the tears of her laughter. "The eggs."

His lips grazed her neck, nuzzled her earlobe, then dried her tears with the warmth of his breath. "Are the eggs really that important?" His hands started a slow, tantalizing journey over the curves and valleys of her body.

Megan felt a fire igniting deep within her, an inferno that only Marc could quench. "What eggs?" she asked, throwing her arms around his neck and fitting her lips to the demanding embrace of his. "What eggs?"

Chapter Nine

An hour later when they wandered back into the kitchen, Megan put Marc in charge of the toast while she scrambled the eggs. Even he could manage that, she decided; the toaster was set, all he had to do was slip in the bread and wait for it to pop up. This time her assessment had been right; Marc handled the entire operation efficiently, and when he placed the four lightly browned pieces of toast on a plate, he was grinning like an expert.

"We work well together," he said, setting the toast on the table and watching her scoop the scrambled eggs out of the skillet and onto a plate. "A good team. Maybe we should think about making it into something more permanent."

"And if a loudmouth like Regis Winthrop comes along?"

Marc shook his head. "Don't mention that man to me." His hands tightened into fists. "If he walked into this room right now, I'd flatten him. There's no way I could ever let someone talk to you like that."

Smiling wryly, Megan put the empty skillet in the sink. "It goes with the territory, Marc. Every feature writer makes enemies. Either you learn to take it or you leave the business." She carried the butter dish to the table and set it in the center. "And I have no intention of leaving."

Marc held out her chair and waited for her to sit. "Why not? No job is worth taking that kind of abuse."

"To me it is, Marc. I like my job too much to quit it because of some immoral twerp. Apparently you can't understand that." She tilted her head back and looked up at him. "There's more to compatibility than toast and scrambled eggs."

Marc sat down opposite her. "We don't do too badly in other departments." His gaze flickered toward the bedroom archway.

"There's a lot of hours between breakfast and bedtime," she said. "Those are the ones that concern me." She salted her eggs and passed the shaker to Marc.

He caught her hand and held it for a moment. "Minor problems. We can work them out."

She shook her head. "You didn't think so in Washington. You sent me to New Orleans and told me to be gone before you got back . . . that we were best off staying away from each other. What changed your mind?"

"The fact that I haven't been able to sleep, that I can't stop thinking about you." He lifted his fork and idly pushed some eggs to the side of his plate. "When I got home, I searched for that in the storeroom"—he motioned to the blue velvet chair—"because I thought it would be a good excuse to see you." He smiled. "I was counting on the universal welcome for a guest bearing gifts."

"Thanks, Marc. I do appreciate it."

"Enough to think about what I said?"

"I'll think about it, but it won't do much good."

"I brought another gift," Marc said, taking the flowered canister from the sofa and placing it at the center of the table as Megan poured the coffee. "These are from Nora. Pralines. When she heard I was coming to New York, she asked if I'd mind stopping off here and giving them to you." He bit off some toast and chewed it. "I told her that you'd mentioned the blue chair at the wedding and that I was having it shipped to you. I didn't mention that I was part of the delivery team."

"Thanks," Megan said. "It wouldn't do any good for Nora to know you were coming here on your own; she'd only start wondering." She sprinkled some pepper on her eggs. This was one relationship she didn't want her grandmother wondering about, because any conclusions she came to would only upset her. "I can't wait to taste the pralines. No one makes them as good as Grandma." Megan knew she wasn't the only one who felt that way; in Baton Rouge her grandmother was famous for her pecan caramels. "I haven't spoken to her since I left. She still doesn't know anything about us." Megan might not be ashamed of her feelings toward Marc, but she didn't want her grandmother to know about them. "Unless you've said something . . . or your parents."

"No." Marc broke off a piece of toast. "What's between us is just between us."

"Your father doesn't think so," Megan said, forking up some eggs.

"Forget about my father." He bit into his toast. "He can't hurt us anymore."

"You don't really believe that, do you? Your father's denunciation bothered me a hundred times more than Regis Winthrop's."

"He's my father, Megan. No matter what he says, no

matter what he does, he's still my father. Nothing can change that." He placed the toast at the side of his plate and wiped his hands on the napkin.

"Exactly, nothing can change that," Megan said thoughtfully. "He'll always be your father." Nibbling on a crust of toast, she remembered how cruelly vindictive Louis had been when he'd called her an uncontrollable liar, worthless trash. No matter what Marc said about working things out, his father would never accept her, never stop trying to hurt her.

Marc's brows knit into his Groucho leer. "Here I am sharing an intimate meal with a beautiful woman and we're talking about my father." He crumpled his napkin, placed it on the table and cleared his throat. "There's got to be something wrong with that. Do you think we could change the subject?" Reaching across the table, he covered her hand with his. "I know we have problems, darling, but let's not look for them, not tonight."

Megan smiled as Marc's hand stroked lovingly over hers. She didn't want to look for problems, but they were still there. Two weeks before, at the lake, Marc had been the one who said they had to talk things out. Now he had changed his mind and didn't want to discuss their problems. Of course, he knew as well as she how his father felt about her and he wasn't about to risk a confrontation. Well, her relatives might not have the Fremonts' social standing, but at least they weren't abusive; she could ask about them. "How are my grandmother and Tim?" A nice safe topic, she decided. Marc was right; why destroy the intimacy of the evening by arguing about his father?

"Fine, although I still think Tim spends more time with his roses than he does with Nora. That greenhouse is his prize possession." Circling her hand, he lifted it from the table and brushed his thumb across her knuckles. "But then I guess it's different with people their age, although my feelings for you seem to grow stronger with each passing moment. I don't think age is ever going to make a difference, not to us."

Silently Megan agreed. She'd never tire of him. The tiny shivers racing up her spine convinced her of that. How could Marc's touch mean so much to her? Affect her so greatly? He was just a man like any other man, but to her, somehow, he was different. An almost imperceptible sigh escaped her lips as Marc smiled knowingly.

They spent the rest of the meal talking about Nora and Tim; Megan was surprised to find how close Marc was to her grandmother. Apparently Nora felt comfortable enough with him to ask him to carry a tin of pralines to New York, and he liked her too much to refuse, even though most men in his position would have considered the role of their housekeeper's delivery boy an affront to their dignity. And then there was his thoughtfulness in bringing her the chair. A pleasurable warmth flowed through Megan as she studied Marc over the rim of her coffee cup. This newly discovered aspect of his personality was one she had never before considered.

The relaxed chitchat over their pralines and coffee reminded Megan of the conversations they had had at the bayou after they had satisfied the intense physical desire that always seemed to flare whenever they saw each other. She smiled to herself—that powerful attraction hadn't diminished, nor had the sense of comfortable understanding she experienced whenever she spoke with Marc. If we were married, we could always be like this, she thought, her eyes darkening with secret longing. She wanted to be with him, never wanted him to leave. If only Marc could stay in New York . . . if only.

"Meggie?" Marc asked, his hand tightening, fingers stroking over hers. "What's wrong, darling?"

"It's nothing," she said. "Nothing really important."
But a sad, knowing smile lingered on her lips. She knew
her feelings for Marc would never change, but neither
would Marc. He was a Fremont first and everything
else, including her love, was secondary. So, there could
never be any future in their relationship. They had
lived in two different worlds and become people who
could never merge because their backgrounds had
shaped them so differently.

After cleaning the kitchen, they returned to the
joyous comfort of the bedroom, but this time they
didn't make love. They just slept, wrapped in the
contentment of each other's arms, and for Megan this
reassuring cuddling was as intimately rewarding as their
passionate lovemaking.

The alarm buzzed, breaking into Megan's dream of
Marc and New York and forever. She mumbled, pulled
the blanket over her head, then reached out to shut off
the alarm. Poking her face out of the cover, she opened
one eye and peered at the digital clock in the radio
alarm on her night table. Six o'clock. It couldn't be, not
already. But it was. Turning toward the window, she
could see the slivers of dawn edging around the sides of
the white louvered blinds. She didn't want to get up
yet; she felt too comfortable. Shifting away from the
edge of the bed, she burrowed her face deeper into the
pillow and stretched languidly. Her bare skin felt sleek
and voluptuous against the fine pink cotton sheet, and a
delicious contentment enveloped her entire being. She
couldn't remember ever feeling quite this wonderful.

Then as she closed her eyes to savor once again the
comforting solace of the moment, she realized that
nothing had really changed. True, she had reveled in
Marc's passion, discovered new dimensions to his personality and had even wished that this new aspect of
their relationship could achieve the permanency of

marriage. But that was just a fanciful dream. Of all the amorous words Marc had whispered in the darkness of the night, not one of them had even hinted at love or marriage, nor had he made the slightest attempt to apologize for his father or say that anything would be different in the future.

She had been so determined not to become involved with Marc again, yet when he touched her, all her steadfast resolutions melted beneath the heated frenzy of their passionate embraces. Was she a fool to respond so eagerly? When he mentioned permanency, was he asking her to become his mistress? Was he using her as Jack Adams had used June? Did he think of her merely as a casual bedmate he had yet to get out of his system or did he truthfully feel something deeper? She needed reassurance, needed to know how he really felt about her.

The musky scent of Marc's cologne drifted up from the pillow, bringing with it erotic memories that started a blushing warmth racing through her body. She smiled and, without opening her eyes, moved closer to the center of the bed, seeking his comforting strength. He reached out and enclosed her in his arms.

"Good morning, love," he said, moving over her and lightly kissing the tip of her nose.

"Good morning," she said softly. He kissed her fingertips, then pressed them against his lips. How wonderful to wake up to Marc's intoxicating caresses.

"You know this is the first night we've spent together," Marc said. "Have I told you how wonderful it is to wake up and find you next to me?" He gazed at her, tenderly yet passionately; and as his body glided over hers, his intentions were clear.

Megan shared his sentiments. There was only one problem; she didn't have the time. "Marc." She pressed her palms against his chest, firmly but gently pushing him away. "I can't. Not now." She squirmed beneath him, avoiding the kisses he dropped on her cheek, her chin, her neck, her breasts. "Please, Marc, stop. I have to get up; I have to go to work."

"Later," he murmured, catching her wrists in one hand and lifting her arms over her head. "Right now we've more important things to do."

"No, Marc." She squirmed and tried to pull her arms free. "I mean it, Marc. I have to get up. I have an eight o'clock conference." She turned her face toward the mattress and wedged her shoulder between them. "Come on, Marc, stop it; let me go."

Marc released her and sat up, pulling the sheet around his waist. His tanned chest throbbed to the racing beat of his heart. His excitement was obvious. "You're serious, aren't you?"

"Very," Megan said, sitting up and reaching for her robe at the end of the bed. "I promised Jerry I'd be in his office at eight o'clock." She swung her feet off the bed. "He has another meeting at ten."

Marc grasped her wrist, pulling her back to him. "So call him and tell him that something came up and you can't make it. There's no rush with the article; in fact, I don't want it coming out too soon."

"I can't do that, Marc. My job is important to me. I've never canceled a meeting before."

"Have you ever done anything like this before?" Marc questioned, his eyes dark with longing. "I mean, is *this* something you do all the time?"

She didn't answer, but when she lowered her head and turned away, Marc released her and swung his legs off the mattress.

"Look, you don't understand." Sitting up beside him, Megan pressed her lips against his back.

Marc flinched from her touch. "I understand perfectly," he said, taking his trousers from the apricot silk chair beside the bed and sliding into them. "We shared something beautiful last night, something that was very important to me, something we have to talk about, but you don't have time; you have to get to work."

"I have no choice, Marc."

"You have a choice. The truth is you've made it, several times, in fact; I've just been too bullheaded to accept it." He slipped his arms into his shirt and, without buttoning it, stormed out of the room. A few moments later the apartment door slammed.

"Marc," she called, "please let me explain." She ran to the door, opened it and peered out into the hall. Deserted, silent except for the wheeze of the elevator carrying Marc away.

She closed the door, chained it, locked the two locks. What was the point, she thought, Marc wasn't there; he had already gone, and without him the apartment seemed empty. Yet he would have stayed . . . if she had forgotten her professional responsibilities and canceled the morning's appointment, he would have stayed. But she couldn't. Much as she loved and wanted Marc, she wanted her job too. She had to be truthful: She wanted everything; she wanted it all.

At seven forty-five, wearing a tan corduroy blazer, a gray pleated skirt and an emerald-green silk blouse, she swept through *Commerce World* magazine's revolving glass doors; three minutes later she entered Jerry's oak-paneled office.

"Megan, sweetheart, it seems like you've been gone forever." Jerry left his desk and smothered her in an overpowering bear hug. "Good to have you back."

"I missed you too," Megan said, kissing him on his bearded cheek. "It's good to be back." Truthfully, she felt more at home at *Commerce World* magazine than she did anywhere else. Here she was the person she wanted to be and here her professional achievements were valued and appreciated.

"Okay," Jerry said, releasing her. "Enough of the

amenities. Let's get down to business. Show me what you've done." Unbuttoning his cuffs, he rolled up his sleeves. His arm seemed bony, his skin too white, as Megan compared Jerry's Manhattan pallor with Marc's muscled tan. "Hey." He snapped his fingers. "Come on, kid, get with it. Stop daydreaming, vacation time is over."

"Vacation, hmm, is that what you think I've been doing?" She waved her manuscript under his nose. "How'd you like to see my itinerary? A hospital facility for children, a malodorous chemical plant, an FDA hearing—writing twenty-four hours a day . . . some vacation." She slumped into one of the brown vinyl armchairs in front of Jerry's desk. "In fact I was thinking of asking for some time off as soon as I finish this assignment." She needed to get away, to do some thinking about Marc, about her, about them.

"Oh? Planning to go somewhere special?"

"I don't know. I thought I might go to India and see Elaine." She named her former roommate, Elaine Akron, who had married an Indian journalist and now lived in New Delhi. "She's been inviting me for months, you know."

"Hmm, got the traveling bug, have you? Larry mentioned that he saw you in Washington." Jerry clasped his hands behind his neck and leaned against his desk.

"Umm," Megan nodded, "he wondered what I was doing there . . . thought I might be cutting into his territory." Why was Jerry mentioning Larry? His nonchalant attitude didn't fool her at all. He never wasted questions; there was a reason for everything he said and did. "I assured him he had nothing to worry about, at least from me."

"Larry also mentioned Fremont and a little incident with Regis Winthrop." Returning to his chair, Jerry picked up a pencil and began idly twirling it between his fingers. "Seems the restaurant fracas topped last week's local gossip charts."

Megan shrugged. "You know about Regis. He never has forgiven me, probably never will."

"I do indeed, but what about Fremont?"

"What about him?"

"Larry said he seemed quite possessive, real macho he-man stuff, and that your relationship just might be a bit more"—he made an undulating movement with his hand—"than casual." Jerry combed his fingers through his sandy hair, adding to its already tousled state. He was one of those people who started the day looking rumpled and finished it looking worse.

"So?" What was Jerry getting at? She'd known him for five years, and until now his most intimate inquiry into her personal life had been, "Did you have a good weekend?"

"So I was wondering," Jerry said, leaning forward across his desk, "if your more-than-casual relationship might interfere with your assignment. Are you, by chance, too involved with Fremont to write an impartial article?"

Standing, Megan walked to the desk and glowered down at Jerry. "Are you questioning my professionalism, my competence?" Flak from Jerry was the last thing she needed now. Her nerves hadn't yet recovered from her early morning bout with Marc.

Completely unperturbed, Jerry looked up at her. "I'm questioning your relationship with Fremont."

Megan backed away and crumpled into her seat. She should have known better than to try to intimidate Jerry; people far more menacing than she had drowned in the attempt. "My personal relationship with Marc Fremont won't influence my article in any way."

"That's all I wanted to know," Jerry said, dropping

the pencil onto the desk and holding up his hands. "You realize that we can't afford to show any favoritism, not with the all-out battle that's brewing between Fremont and Nessac. I don't want *Commerce World* caught in the middle. If our motives are questionable, we lose our credibility, and in this business, that's everything."

"There won't be any problem," Megan assured him, "no problem at all."

"Fine," Jerry said, "now let's get down to work." He picked up her manuscript and began thumbing through it.

They worked on the manuscript for two hours, during which time Jerry made suggestions about some areas he thought should be expanded and others that had to be cut.

"Good stuff," he said, "plenty of meat. The Las Vegas presentation should wrap it up, and then we'll pull it all together."

When Jerry dashed off to his ten o'clock meeting, Megan returned to her own office. Office? Ha, cubicle was a more fitting description, she decided as she entered the nine-by-nine room with its gray-green plywood and white frosted-glass walls. Still, she loved every crowded inch of it, and pride glowed within her each time she saw her nameplate on the door.

Once seated behind her desk, she started checking through the mail she had received during the two weeks she had been away. A letter from the author of a computer sales book thanking her for a good review. Some advertisements. Research information she had requested. Bills. New books to be considered for review. She read over the advertisements, saved some, tossed most into the wastebasket, checked the bills against her credit card vouchers and earmarked them for the accounting department. Then she began thumbing through the books. It was good to be back, good to be in her own office, surrounded by familiar things, familiar people.

Sighing pleasurably, she took out the article and began considering the changes Jerry had suggested. Although she agreed with most of them, there were a few about which she wasn't so certain. Deciding that she'd have to review her notes, she took out her tape recorder and began listening to the tape she had made after the FDA hearing.

When she was midway through the tape, the phone rang. Pressing the flashing red button, she answered it. "Hello."

"Meeting over?" Marc asked, a layer of southern silk coating the underlying sarcasm in his voice.

"Yes, I told you that Jerry had another meeting at ten o'clock." Why was he calling? She hoped that he wasn't going to start badgering her again. Still, it was good to hear his voice, to know that he wasn't as angry as she had supposed.

"You did, didn't you? That's why I waited to call." He hesitated for a moment, and when she remained silent he continued. "What are you doing now?"

"Working." She toyed with the telephone's coiled wire, stretching then releasing it.

"I'm at my broker's now. I'll be leaving in a few minutes. Will you have lunch with me?"

Megan considered his invitation. The emotional part of her wanted to have lunch with Marc, but the professional side wanted to get on with her work. "I don't know, Marc. I have so much to do."

"You have to eat, don't you? Or have you given that up too, as part of your new professionalism?"

"Of course not, it's just . . ." Oh well, she had tried to say no, hadn't she? "All right, where and what time?"

"I'll make reservations and pick you up in about half an hour."

Megan checked her watch. "Eleven-thirty. I'll meet you downstairs. You know the building? In Rockefeller Center?"

"Right. See you then." The line went dead.

Megan clutched the silent receiver for a few seconds, then hung up. Why did Marc have to keep making snide remarks about her work, acting as if she were wrong to place such importance on it? Couldn't he see how much it meant to her?

"Megan?" A young brunet hitched her horn-rimmed glasses higher on her nose and peered through Megan's open door. "Got a minute?" She straightened the collar of her denim jumpsuit.

"Just about. Come on in, Lucy." Lucy Baldwin was this year's fellowship student, and Megan had become her mentor. "What's up?" Megan motioned her to the gray vinyl armchair beside her desk.

Lucy shook her head and remained standing. "Jerry's letting me do this book review." She held up a paperback advance copy. "And, well, to tell you the truth, it's absolute drivel—total nonsense, a complete rip-off."

Megan smiled to herself. Only an idealistic nineteen-year-old scholarship student could get so incensed over a book entitled *Charting the Markets*. "You didn't like it," she said.

"It's nothing, not one new idea, just a bunch of meaningless charts taken from other sources." Standing beside Megan, she began flipping through the pages. "See what I mean? Not one original idea. And they're charging twenty-five dollars. It's a rip-off, a complete rip-off."

"Well," Megan said, "you can't say that, not in those words, I mean."

Lucy picked up the book and plopped into the chair. "I can't say that, not in any words. I have to give it a good review."

"A good review? After what you've said about it? How on earth can you?" Megan eyed Lucy quizzically; something more than youthful idealism was bothering the young girl.

"The author is a friend of Jerry's. A very good friend, if you get my drift."

Megan leaned across the desk and peered at the author's name. Ariel Logan. Good friend, indeed; current mistress was a more accurate description. What a sneaky thing for Jerry to do, Megan thought, laying this book on a neophyte like Lucy. "I see what you mean," she said, smiling. "Still, you have to be truthful. Jerry wouldn't want you to lie. Our readers come first."

"But what about my job? I can't tick Jerry off. I was counting on working here after I graduate. Like you."

Megan was too fond of Lucy to let her get herself into a nervous uproar by trying to please Jerry, Ariel, and her own conscience. "Not even Jerry can argue with the facts," she said, rolling a sheet into her typewriter. "Pull your chair over here and I'll show you how to write a completely objective book review that tells the reader not to waste his money."

They had finished a page and a half of rough copy when the phone buzzed.

"Get that, will you?" Megan asked Lucy. She continued typing while Lucy reached for the receiver.

"Miss Mahlar's office," Lucy said, then listened for a moment. "It's Fran at the reception desk. There's a man down there. Marc Fremont. Says he has an appointment with you."

"Oops." Megan checked her watch. Eleven-forty. "I forgot all about it."

"Fran wants to know if she should send him up."

"Yes, please. I'm ten minutes late already." She switched off her typewriter and turned to Lucy who had just hung up the phone. "When is this due?"

"ASAP."

"As soon as possible," Megan translated. "One of those, hmm? And Jerry doesn't like to be kept waiting."

Lucy nodded in agreement.

"Look, I have this lunch date that I just can't break, but I'll make it fast." She checked her watch. "Say half an hour. Then we'll get back on this thing, get it finished in a couple of hours and you can have it on Jerry's desk first thing in the morning."

"Gee, thanks, Megan, I really appreciate this. . . ." Lucy's voice trailed off as she looked toward the doorway and saw Marc, handsome as ever in a camel's hair sport jacket and dark brown pants.

A fresh, open-necked white silk shirt accentuated his tan. Obviously he'd gone back to his hotel after leaving Megan. "Hi," he said. "Sorry to interrupt, but we did have an eleven-thirty luncheon date, didn't we?"

"We did," Megan agreed, reaching for her tan corduroy blazer and her beige leather shoulder pouch. "Unfortunately, Lucy and I got sidetracked on a tricky project." She smiled apologetically. "Lucy Baldwin." She motioned toward Marc. "Marc Fremont."

"Hello," Marc said, flashing a Rhett Butler smile and offering Lucy his hand. "I'm very pleased to meet you."

"Hi," Lucy replied, her complexion pinking beneath his warm gaze.

Megan smiled to herself, feeling she could read Lucy's lovesick thoughts—envy, desire, adoration. Marc was still the physical embodiment of the dark-haired prince every young girl fantasied about.

"So this is where you work," Marc said, surveying the tiny office.

His tone was so openly condescending that for a moment Megan wanted to say that the office was only temporary, that she'd be moving to larger quarters as soon as the decorators had finished. Stop it, she warned herself. Stop letting him twist you in circles; stop trying to make yourself into something you're not just to please him. Two minutes ago you loved this place and now . . . "It's not very much, but it's all mine," Megan quipped arrogantly.

"Mmm," Marc said thoughtfully.

For a brief moment, Megan didn't know whether it was an impressed "mmm" or a critical "mmm." Definitely a critical "mmm," she decided. True, her office wasn't nearly as elegant as his, but then she wasn't chairman of the board. "Would you like a short tour?" Maybe if he saw how much individual effort went into each issue of *Commerce World*, he'd understand her dedication.

"Very much," Marc said, "after all, you're thoroughly familiar with where I work."

"Thoroughly," Megan agreed, motioning him out of the office.

"I'll see you later," Lucy said.

"Count on it," Megan replied.

"Nice meeting you, Lucy," Marc said.

"Likewise." Once again the freckles on Lucy's cheeks were bathed in a pink background.

Megan gave Marc the five-star tour—editorial offices, art department, accounting, advertising; and everywhere she introduced him, she noticed those same envious stares. No doubt about it, Marc Fremont was an attractive man, in New York as well as Louisiana.

"We'd better be going," Marc said, after about fifteen minutes. "I've made twelve o'clock reservations at Armand's." He seemed bored and totally unimpressed with anything she had shown him.

"Oh, Marc, I can't possibly go to Armand's," she

said, picturing the measured elegance of the exclusive French restaurant. "They take forever and I promised Lucy I'd be back in half an hour."

Marc's lips pressed tautly together and a telltale muscle throbbed in his jaw, but he turned to a copy editor at a nearby desk, asked to use the phone and canceled their lunch reservations. "Where would you like to go?" he asked, leading her to the elevator.

"There's an outdoor café in the lower plaza where we can get a quick sandwich," Megan said, stepping into the elevator.

"If that's what you want." He jabbed the lobby button, his brusque manner indicating that the outdoor café wasn't what he wanted.

The elevator descended quickly, and they exited at the lobby. Marc slipped his arm around her waist and propelled her toward the glass doors opening onto the street. "Lead on," he said. "This is your town, your game." His cynical tone left no doubt that he felt Megan was being unreasonable.

"Look, Marc, try to understand." She halted in the middle of the lobby in an attempt to emphasize her point.

Another elevator door slid open and three dark-suited businessmen exited and excused themselves as they swerved to the right to avoid Megan and Marc.

"I am trying," said Marc in a voice loud enough for anyone nearby to hear. "I've been trying ever since I saw you at Nora's wedding, but every time I think our relationship has reached a level of some importance, you show me exactly how wrong I am and I explode, like this morning when that damned alarm went off and you hopped out of bed like a rabbit who's seen a fox."

The three men paused at the door—they had heard Marc's outburst. They eyed Megan, up, down and up again. After several seconds they grinned sheepishly and left.

She flushed at the appraising, knowing stares of the men—at what they were surely thinking. She turned away. "Please, Marc, let's go." Why did she always feel this shame whenever she was with Marc? Why couldn't she accept their relationship as openly as he did?

"Sorry," Marc said, "I didn't mean to embarrass you." He led her through the glass doors out onto the tree-lined ramp leading to the sidewalk.

You may not mean it, Megan thought, but somehow it always happens.

They strode past an atrium with tall maple trees and a fountain at its center. Most New Yorkers were so wrapped up in their own thoughts or conversations that they hurried by without even glancing at the colorful garden displays that changed seasonally. Only the tourists stopped to admire the scenery and snap photos.

"It's all right," she said. "If I can take Regis Winthrop, I should be able to tolerate a few fraternity-house leers."

"You shouldn't have to take any of it."

She looked at him and arched an eyebrow.

"All right," he said. "I'll try to see things your way. Dammit, Meggie, I'm always exploding at you, then two minutes later I want you back. It's getting to be a habit."

Megan smiled, but said nothing. Marc had become her unquenchable addiction years ago.

They approached the corner and blaring car horns drowned out her words as a yellow taxi cut around a red sportscar.

"How can you stand this?" Marc said as passersby jostled and crowded them against the side of a building.

"You get used to it. Truthfully, I hardly even notice the crowds anymore."

She sidestepped a bearded young man wheeling two huge cartons toward a delivery entrance. "Ah, here we are." She pointed to the outdoor tables in the lower plaza where in cooler weather skaters breezed over the ice. Megan usually tried to avoid their cheerful images. To her, ice would always signify pain.

They sat at a table near the edge of the rink. Tourists strode by, pointing at the buildings, the gardens, the statuary and a carefully arranged semicircle of music stands and chairs. The café was crowded, streaming with out-of-town visitors and plaza workers on their lunch breaks.

Marc ordered two coffees. Megan had an egg salad sandwich; Marc had ham and cheese.

"So," Marc said, "how'd your meeting go?"

"Fine. Jerry had some good suggestions. He usually does." She curled her hand around her coffee cup. "How was your session with your stockbroker?"

"Very profitable. I got most everything I wanted." He grinned intriguingly. "I think some people are in for a very unpleasant surprise."

"Oh, something I should know about for my article?"

"Soon, but not yet, not quite yet."

The café tables were filling rapidly. Megan watched a young couple wearing matching chino shorts and white T-shirts sit down at the next table. The boy leaned forward, ruffled the girl's long blond hair and kissed her lightly on the cheek. A caring, sharing love that created for them their own private world. Megan envied their closeness, their need for one another. Feeling like an intruder, she turned away. Marc's eyes met hers as he reached across the table and covered her hand with his. For a moment she felt as if their thoughts were merging, memories of the bayou, of the cottage at Lake Pontchartrain, and just the night before at her apartment. There were times when they too were alone, deliriously happy in their own private world.

"Meggie, I have to go back to New Orleans tonight. Come with me."

Megan pulled her hand free, fingered a pink paper sugar packet and tapped it on the table. "I can't, you know I can't."

"Why not? Because of that damned job? Is that what's so important to you? How can that be?" He pulled the packet out of her hand and tossed it on the table. "Good God, it's such a nothing situation, no prestige at all; my dressing room's bigger than that cell you call your office."

Megan stared at him and shook her head. When he spoke so disparagingly of her work, something deep within her tore and broke apart—her love, crumbling beneath the pressure of his disdain. Looking at his cruelly arrogant face, she couldn't find the slightest trace of the man who had held her in his arms the night before. How could she love a man who didn't respect her, who didn't value the work that was such an important part of her life?

"There's more to a room than just its size . . . people, the work that's done." Without waiting for his response, she turned away and watched as four men carrying instrument cases walked to the music stands near the statue of Prometheus.

"I'm not the only one who judges a position's importance by the office it's given. *Commerce World*'s president doesn't work in a two-by-four cubicle."

The string quartet began tuning up, a grating, cacophonous sound that punctured Megan's thoughts. "Then what you're saying is that Nora and Tim aren't nearly as important as your parents. . . . After all, a small gardener's cottage can't measure up to Fremont Oaks."

"Dammit," Marc said, shifting his chair closer to the table as some children scampered past to join the crowd gathering near the musicians. "Stop twisting my words. You know that's not what I mean."

"Unfortunately," Megan said, "I think that's exactly

what you mean." She pushed back her chair and stood. "It's what your father meant; you were raised by him, why should you be any different?"

"So," Marc said, moving to her side. "If I'm like my father, then you must be like your mother. Is that what you're saying?"

Megan's hands tightened into fists that pressed against her hips. She wouldn't slap him, wouldn't make a scene. "Oh, Marc, how could you? How could you?" Her voice broke as she snatched up her handbag and strode quickly away, despising herself for breaking down and letting Marc know how much his remark had hurt her.

"Meggie." Marc fumbled in his pocket, placed some bills on the table, then started after her and grabbed her arm. "I'm sorry, I never should have said that. It's just that I hate when you compare me to my father. I'm not like him; you have to believe me." He brushed his hand across her cheek, then through her hair. "And I've never compared you to your mother. You know that, don't you? It was a cruel thing for me to say, but I guess I just wanted to hit back at you, to hurt you the way you'd hurt me." Two teenage girls walked by, bumped into Marc, mumbled, "Excuse me," and then looked back, giggling. Marc muttered beneath his breath and, still holding Megan, ducked into the deserted delivery entrance of a gray granite skyscraper. "Will you forgive me, please?"

Megan shook her head. There was so much to forget, so much to forgive. Their backgrounds, their lives, everything about them was so different, and yet . . .

"Meggie, don't do this to me, say something."

"There's nothing more to say, Marc. You said it all. Our lives are different, we think differently; an unmatched pair, that's us."

"Unmatched? You can't mean that. Not after last night."

"What was so special about last night?" Megan tried to affect a casualness she didn't feel, but what was the point of prolonging a hopeless situation? "We're two unmarried adults. These things happen. We haven't harmed anyone." Not wanting to think about how much she loved him, she tried to block what she was saying and strained to hear the music from the string quartet, but even their melodious tones couldn't soothe her anguished heart.

"That's right," Marc agreed. "We're both adults now and last night didn't harm anyone. . . . In truth, it was more beautiful than ever because you told me you loved me," he whispered softly, framing her face with his hands. "Last night you told me you loved me." Placing his thumb under her chin, he lifted her face toward his. "The truth, Megan, were you telling the truth? Were you?"

His eyes reflected the pain she was feeling, and she couldn't be falsely casual, couldn't lie anymore, not even to salvage her pride. "Yes," she whispered. "I love you, Marc. I've always loved you . . . ever since that very first time . . . I've never stopped."

"Thank God," he said, dipping his head and grazing his lips over hers. "Then you'll forget about this magazine nonsense and come home with me."

Forget about the magazine? Come home with him? She couldn't. She might love him, but other things in her life mattered too. Eight years ago she had been forced to forget Marc and concentrate on her career. Although she had never really forgotten him, her career had become very important to her and she couldn't give it up, not now. "I can't, Marc, I just can't." She pressed her hands against his chest and looked up at him, realizing that it was futile to deny her feelings for him, but at the same time determining to resist them since so much more was at stake.

"Why not? If you love me?" Catching her hands in

his, Marc brought them to his lips. "Don't you know how I feel about you? How I've always felt? Why is your job so important?" Bending her fingers over his, he kissed the curve of her knuckle. "I was a fool to blow up in Washington. I should have kept you with me."

"No, you couldn't. This is where I belong, where I have a life of my own, a career."

"But if you want to be with me . . ."

"Not in Louisiana. Why don't you stay here?" she asked, voicing the thought that had been simmering in her mind. But even as she spoke, she knew he wouldn't consider her suggestion. Louisiana was a part of him, his heritage of life, the heritage that would always keep them apart.

"Don't be ridiculous," Marc said, releasing her hands and stepping back. "You know I can't do that. My family, the company, everything that matters to me is back there."

"Exactly," she said, keeping her composure despite her aching heart. "Everything that matters to you." Everything that I hate, she thought. "Good-bye, Marc. I did love you. I never lied to you about anything." She turned and began walking rapidly back to her office, hoping that he would follow her, hoping that he would say—say what? She herself didn't know, because at that moment their worlds were farther apart than they had ever been.

Marc didn't follow and Megan, despite her turmoil, spent the rest of the day working on Lucy's book review and the changes in her article. By nine o'clock that night, when she finally left her office, both features were shaping up nicely.

The next morning she checked with the art department and asked them to send a photographer to Louisiana. There were some photos she definitely wanted to highlight her article. After making the corrections Jerry had suggested, she checked back with him.

"Great," he said. "I think it reads much better this way. Now all you have to do is get the scoop from Vegas and we'll be ready to roll."

"That's right," Megan agreed, "the scoop from Vegas will tie everything up. After this weekend I'll be all finished with Marc Fremont."

Chapter Ten

L as Vegas was the last place in the world Megan would have chosen for a security analysts' convention. After all, these research experts earned their living trying to convince investors that buying stocks was a science and not a gamble. Yet when the bellman took her luggage and led her through the lobby to the elevators, she noticed some comforting similarities to the world of finance: The hotel's atmosphere was no less frenzied than the stock market's, and the blackjack players studied the cards just as intently as brokers charted the fluctuating Dow.

Slot machines clattered everywhere, in the brightly lighted casino, the red velvet lobby, the noisy corridors, even in the lounges. Megan half expected to see a row of them standing imposingly in her room, but she was gratified to discover a differently sybaritic decor dominated by a white-satin-covered circular bed resting on a raised platform. Flocked wallpaper in a feathery lilac and gold design covered the walls, and lavender brocade draperies shut out the Strip's neon world.

She kicked off her shoes, shrugged out of her jacket and unbuttoned her blouse while walking into the mirrored dressing room. The trip in from New York had made her feel grubby and creased. She'd have to shower and change because she had dinner reservations for eight o'clock. She checked her watch. Six. Still plenty of time. She unzipped her skirt, changed into her maroon silk caftan and turned on the gold-plated faucets in the sunken marble tub.

Packets of bath salts lined one corner of the marble vanity and Megan selected a lilac scent. She slipped into the bath, leaned back, and relaxed in the warm, fragrant water. The huge tub was actually a spa, and when she flipped a knob, air began bubbling through the sides and bottom of the smooth marble surface. "Mmm," she murmured contentedly, closing her eyes and sinking lower until the bubbles tickled her chin. "Luxury, sheer luxury." Scooping up a handful of bubbles, she blew them into the air and watched them float away. She felt pampered, voluptuous and very feminine. Inexplicably, her thoughts drifted to Marc.

Marc. The mere memory of his touch started a sensuous ache prickling deep within her. Had she been a fool to admit that she loved him? No, she told herself. He had to understand that what she felt for him was stronger than a fleeting sexual attraction. She couldn't deny that she loved him, but neither was she naive enough to believe that love conquered all, at least not in this instance when there were so many other problems to consider.

Marc's roots were at Fremont Oaks and he would flourish there, but for her it was poison; she would wither and die on the vine. Shivering at the prospect, she reached for a thick white towel from the heated rack at the side of the tub. She'd been so involved in her own thoughts that she hadn't realized the water had cooled. She'd have to get ready quickly if she wanted to be on time for dinner.

Late that afternoon, while she'd been registering, she'd met Linda Woldin, a Chicago commodities broker she'd known since college; they'd been delighted to see each other and had made reservations for the dinner show. Linda had warned her to be prompt because no food was served during the show.

Tossing the towel on the antique white dresser, she sat on the lavender velvet vanity bench and began pulling on her panty hose. Her nail caught in the nylon and a run shot up her leg. She crossed to the dresser, took out another pair and began pulling it on very carefully. She'd brought only two pairs with her, one to wear and one to wash. Now that she had snagged one, she'd need to buy another. No problem, she decided. She'd browse through the shopping arcade after dinner. There wasn't anything you couldn't buy in Vegas if you had the money.

Plush oyster carpeting pampered her toes as she opened the mirrored wardrobe and took out a lightweight, black knit dress with snug-fitting wrist-length sleeves and a V neck that buttoned down the front. Three gold chains of varying lengths and textures circled her neck and high-heeled black silk sandals lifted her legs attractively.

A small, secret smile tilted the corners of her mouth when she checked herself in the mirror. The supple fabric flowed loosely over her body, yet clung to and accentuated every curve between her shoulders and the mid-calf hem. Just a bit more color, she thought as she applied a touch of eye shadow. There, perfect. The striking black knit ,provided the ideal foil for her tousled auburn hair and vivid green eyes.

She had agreed to meet Linda in the dinner theater, and when she approached the maître d', he showed her to a small table on the third tier of a restaurant which had been built around a large, semicircular stage. Multi-armed brass chandeliers with star-shaped bulbs glowed from a glittery ceiling, and plush red carpeting covered the floor. Almost every table in the huge room was occupied, and a conversational roar combined with the clatter of china and silver to create a deafening crescendo.

"Hi," the slender, thirtyish brunet seated at the table said, peering at Megan over the top of the gold-rimmed glasses that had slipped halfway down her nose. "For a while there, I thought you weren't going to make it." She set her cigarette in the ashtray and held out her hand.

Megan returned Linda's handshake and sat down. "I took a bath and almost forgot to get out. Have you seen the tubs?"

"Um, sheer luxury, but then again, this whole place is fantasyland."

A slightly stout waiter in a short black jacket handed them menus and asked if they wanted cocktails. Both women ordered mineral water with a twist of lime.

"So, what have you been doing with yourself?" Linda asked.

"Well, right now I'm writing a feature on Fremont Industries. That's the main reason I'm here, although I will be covering some other sessions for *Commerce World.*"

"Fremont, hmm? The Nessac thing, isn't it?"

"That's right. The takeover attempt is a hot issue right now."

"As far as I'm concerned, the Fremonts deserve everything they get. Fremont Industries is a public company, but that family acts as if it were some sort of feudal kingdom. They haven't raised the dividend in years, and then there's that scam the old man tried to pull."

"Scam? What on earth do . . ."

Linda held up her hand to hush Megan when the waiter returned for their dinner order. Megan followed his suggestion and selected an endive salad with squab and wild rice. Linda, explaining that she was dieting, had a well-done hamburger patty, sliced tomatoes and cottage cheese.

"Well, this is just a rumor, mind you. The Fremonts were powerful enough to hush things up, and they're probably hoping it will stay that way, at least until they can sweep Nessac from their door. But if the DC grapevine holds true to form, the story will be all over Wall Street by next week. Anyway, I have a friend in Washington who's chummy with a guy from the SEC, and it seems they're investigating a particularly sweet deal of Louis's. Apparently he sold some stock at a profit three months ago, then bought it back last month . . . five points lower." She smiled and winked behind her brown-tinted lenses. "He reported the sale but not the buy-back. How's that for a scoop?"

"An illegal insider transaction." Megan's carefully controlled features concealed her inner surprise. "An SEC investigation." That was an unexpected scoop. Corporate officials like Louis Fremont had to report all stock purchases and sales to the SEC, and their profits had to be shared with the corporation so that the minority stockholders would benefit equally.

"You got it, kiddo, and a little scandal like this is just the break Nessac has been waiting for. Papa Bear stoking his own fortune while the minority shareholders aren't even collecting decent dividends. Fremont stock will plummet and Nessac will be able to make a tender offer for a fraction of what it's worth." She sat back and fumed as the waiter set their dinner plates in front of them.

And very few people have any idea of how much Fremont Industries is actually worth, Megan thought to herself. All that cash from recent land sales just sitting there. Once the word got out, Nessac wouldn't be the only wolf huffing at the door. Every cash-hungry conglomerate would be clamoring to get in on the act. And she had all the information. Her feature would be a smash. *Commerce World* would scoop everybody. Slicing into her squab, she wondered what Louis Fremont would have to say about breeding when he was brought up on stock manipulation charges. Then she thought of Marc, and somehow the prospect of revenge wasn't nearly as exhilarating as she had expected it to be.

Having said what she had to say, Linda lost interest in the Fremonts and the two women spent the rest of the meal discussing how high the Dow would go by the end of the year and whether the unstable situation in the Mideast would affect the price of gold.

Megan enjoyed Linda's company and was so impressed by her financial expertise that she decided to ask Jerry if he'd consider letting her write a profile on Linda for a future issue. In Megan's opinion, commodities were too risky for most people and she respected Linda's policy of warning prospective buyers to evaluate their purchasing decisions carefully since they could easily lose their entire investment. During her career as a financial writer, Megan had met too many brokers who were more concerned about their own commissions than the investor's money, so she admired Linda's practical yet compassionate attitude.

They had finished dinner and were enjoying their coffee when the maître d' approached their table. "Miss Mahlar, Mr. Fremont would like to invite you and your friend to join him for an after-dinner drink at his table." He motioned to a first-tier banquette overlooking the stage where a smiling Marc nodded and waved to them.

"Well, speak of the devil," Linda said, looking

slightly perplexed. "I had no idea he was a friend of yours, or is this just because of that feature you're writing?"

"Both," Megan said. "My grandmother is his family's housekeeper." She nodded to Marc as she continued sipping her coffee. She couldn't see him, not now, not after what Linda had just told her about his father.

"And you're writing this article?" Linda looked even more perplexed. "Isn't that a sticky situation?"

"It's a long story." Megan's hands circled the white china cup as she placed it carefully on the table. She'd have the maître d' thank Marc and tell him that they were perfectly happy with their own table. "Too long to go in to now."

"I'll bet it is," Linda said, grinning. "Well, I never turn down a free drink, no matter who's buying." She pushed back her chair and stood. "Besides, those seats are much better than ours. I think we'd actually be close enough to see the performers' faces." Her smile broadened. "Or whatever."

There wasn't any way Megan could refuse to accompany Linda, so she followed quietly behind as the maître d' led them to Marc's table. For some reason, Megan had assumed that Marc would be alone, but when they approached the banquette, Louis Fremont, Jack Adams and Frank Dunston stood up. All the men wore tuxedos and Jack Adams' white shirt had a ruffled front. Forced smiles wreathed their faces and none of them seemed particularly happy to see Megan. Their expensively gowned wives remained seated, but their welcoming smiles seemed genuine.

However, once the introductions were completed their attitudes became so coolly indifferent that Megan decided she hadn't a friend among them. Rejection again. Her back stiffened in self-protection. She didn't need them; she didn't need anyone, not anyone at all.

"There are bound to be questions after my talk,"

Marc explained to Megan and Linda, "so I decided to take along some legal and financial help." He indicated Dunston and Adams. He helped Linda into the seat next to Cara Adams, seated Megan beside himself, asked what they'd like to drink, then ordered a coffee liqueur and a créme de menthe. His manners matched his attire—both were impeccable.

Jack Adams had his arm around his wife's shoulder, and Megan couldn't help thinking that if she didn't know better he'd appear to be the picture of a very devoted husband. As he adjusted Cara Adams' black lace shawl and whispered in her ear, Megan realized that his wife obviously hadn't the slightest inkling of her husband's long history of office affairs and probably trusted him implicitly. Adams had duped everyone. What a colossal creep, Megan thought, frowning as she watched his hypocritically solicitous behavior.

"Meggie, how nice to see you again," Denise Fremont said in a benevolent but patronizing voice. "And you're looking lovelier than ever. Nora must be so proud of you. Are you and your friend here on vacation?"

"No, as a matter of fact, we're both here for the convention," Megan stated briskly, her fingers curling on her lap.

"Oh?" Marc's mother lifted her eyebrow in surprise. "I thought Nora said you worked for a magazine. Isn't it *Vogue* or *Bazaar* or something like that?"

"No, dear," Louis Fremont said, patting his wife's hand and smiling snobbishly. "It's a financial journal . . . money, investments, commercialism. Hardly your type of reading."

Megan traced the small gold clasp on her black silk purse and tried to contain her resentment. *Hardly your type of reading.* What a pompous prig, she thought as she felt her blood begin to boil. Louis's condescending tone of voice seemed to imply that financial literature was too crass for his wife's delicate eyes. Damn the man. He was so smug, so sure of himself, and he always seemed to find a way to make her feel inferior. Her anger rose within her and she couldn't wait to write her story, tell about the insider sale, smear his despicable arrogance all over the front cover of *Commerce World*.

"No, I don't mind the weather in Chicago," Linda was saying. "From what I've heard, New Orleans rain is a good match for our wind. Besides, Chicago's where the commodities exchange is, so I couldn't work anywhere else."

The waiter returned with their drinks. "Last order," he said. "We don't serve during the show."

Louis ordered another round and then asked Linda her opinion of soybean futures as an investment. The other men listened attentively. Cara, Marc's mother and Elaine Dunston shifted their chairs and chatted with each other.

"So," Marc said, turning to Megan. "You're here for the convention. Will you be staying all three days?"

"That depends. I'm on a deadline and I may not be able to spare the time." At the center of the table, a thick white candle encased in a shield of amber glass flickered briefly, and Megan traced the shadows it cast on the red linen cloth.

"It seems I've heard that before. In fact, you never seem to be able to spare the time . . . when it comes to me, that is."

"Writing for a magazine is a demanding job, especially a financial journal. You can understand that. Today's money-making news is next week's confetti. Deadlines have to be met or we might as well not bother."

"But you seem to have time for everyone else, for June Clayson and that girl you were helping with a book review."

"Lucy." Megan nodded. "I like to help people."

"What about me?"

"You don't need my help. You've got all the help you could possibly use." She glanced at the three men chatting with Linda. "Far more than most people can afford."

"There are some things in life more important than business and work."

"More important than *my* business and *my* work; that's what you mean, isn't it, Marc? The same standards don't pertain to yours at all, do they?"

"Damn you. Listen to me." Marc's fingers bit into her arm as he turned her toward him. "Why must you be so pigheaded?"

"Pigheaded?" She stared at him defiantly. "I'm merely doing my job, Marc. Just as you're doing yours."

"I doubt that," he replied tersely, his lips barely moving.

"Exactly what is that supposed to mean? *Commerce World* doesn't pay me to just warm a desk, you know."

"Just how much do they pay you? Enough to give up everything else in life?" Marc snapped, his disdainful question whipping over her. "Judging by what I've seen, I sincerely doubt it."

Megan ignored him and sipped her liqueur. She was tired of defending her job to him. If he didn't understand its importance to her by now, he never would.

In the pit beneath them, the orchestra began tuning up, a whining, clanging jangle of strings and percussion. "I'm not finished with you," Marc stated, releasing her abruptly as the lights dimmed and the room grew silent. "We'll talk later." The music rose again, a soft, undulating mideastern melody punctuated by cymbals and drums. Marc's arm rested on the back of the seat, just above Megan's shoulder, where she was intensely aware of it.

The dinner show was billed as *Scheherazade's Fanta-*

sy, an Extravaganza of Love. The curtain opened to reveal a stage decorated like an ancient Arabian palace. Pink, turquoise and gold draperies hung between filigreed Moorish arches. Multicolored incense smoked from a row of brass hookahs assembled before piles of richly embroidered throw pillows. A unanimous "ah" rose from the audience.

The wavering music drifted between the vivid mist and spun around the room. Then the tempo increased and twenty bare-chested, sword-slashing male dancers wearing red fezzes bounded onto the stage and began doing a cartwheeling ballet. Their movements slowed when a darkly handsome man in a white headdress descended on an Oriental carpet.

It's beautiful, Megan thought as the men leaped across the stage and reclined on the pillows. Like something out of the *Arabian Nights* book I used to pore over as a child. The remembrance of those happy childhood hours brought a small, silent smile to the outer edges of her mouth.

The music slowed, became more undulating, the percussion farther apart. A line of ballerinas wearing opaque pastel veils and rows of gold coins pirouetted to the center of the stage, their hands rippling and torsos arching, beckoning to the men, then backing away. One tall brunet, clad completely in white, separated from the other women and swayed before the dark-haired man sitting cross-legged on the carpet.

The mist from the hookahs shrouded the stage in a gauze as colorful as the dancers' veils, and the ballerinas dipped and turned, weaving in and out of the fog, their gold coins jangling as their arms invited the men and then withdrew.

Tension rustled through the theater as the spectators shifted in their seats. The sensuality exuded by the music and the dancers mesmerized the audience, drawing them into the erotic scene being enacted on the stage. Megan arched her back and rotated her foot as if it had fallen asleep, while Marc dropped his arm, drawing her to him. Their thighs touched and his warm flesh seemed to burn through the barrier of their clothes, but Megan made no attempt to move away. She could barely breathe.

Lifting their veils to cover their faces, the ballerinas backed away from the men and edged toward the front of the stage. Megan's fingers tightened around her glass and she drained it, as if drinking the dark brown liquid could shatter the eroticism of the moment.

Marc's arm slipped lower, circling her waist; his hand rested lightly on her thigh, pressing it tightly against his own. The heat from his body passed through to her and she felt enveloped by passion, the music, the dancers, Marc.

The ballerinas circled at the front of the stage, their bodies swaying, arms waving in time to the music, beckoning to the men behind them and the audience in front of them. Megan closed her eyes and ran her tongue between her parted lips. She couldn't stay seated. The sensuous dance tugged at the core of her femininity and she wanted to kick off her shoes, wrap herself in a diaphanous robe and open her arms to the man she loved. She ran her fingers over the V at her neck, trying to loosen it and let some cool air dissipate the heat blazing through her veins.

"One day, I'd like to see you dance like that for me . . . just me," Marc whispered softly into her ear, pushing her hair back behind her ear and nuzzling his cheek against hers.

Megan straightened her back and shifted in her seat, her tense body aching with erotic desire. She sighed helplessly as Marc's fingers drifted to the open V of her neck, tracing its outline and making her skin tingle at his touch.

The others at the table, equally entranced by the show, saw and heard nothing but the music, the dancers and the private fantasies of their own imaginations.

"And when you do," Marc said, his other hand stroking slowly up her thigh until his palm flexed against her stomach, "I'll take off those veils, one by one. . . ." His voice deepened in a familiar promise. "Until at last there's nothing between us . . . only you . . . only me."

His words painted a picture in her mind and she could see herself standing before him, swaying, inviting. Her skin tingled with the expectation of his touch and she knew that if he kissed her now . . . if they were alone . . . Lifting her hands, she pressed her fingertips over his mouth to silence him. Marc stirred her sensuality as no other man ever could.

He kissed her fingertips, his tongue circling her nails lightly and dipping in between, his blue eyes darkening in passion. When she pulled her hand away and clutched it in her lap, he tightened his grip on her waist, smiled and repeated, "Just for me, Meggie, just for me."

She shivered at the warm sensuality in his voice and, turning toward the stage, tried to concentrate on the ballet, but she was uncertain of where the fantasy ended and she and Marc began. The music reached a deafening crescendo and the dancer in the white fez caught the prima ballerina's hand, drew her to him for a moment, then released her while she spun around him in a spiraling whirl that ended with her kneeling at his feet. Touching her hair tenderly, he swung her into his arms and carried her to the carpet.

"I want you, Meggie," Marc whispered. "I want you right now." His warm breath teased the shell of Megan's ear and he smiled confidently as she trembled with a yearning she couldn't control. Her body was pressed so close to Marc's—so intimately aware of his nearness—she found it impossible to tell where their separate flesh began or ended. "Do you have any idea of how much I want you?" he demanded, his voice husky with need. "Tell me, do you?"

An intensifying hunger pulsated deep within her and she tensed and quivered as she bit her lip to keep from crying out. Marc couldn't possibly want her any more than she wanted him.

The carpet lifted, circling the stage while the two dancers held each other tightly and waved to the audience. The music softened, the lights brightened and the audience, as if waking from a dream, rose to their feet and applauded. "Beautiful," Marc said. "Absolutely beautiful. The perfect way to begin an evening."

He stroked Megan's nape, turned her face toward his; and as their eyes met, she couldn't be sure if he meant Scheherazade's fantasy of love or the very personal fantasy he had drawn from the shadows of her mind. She remained seated and watched the crowd winding through the tables and heading toward the exits. Marc wasn't touching her any longer, but she could still feel the silent pressure of his body reaching out to claim her. *I want you, Meggie.* Once again she trembled in anticipation.

"I've never seen anything so utterly romantic," Cara Adams said. "That lovely dancing, those movements . . . When she knelt . . . why it makes me want to get married all over again." She kissed Jack on the cheek.

"Well, this is certainly the place to do it," Elaine said. "Did you notice all those chapels as we drove in from the airport?"

"Oh, dear, they're so tawdry," Mrs. Fremont said. "I can't imagine anyone I know getting married in a place like this."

"Don't worry, my dear," her husband said. "I'm quite sure no one you know ever will."

Frank Dunston checked his watch. "We'd better get a move on. We've got reservations for Wayne Newton's midnight show." Placing his arm around his wife's waist, he started moving toward the exit.

"Would you girls like to join us?" Cara Adams asked. "I'm sure there won't be any problem. Jack knows the manager."

"Sorry," Linda said. "I'll have to take a rain check. I've got an eight o'clock breakfast appointment with Phillip Rensaler. I've been trying to get a guest shot on his TV show for the past two years, so I can't afford to show up with a cottony brain." She joined the line heading toward the exit.

"Same for me," Megan said, eager to get away from Marc before she was trapped in the sensuous web he was weaving around her. "I'm too exhausted to sit through another show." A cold shower, that's what I need, she decided.

"I think I'll pass too," Marc said, his gaze moving over Megan in a possessive way that seemed to bare her thoughts as well as her body. "I've had enough of crowds for tonight."

"Well, let's plan to meet later in the lounge," Louis Fremont said.

Marc stopped to talk to his father while Megan joined the line leaving the dinner theater.

"Excuse me." A short round man wearing wire-rimmed glasses pushed in front of Megan and held her back while a group of his friends cut into the line.

Marc quickly grasped her waist to steady her, bringing her close to him. Held tightly to his chest and hips, she could feel the lean masculine strength of him pressing against her soft femininity. Too tempting, much too tempting. Closing her eyes as the touch of his body brought back memories she wanted to forget, she pulled away from him and slipped into a group near the back of the line.

When she finally reached the exit, Megan found herself surrounded by a throng of strangers. Stepping away from the crowd, she turned just in time to see Linda disappear into the elevator.

"Meggie," Marc called from the fountain at the center of the lobby.

For a fleeting moment she considered ignoring him, then she rejected that idea. Stop it, she ordered herself silently. You can't behave like a schoolgirl for the rest of your life. You'll have to learn to deal with Marc just as you've learned to deal with all your other problems. Smiling confidently, she waved back and waited until he had reached her.

"Can I buy you a drink? The lounge isn't too noisy now."

"Thanks, but I have to pick up something at one of the shops." She pointed to the wide, curving stairway that led to the shopping arcade. She'd buy the panty hose and return to her room—alone.

"I'll come with you if you promise to join me in the lounge afterward." He fell into step at her side.

"I don't think so, Marc. I'm really very tired." She shivered as they passed beneath an air-conditioning vent, not merely because of the cool air.

"Just one drink," he said. "I promise not to talk about our jobs or our families, and you can leave whenever you want." The air conditioning blew across his bluntly cut hair and a few black strands curled loosely over his forehead.

Without thinking, Megan brushed them back. "I'm sorry," she said, pulling away as if she had burned herself. She felt like kicking herself for what she had done, but it was almost a reflex action that she hadn't been able to stop.

"I'm not," he said softly. "I like when you touch me

and I like touching you." Marc gripped her wrist and slowly kissed her fingertips. "One drink," he murmured against her palm. "What harm can it do?"

Just one drink. He made it sound so casual, Megan thought. And why not? After all, as Marc had said, what harm could one drink do? "We'll see," she said, pulling away and continuing down the stairway. No matter how insecure she felt, she couldn't spend the rest of her life avoiding Marc.

The shopping arcade was the quietest place in the hotel since most people were busy losing their money upstairs and had very little to spend there. Megan's heels clicked over the marble floor as she glanced through the plate-glass windows. She needed only panty hose, but she couldn't resist the lavish displays.

"See anything you like?"

"Everything," she exclaimed, pausing to study a flowing white chiffon gown with thin rhinestone straps. She'd love to buy it, love to feel the luxurious fabric against her skin.

"Everything?" he repeated, a bright glow lightening the deep blue of his eyes.

"I love beautiful things," she said almost to herself. Beautiful feminine dresses to make up for years of cutoffs and hand-me-downs.

"So do I," Marc whispered, lifting her hair and caressing the nape of her neck. "Tell me what you like and I'll buy it for you . . . anything at all." He indicated the expensive gowns and lingerie.

Anything at all. Of course. Marc could buy anything he wanted. What a wonderful feeling that must be, she thought, remembering how carefully she had to budget her paycheck. If it weren't for the investments she had made based on Jerry's advice, she would never have been able to afford her apartment or the designer clothing she'd become addicted to. Still, she knew that all her earnings combined would never put her in

Marc's league, either financially or socially, because inherited wealth was in a class of its own. People just thought differently when they had been born to money and had never known what it was like to scrimp and save.

Suddenly she felt that Marc was telling her that if she forgot about *Commerce World* and returned to Louisiana with him, he'd buy her whatever she wanted—all the things *she* couldn't afford. Another put-down, another way of showing her how unimportant her job was. She'd rather die than accept a gift from him; rather be dead than admit her job was any less meaningful than his.

"Anything I want I can afford to buy for myself," she said belligerently. "I don't need your charity, not anymore."

"Charity?" For a brief moment Marc appeared stunned, then his complexion's hue deepened as he grabbed her shoulders and pressed her against the plate-glass window. "You little idiot. You've become so blind, so power hungry, that you can't even see what I'm trying to do." His fingers tightened for a minute, then he released her and strode away. "Oh, what's the use?"

"Marc, wait," she pleaded. He seemed so disgusted with her, so hurt; maybe she had misjudged his motives. It was all right for her to be upset with him, but she hated having him angry with her—she didn't deserve it.

"No. I'm through waiting. I've waited long enough. Eight years ago I felt like a heel for making love to you before you'd had a chance to experience life. Well, now you've done it all. You're grown up enough to know what you really want. So you make the choice, your career or me." He stared at her, waiting for an answer.

"I . . . I . . ." Looking into his dark eyes, she saw the reflection of her own image. The music from the fantasy spun through her mind and for a moment she longed to shut out the world, sway before him and kneel at his feet. No, that's all that was—a fantasy. This was the real world and if she knelt at Marc's feet, he'd walk all over her, then toss her away when he'd finished with her, leaving her with nothing. "I can't, Marc."

For a moment Marc was silent and his eyes searched her face as if her features might reveal some secret insight her words had concealed. "I see," he said, his voice deep and bitter. "I take it all back, Meggie. You haven't grown up at all." He shook his head. "People don't mean any more to you now than they did eight years ago." Then, without another word he trotted up the stairway. He held his body ramrod straight and he didn't bother to glance back at her.

Megan peered into the store window, but the tears in her eyes made window-shopping impossible. Marc's accusation had hurt her more than she cared to admit. How could he say that people didn't matter to her? She brushed a falling tear from her cheek. What had she ever done to hurt him, except insist that her career was as important as his heritage? She just couldn't understand his attitude.

Instead of buying only the panty hose, she wandered through the shop, looked at the lace-trimmed silk lingerie and found it irresistible. When she returned to her room forty-five minutes later, she had purchased a pleated seafoam nightgown, two beige satin teddies, a ruffled gray chiffon blouse and four pairs of panty hose. Impulse buying, but shopping was supposed to boost a woman's morale, she thought as she carried the boxes inside. Well, she had bought enough to rejuvenate three women. So why wasn't she happy? Why did she feel so utterly empty?

She tossed the shiny white boxes tied with gold ribbons on the bed and frowned. She knew she hadn't really needed anything except the panty hose, and had probably spent more than she could afford, but she always bought clothes when she was upset. In fact it had taken all her willpower to resist the flowing chiffon gown with the rhinestone straps.

Buying new clothes usually cheered her, she thought, clutching the nightgown to her neck and checking her reflection in the dresser mirror, but the way she felt now, acquiring the entire store wouldn't have cured her depression. And her miserable mood was entirely Marc's fault. She didn't like the accusations he kept hurling at her because they made her feel hard and insensitive, and she wasn't—she knew she wasn't.

She had changed into her maroon silk caftan and was running some water into the tub when a knock sounded at the door. When she answered it, a red-jacketed waiter carried in a large tray and set it on the voile-skirted table by the window. Marc followed behind him. His tie was off and the first few buttons of his light blue evening shirt were open.

"I didn't order anything," Megan protested, her eyes following his movements around the room.

"I did," Marc said, taking off his jacket and dropping it over the back of a lavender velvet chair. "Why don't you just leave everything," he told the waiter, handing him several folded bills and nodding toward the open door.

"Thank you, sir." The waiter palmed the bills and quietly closed the door.

"Marc, I don't know what you think you're doing, but . . ."

"You promised to have a drink with me, remember?"

"But you said . . ."

"I meant it all, every word of it. You're an obstinate little fool." He began uncorking the champagne the waiter had left. "But I'm a terrible loser, so why don't we have that drink you promised me and see what happens?" The cork popped and Marc poured the foaming liquid into the two chilled glasses beside a platter filled with cold hors d'oeuvres and petits fours.

"I never promised to have that drink."

"You never said no. Don't you remember, you said you'd think about it. I was the one who exploded and walked away. Well, I've had a change of heart. Why look for problems? Take what you can get." A confident smile curved the corner of his lips. "To a pleasant evening," he said, handing her one glass and lifting the other in a toast. "With no business discussions."

Megan's fingers tightened around the stem of the glass as she watched Marc walk to the bed. She didn't want to be happy that Marc was there, but she couldn't control an involuntary surge of joy. Why deny it? Hadn't Marc come there bearing a smile and champagne? "Marc," she said, "I'm sorry for what I said before . . . downstairs. . . . There's just so much . . ." She wanted to explain how his offer to buy her expensive clothing had insulted her and made her want to retaliate . . . but yet . . . what could she say? She herself didn't understand their deep, unrelenting emotional involvement.

"There's always been so much," Marc said softly. "Too much to forget."

Too much to forget. How true, Megan thought. Yet she was forgetting, wasn't she? She despised herself, despised her inability to stay angry with Marc.

"Mind if I see what you bought?" he asked, indicating the packages, then pulling on a ribbon without waiting for her answer.

"Yes, I do mind," she said, snatching the package away in an effort to combat her own spineless reactions to Marc. "I also mind the way you came barging in here without even asking my permission, acting as if you owned the place." She gathered up the rest of the packages and put them on the dresser. She had to make him leave before she begged him to stay. "Now that we've had that drink," she said, holding up her half-full champagne glass, "I wish you'd leave." A change of heart. . . . Take what you can get. Wasn't that what he had said? Well, she wasn't going to allow it, wasn't going to let Marc continue orchestrating their relationship to suit his varying moods.

"Did you have other plans?"

"As a matter of fact, I was just about to—" She clapped her hand over her mouth, then raced into the bathroom as she remembered the water flowing into the tub.

The water had reached the top and was pouring into the overflow drain. She placed her champagne on the vanity, then knelt to turn off the faucet.

Marc strode quickly after her, then stopped, his hands resting on the doorjamb. "Forget that," he said. "I want to talk to you."

"But, Marc, the water . . ."

"This is more important," he insisted, setting his glass down beside hers.

"All right," she said, pivoting on her knees and turning toward him. "Why is it so important? Tell me, Marc, why is it so important?" Her lips parted as she grasped the side of the marble tub and looked up at him.

Stepping closer, Marc clasped her shoulders before she could get to her feet. "Meggie," he said, kneeling beside her and framing her face with his hands. "Don't you know? Don't you know what you mean to me?"

Megan shook her head, wanting to believe, but so afraid to take the risk.

"Every time that dancer moved across the stage, I kept seeing you swaying for me, wanting me, welcoming me into your arms." His head dipped as his mouth sought the warmth of hers.

Megan closed her eyes, recalling how she had lis-

tened to the music and longed to do exactly what Marc
was asking. Even more, she yearned to be sensually
seductive, to show Marc that she wasn't a teenager
anymore, that she was a woman, with a woman's
desires and a woman's needs. She inched away from
him, remaining tantalizingly out of his reach until her
back finally rested against the thickly carpeted floor.
Last week, at her apartment, Marc had stroked her into
submission, but that wasn't what she wanted now.
Tonight she had to be certain of her own feelings, her
own power as a woman.

"Meggie?" He held himself away from her and
looked at her quizzically.

Steam rose from the tub, and in the shadows of her
mind Megan heard the undulating music and remembered how the sensuality of the dance had made her
yearn for Marc. Despite the problems keeping them
apart, nothing could diminish the joy she felt when
Marc held her in his arms.

The carpet beneath her was a velvety cloud. Marc
was so arrogantly dominant that he always controlled
the situation, but once again her independence struck
and made her want tonight to be different; tonight *she*
wanted to make love to *him*. She fumbled with the belt
on her robe and untied but didn't open it. Then, slowly,
deliberately, she reached up and began unbuttoning
Marc's shirt, pulling it out of his trousers and over his
arms until it formed a silky blue puddle on the oyster-
white carpet. Keeping one palm pressed against his
chest, she leaned on the other hand, lifted herself up
and urged him steadily back until their positions were
reversed.

For a long, silent moment Megan rested above Marc,
mesmerized by the passionate desire burning in his
eyes. A hungry yearning ached so deeply within her
that she held still while they gazed at each other,

prolonging the anticipatory elation that was so near yet so far. Finally, as his blue eyes blazed with fire and his smile curved with the joy of promised pleasures, a rush of ecstasy went surging through her body. She traced his features, then trailing along his jaw and neck, she probed the muscles of his shoulders and chest. When she brushed lightly over his trousers and began toying with the clip on his belt, he groaned, fastened his lips on hers and rolled her roughly onto her back.

"No." She held him away from her. "Don't you remember the dancers?" She smiled seductively as the corded muscles in his back quivered beneath her teasing embrace.

"Meggie. . . . Please. . . ." Marc's voice was a husky plea as he tried to force her back.

"Umm," she said, shying away and kissing his jaw, his neck, nibbling at his chest.

"I can't take any more," he groaned, parting her robe, then kicking off his shoes and the rest of his clothes. "Meggie," he breathed, burying his face between her breasts and inhaling the sweet moisture of her skin. "Don't torture me."

Tangling her fingers in his hair, she pressed him closer as his hands and mouth continued their tantalizing exploration of her flesh. Her bones melted beneath his touch until at last her body writhed in an agony of unfulfilled desire.

"Welcome me, Meggie," he groaned as his hands caressed her thighs. "Welcome me, darling."

"Oh, Marc, I want you so much," she said, stroking impatiently over his back. "So very much."

"Oh, Meggie, sweetheart." His mouth dug hungrily into hers as he shifted his body and satisfied her desperate ache. "You have me, darling, you have me . . . forever."

Her lips parted, her tongue sought his and she held

him closer until at last the mindless joy building within her erupted into a glittering ecstasy that swept away every other thought and feeling.

Their world became a rolling, racing rocket that tilted and soared on the edges of reality until finally it spun out of control and erupted, leaving them drifting amid the glowing stars of outer space—falling—gently, softly falling. Megan's voice echoed strangely in her ears as she cried out in pleasure and curled her fingers around Marc's perspiring shoulders.

Clasping her tightly, Marc trembled against her breasts and sighed. He waited for a few moments while their breathing eased, then rolled onto his back and cradled her in his arms.

"Do you feel like a sultan?" she asked, burying her face in his chest and inhaling the spicy-clean scent of his cologne.

"I feel like I never want to leave you," he said, brushing her hair back from her face.

"Don't." She drew small, worried circles on his chest. "Don't leave me the way you did downstairs, and don't send me away like you did in Washington," she pleaded as the frightening insecurities of the past crept into her thoughts and eroded her self-assurance. "Please, I need you so much." Why did she feel so ambivalent around Marc? So confident one moment and so fearfully uncertain the next. "Don't keep coming back and then leaving again. I can't take it."

"If you need me, why won't you stay with me? Why won't you come to Louisiana with me?" Still stroking her shoulder with one hand, he sat up, flipped the drain on the tub and began filling it with warm water. "If it weren't for this convention, would it have been another eight years before we saw each other again?" He switched on the air bar and bubbles broke through the water's surface. "Would you have stayed in New York and I in Louisiana?"

"You don't understand, Marc. It's different for me than it is for you."

"How different?" Scooping her into his arms, he stepped into the tub, lowered her into its bubbling warmth, sat down beside her and began soaping her body. "How is it different for you than it is for me?" he asked in a husky whisper.

His soapy hands, sliding down her breasts and over her stomach, made it hard for her to think straight. "For a man it's just . . ." She stopped and shook her head, too embarrassed to explain the deep emotional commitment she felt during their lovemaking. He couldn't possibly understand; no man could.

"Are we back to heritage and jobs? Are you saying that I'm too rich to be human, to be hurt, to be in love? Well, you're wrong," he said, delicately circling her thighs. "It's not just casual sex I want from you. I can get that by picking up any phone in this hotel. What I want from you goes much deeper, and we could have it, too, except that you're holding something back, something that keeps coming between us."

Megan turned to him and hesitated for a moment. Marc was right, but how could she tell him that she was afraid to trust him, too badly burned to ever put her fate in his hands again. She looked down, breaking the contact of their eyes. She needed her independence every bit as much as she needed his love.

"Still shy?" Marc asked, handing her the soap. "Well, I can think of a very pleasant way for us to become better acquainted." He smiled and began guiding her hand over his chest and stomach.

"More pleasant than this?" she asked, nibbling on his ear as her soapy fingers slid sensuously over his body.

Drawing her closer, Marc settled her on his lap and within a few moments Megan forgot everything except the delirious joy that was surging through her body.

Much later, when they had toweled each other dry and were lying in bed sipping champagne, Megan's doubts returned, but she was too pleasantly exhausted to voice them and soon fell asleep cradled in the warm security of Marc's arms.

The next thing she was aware of was Marc shaking her shoulder. "Meggie, wake up."

"Mmm, no, go away." She was too tired to open her eyes and she cuddled closer to the warmth of his body.

"Listen," Marc said, "I'm going back to my room. I can't show up for my morning conference in a tux. I'll see you after lunch. Wait for me." He brushed back her tousled hair and kissed her on the forehead.

"Mmm, okay," she said, but she didn't really understand that Marc had gone until she awoke early the following morning. She smiled to herself as she remembered last night, and much as she would have enjoyed waking up in bed with Marc, she knew that he had left her only to change his clothes. She'd see him again. Soon. Probably in less than a few short hours. Feeling totally contented, she rolled onto her stomach and went back to sleep.

Chapter Eleven

$\mathcal{D}$ark silence shrouded the room until a door slammed across the hall, shattering Megan's sleep. Slowly, she opened her eyes and looked around. Lilac swirls—white satin—not my apartment, she thought. Where . . . ? Then she remembered, remembered everything down to the most intimately sensuous detail.

Stretching languidly, she ran her hand along the side of the bed where Marc had slept. He was gone now, but that was all right; he had kissed her, whispered that he'd see her after lunch. Smiling voluptuously, she clasped his pillow, snuggled into it, sighed pleasurably and began planning her day. She had a ten o'clock seminar, then the Fremont Industries' luncheon, after which she'd probably spend some time with Marc before going to her two-thirty Treasury Bond futures conference. A busy but pleasant day, the kind she liked best. Idly, she wondered if she'd have a chance to incorporate Linda's information about Louis Fremont into her manuscript, wondered if she should. After all, it was bound to hurt Marc in his efforts to ward off Nessac's takeover attempt.

Still, she had her professional ethics to consider, her promise to Jerry. A nagging unease tugged at the corners of her mind as she slipped into her robe and went into the bathroom.

Two thick lavender towels lay on the floor where she and Marc had dropped them just after they had dried each other and before he had carried her into the bedroom. As she knelt to pick them up, she found a morocco leather billfold on the floor between the vanity and the tub. Marc's, she thought. It must have fallen out of his pocket when . . . She blushed, a warm haze enveloping her body as she remembered the hasty way he'd torn off his clothes.

She picked up the clip and held it for a few minutes. He'd be sure to miss it—wonder if he had lost it; she had to get it back to him. She reached for the phone built into the marble wall above the vanity and asked the operator to connect her with Marc's room. The phone rang three times before a woman answered.

Sickening jealousy coiled around Megan's heart. Her voice gagged in her throat and she couldn't speak. What was a woman doing in Marc's suite? Don't jump to conclusions, she warned herself, remembering the eight years they had lost because of a foolish mistake. The woman could have been a chambermaid or a secretary; there were any number of possible explanations. Unfortunately, none of them satisfied her. Sharply edged guilt slashed at her suspicion and mistrust as she berated herself for doubting Marc. Trust, she told herself, trust; she had to learn to trust Marc. Perhaps it was possible for some women to love a man without trusting him, but she couldn't, she couldn't at all.

"Hello," the woman repeated. "Is anyone there?"

"I'd like to speak with Mr. Fremont, please." Megan's voice echoed in her ears, firmly businesslike, betraying none of the fearful emotions cowering deep within her.

"One minute, please."

Megan overheard some mumbled conversation while she waited, then a low voice grumbled, "Louis Fremont here."

"I'm sorry," Megan said, wishing she had never called. "I wanted to speak with Marc."

"He's not here. Who is this?"

"It's not important. I'll call back later," Megan said, hanging up before Louis had a chance to repeat his question. For a few trembling moments, she chided herself for being so infantile; then she realized that there wasn't any way she could have told Louis about the money clip. . . . She could never explain how she had gotten it.

Still, she had to find a way to get it back to Marc. He had promised to see her after lunch. Of course, she'd take the clip with her and give it to him then.

After showering, she dressed in a coffee-colored linen suit, then attended a seminar by the guru elf of Wall Street. Stock market elves weren't anything like the magical people Megan remembered from her childhood fairy tales; they were investors who studied graphs of past performances and bought or sold stocks according to the technical fluctuations of the market.

Right now, Megan wished that all Fremont Industries' stockholders could be fairy-tale elves to whom her article, and her exposé on insider manipulations and hidden cash holdings, wouldn't matter at all. Her renewed personal relationship with Marc had made her own attitude about writing the article so ambivalent that she didn't want to think about it, yet she couldn't avoid it. The conflict between Marc and her career crowded all other thoughts from her mind, and when the guru's speech was over and the audience began applauding, she had only the faintest inkling of what he had said.

The Fremont Industries' luncheon was to start at noon, and Megan's technical seminar ended just in time. Megan headed for the conference member's booth just outside the dining room's double glass doors. She was given a white plastic packet containing much of the same information she had received from Steve Butler; and a small red card stapled to the packet informed her that she was seated at a table not far from the dais.

Soft music from overhead speakers mingled with the guests' conversation as she jostled her way through clusters of dark-suited men and women. The large round tables were set with red linen cloths, silver cutlery, pink and red mums in crystal bowls and fresh fruit appetizers in pineapple shells. When she reached her table, she found that several writers from most of the other well-known financial journals and magazines were already seated and the topic under discussion was Fremont Industries.

"The buzz is that Fremont's going to try to quash Nessac today," Charlie Ronkerman from *Business Life* said, lifting his bushy gray eyebrows and puffing on his pipe. "The question is how? Some new product they're working on? Raising dividends?"

"That's just a bunch of corporate hype," Pauline Symonds of *Investment Weekly* said, flipping her long blond hair over the collar of her light blue suit. "Nessac filed with the SEC today and ran a full-page ad on the financial pages, offering to buy all available Fremont stock at forty dollars a share. It's trading at thirty-two, so I don't see much chance of Fremont holding on.

Ah . . ." Her doe-eyed gaze shifted beyond Megan. "Here comes our host." She whistled softly. "Now I wouldn't mind one bit if he tried a little personal persuasion on me."

Megan followed Pauline's glance and saw Marc, his father, Jack Adams, Frank Dunston, Steve Bennett and three other men making their way to the dais. Not exactly a Megan Mahlar fan club, she thought. Well, knowing that Marc loved her went a long way toward eradicating the hostile feelings of the others. She straightened in her seat, telling herself that and trying to ease her discomfort.

"Hmm," Charlie snorted, answering Pauline's comment. "*Women.* Great investment advisors you are. A good-looking guy can sell you anything."

Pauline took a cigarette from the white china holder at the center of the table, then leaned toward Ronkerman and waited for him to light it. She inhaled deeply, then tilted her head back and let the smoke drift toward the ceiling. "Cool the macho bit, Charlie. My business sense is as sharp as any man's and so are my more physical needs. But like any professional, I never let one influence the other."

Never let one influence the other, Megan repeated silently as she watched a smiling Marc shake hands with the people crowding around him. His charcoal-gray pinstripe wasn't much different from any other suit in the room, but the man wearing it exuded an aura of assured elegance that seemed to dominate everyone around him—a masterful confidence entwined with an amiable smile.

Megan grew warm as her thoughts drifted back to the night before and she recalled the insistent passion that lay hidden beneath the businesslike demeanor of his expensively tailored suit. Could she really write an article exposing Fremont Industries' weaknesses after spending the night in Marc's arms? Merely thinking about it seemed like a betrayal of the words she had whispered in the darkness. But how could she not write it if she valued her career as a journalist? Either choice left her a loser and the dilemma seemed unsolvable.

The chicken crepes were cold—two thick, tasteless pancakes swimming in a congealed white sauce. The usual convention fare. Pushing it aside with a slight grimace, Megan satisfied herself with the Bibb lettuce salad and a small French roll. At least that part of the meal was supposed to be cold.

After the waiters had served coffee, the program chairman introduced Marc, who began detailing Fremont Industries' growth from a small family company to a large, publicly owned corporation.

He's so sure of himself, Megan thought as she looked up from her yellow notepad, so calmly dominating, not a trace of the self-deprecating uncertainty she had seen at the beach house. She glanced around the room. Even these jaded Wall Street realists were impressed. He seems so strong, so reliable—they want to believe him. Marc tapped on the lectern to emphasize a point and the audience nodded in agreement, a concrete example of his charismatic power.

"And we're still growing," Marc continued. "So, I'd like to take this occasion to introduce our latest product, resulting from more than ten years of research. GROMAX, the first environmentally safe fertilizer incorporating an insecticide as effective as DDT."

He paused while an excited murmur passed through the audience. Everyone at Megan's table began scribbling on notepads as black-jacketed waiters wove through the room handing each woman a long-stemmed red rose and each man a white carnation. The gold ribbon tied around the flowers said, *Fremont grows again, with* GROMAX, *the fertilizer of the future.* Megan recalled that during her laboratory tour, Ty had told her that the fertilizer plant was off limits; no doubt they'd been producing GROMAX.

Happiness for Marc brought a glow to Megan's cheeks as she accepted her rose. *Ten years' research.* She knew how much this moment must mean to him, especially now, in light of Nessac's takeover attempt. A smile wreathed her lips as her gaze shifted back to the podium.

"And," Marc added when the room had quieted down, "I've one other statement." He paused briefly, using the time to reestablish eye contact with the audience. "After spending some time in New York, I'm pleased to announce that Fremont Industries, with the assistance of Helderstone Brothers brokerage firm, is offering to purchase one million shares of Fremont Industries' stock at a price of forty-five dollars a share."

For a moment dazed silence greeted this statement, then everyone seemed to be speaking at once. Marc smiled as the program chairman rapped his gavel and asked for quiet. His efforts were futile. Marc's startling announcement had generated an irrepressible excitement. Megan leaned back in her chair, dazed by Marc's announcement, but definitely pleased.

"Talk about best-laid plans. . . . This really puts a crimp in Nessac's," Charlie said, setting his pipe in the ashtray. "It certainly caught me by surprise. I've seen their balance sheets; where the devil is Fremont getting that kind of money?"

"Bank loans probably," Pauline said. "Helderstone has good contacts."

Megan thought about, but didn't mention, the recently acquired cash reserves resulting from the land sales. It would be public knowledge soon enough, but for now it was her exclusive information. She tapped her finger against her lips as the realization came to her. No wonder Marc had been so concerned about her article's coming out too quickly. If Nessac had learned about his plans before this afternoon, they probably would have made their own offer sooner, which could have cost Fremont Industries the first round and perhaps the entire battle.

GROMAX was temporarily forgotten as the question-and-answer session centered around Fremont Industries' offer to buy back its own stock. Marc answered some questions while referring others to Jack and Frank. Megan took rapid notes, realizing that with a dual takeover battle her article was now more timely than ever. After fifteen minutes, the chairman called an end to the questions and hustled Marc and his entourage out a back door before Megan had a chance to speak with him.

I've got to get to him, she thought, elbowing her way through the crowd as she tried to follow him. The rest of the audience was aimed in the opposite direction and she squeezed against the wall as two men engrossed in conversation shoved past her, realized what they had done and turned to apologize. "The exit's that way," the shorter man said, eyeing her oddly while making it perfectly clear that he resented having to tell her something so obvious. Megan nodded and continued in the opposite direction while the man shook his head in annoyed disbelief. "Women," he muttered to his companion. "Who can understand them?"

Megan shrugged off his comment. If she had been a man, he would have thought she had a good reason for bucking the crowd, but since she was a woman. . . . She smiled wryly as she rounded the dais.

The door through which Marc had gone led to a steamy kitchen, and as she crossed between the chopping block and the sink, a man in a stained white apron looked up from his pots to tell her she didn't belong there.

"I'm with Mr. Fremont. Which way did he go?"

"That way," he said, wiping his hands on his food-splattered white apron and pointing to a stainless steel door that swung out into a carpeted hallway with a series of oak doors on either side.

Megan saw that a door midway down the hall was open and an angle of light streamed out onto the maroon hallway carpeting. Masculine laughter—ice clinking into glasses. They must be in there, she decided.

"I thought it went pretty well," Marc was saying. "We took the wind out of Nessac's offer." His confident voice reflected his satisfaction. "Now we just have to hope they don't try to get back in the race by topping our offer."

"I'd feel better if we could have bought more than a million shares," Jack Adams said. "There's five million outstanding and some shareholders might turn to Nessac after our offer runs out."

Megan tapped lightly on the half-open door. No one answered. They hadn't heard. She wondered if she should just walk in. No, she decided; considering the men who were with Marc, she'd rather walk into a nest of vipers. She knocked again, harder this time, hoping Marc would be the one to answer.

"I know," Marc continued, obviously unaware of her presence, "a good percentage of the stock is still family owned, but we lost control when we expanded and went public. We've got to rebuild shareholder confidence. That's why I pushed GROMAX; I'm hoping some shareholders will keep Fremont stock on the basis of its growth potential."

"Nobody's going to hold the stock if we don't get a favorable write-up in *Commerce World,*" Louis said.

"Don't worry, we will," Marc said. "I've got *that* situation well under control."

Megan's hand remained poised over the door. Under

control? What did Marc mean? Unavoidably, her thoughts flickered back to the night before. He couldn't have, he just couldn't.

"Hmm," Louis said, "I don't know why you agreed to that article in the first place. It was that Mahlar girl again, wasn't it? She called you this morning while I was dictating to that hotel stenographer. Wouldn't give her name, but I'm sure it was she. You never met us at the lounge last night. I can guess where you were. Did you have to get involved with her again? Hasn't she cost us enough already?" His voice was bitterly condescending.

"What's between Meggie and me is private. I had no idea she was going to write the article, Dad. It was as much a surprise to me as it was to you. I agreed to it because we had to fight Nessac's publicity with a dose of our own."

"Miss Mahlar? Miss Prim and Proper?" Jack Adams said, chuckling ribaldly. "Well, what do you know about that? I had her pegged as a troublemaker the minute she came in with that damned tape recorder."

"Watch it, Jack," Marc said tautly, then hesitated for a few moments before speaking again. "I told you not to worry, Dad. I've taken care of things. Believe me, Meggie's not going to do anything to hurt us. Now, the subject is closed and I don't want to discuss it again." A glass slammed on a tabletop, emphasizing Marc's statement.

Megan lowered her hand and shut her eyes. How could she have been so foolish? All Marc's lovemaking and talk about her giving up her career was a pack of nonsense, nothing more than an insincere attempt to guarantee a favorable article for Fremont Industries. He was so sure of himself, of his power to control the situation, to control her. He really believed that she was still the same gullible female she had been eight years before; despite everything she had told him, he didn't for one minute believe that she had changed. Well, she'd show him exactly how wrong he was; there wasn't anything weak about her, not now.

Flinging the door open, she strode quickly into the room and stopped directly in front of Marc.

"Meggie." Marc's broad smile was so warmly welcoming that it nearly melted the ice around her heart, nearly but not quite; she knew it was as cruelly false as all his other smiles, kisses and caresses.

"Marc, I have to see you privately." She ignored the other men, but she could sense their demeaning smirks and their ugly suspicions.

"No problem, Marc," his father said. "We were just leaving anyway. I promised your mother we'd stop off in Los Angeles on our way home. I don't suppose you'll be going with us?" His words were casually indifferent, but his cynical tone made Megan feel crawly, as if she were dirty, as if she needed a hot shower with antiseptic soap.

"No," Marc said, moving closer to Megan, but not touching her. "I don't think so. I'll see you back in Baton Rouge."

"Fine. I'll tell your mother." Louis nodded to Megan and left the room. Jack, Steve and Frank followed his lead.

Marc trailed them to the hallway, spoke quietly for a few minutes, then closed the door and returned to Megan. "I was looking for you at the luncheon," he said, smiling and holding out his arms.

"I was there," she said, deftly twisting out of his reach. "I was also outside"—she indicated the closed door—"for several minutes before I came in."

"Oh?" Marc said, his manner suddenly wary.

"I knocked, but you didn't hear me."

"I guess we were too busy celebrating. The talk went over well, don't you think?"

"I think most of the audience was convinced of your

integrity." Turning away, she fingered the Boston fern
on an alabaster pedestal between two green velvet
Queen Anne chairs.

"Most, but not all?" Marc said, coming up behind
her, close, but still not touching.

"Not all," she agreed.

"Not you?"

No, not me, Megan thought, definitely not me.
You've hurt me for the last time; I'll never believe you
again. Biting her lower lip, she swallowed her sorrow
and summoned her pride. "You left your wallet in my
room," she said, taking the morocco leather billfold out
of her canvas satchel and handing it to him. "I wanted
to return it." Stepping to her right, she tried to pass him
and head for the door.

Without thanking her, he shoved the billfold into his
pocket and grabbed her arm, halting her flight. "You
wanted to return it? Just like that? What the devil is
wrong with you?"

"Wrong with me?" Megan said, trying to twist free.
"Why, nothing at all is wrong with me. In fact, you
might say that I've finally come to my senses."

"Finally come to your senses? Well, as far as I'm
concerned, you're not making any sense at all." He
drew her closer until their thighs and hips touched and
her breasts were crushed against the firm strength of his
chest. "And I've no intention of letting you go until you
do start making some sense."

"Let me go. You're hurting me."

"Tell me, Megan," he demanded, ignoring her request and pulling her so close that their heartbeats
merged, wildly punctuating the stony silence of the
room. "You're not going anywhere until you tell me
what brought this on."

"What brought this on?" Megan tilted her head and
looked up at him. "I told you I was outside this door. I
couldn't help listening." She choked back the lump

rising in her throat. "I heard you talking to your father. Telling him not to worry, that I was under control." She shook her head in disbelief. "Oh, Marc, how could you? How could you talk about me like that?" Lowering her head, she willed herself not to cry. She'd never let him see how much he had hurt her, not this time.

"What did I say?" Placing his thumb beneath her chin, he tilted her face back up toward his. "I merely assured my father that the article was going to be favorable. It is, isn't it?"

"Don't be so sure. I can still hear Jack Adams cackling over the prim and proper Miss Mahlar." She freed herself from his grasp and backed away. "You told him about us, didn't you? That's such a low thing to do, Marc. How can I say anything good about Fremont Industries if you could treat our relationship like locker-room gossip . . . crow about it with a lech like Adams."

"Tell Adams about us? What kind of a man do you think I am? He was just guessing. You know how his mind works. I meant what I told you, Meggie . . . every word of it." His hand slid beneath her hair, gently tickling her neck as once again he pulled her toward him. "What's between us is just between us; it's something special." His fingers combed through her hair, curving it behind her ears. "It's always been special, you know that, don't you? So why do you keep putting up these roadblocks?"

"It's special, all right. You think I'm like my mother. Good enough to sleep with, but not good enough to marry. Two kinds of women; that's what your father thinks, what Jack Adams thinks, and you're no different." She tossed her head, tilting it away from his sensuous touch. At last she had voiced the fearful accusation that lingered in her thoughts, the deadly poison, destroying the love she felt for Marc.

"Marry, hmm?" Marc said thoughtfully. "Well,

Meggie, I never knew your mother and, truthfully, I've never thought about her one way or the other, but marrying you is no problem at all." Cupping her elbow, he hustled her out of the room. "No problem at all."

"Where are we going?" She placed her feet firmly together, standing rigidly, refusing to move.

"Just stop arguing and come with me," he said, propelling her through the lobby, past the red velvet settees and the registration desk. He led her out the door and handed his car keys to a young red-jacketed parking valet.

"Marc."

"Quiet. This time there aren't going to be any mix-ups."

The valet delivered the car, and when Megan was settled in the passenger seat, Marc got behind the wheel and started driving along the Strip toward the downtown area. His lips were tightly closed and he refused to answer Megan's questions about their destination until he pulled into a multi-tiered parking lot beside an aqua-toned building.

"Get out," he said, opening her door as a young couple in jeans emerged from the building holding a piece of paper and clinging to each other lovingly. "We're getting married."

"What?" Megan stared up at him, too shocked to move. Getting married? "But . . ." She couldn't believe what he was saying. She couldn't marry Marc; she had her career.

"No buts," he said, helping her out of the car. "That's what I wanted to do eight years ago, what I would have done if you hadn't been so set on getting to New York." Marc pulled her into his arms, holding her tightly, as if he would never, could never let her go.

"We can't get married." She stammered in disbelief, her green eyes huge in her pale face as she pressed her fingers against her temples trying to make some sense out of what she was hearing. "You heard your father. You know how he feels about me."

"*Forget* about my father," he snapped. "*Forget* about your mother. I told you, this is just between us. Meggie, just between us."

His gaze captured hers and her heart expanded joyfully as she saw her own tender love reflected in their depths. She wanted him so much that she couldn't speak, couldn't ask him, couldn't tell him.

"Do you *want* to marry me?" he asked as he stroked over her shoulders and down her arms, holding her to him as if he couldn't bear being parted from her. "That's the only thing that matters now. . . . Don't think about anything else . . . don't talk about anything else. No questions, darling, just an answer, one answer. Meggie, sweetheart, do you want to marry me?" Pulling away, he caressed her with his eyes, staring at her so intently that she felt as if he could see into the depths of her soul.

Marry Marc. Be with him forever. That was all she had ever really wanted from the very first moment she had gone into his arms and felt the firm warmth of his lips parting against the sweet welcoming of hers. Her life in New York and her career faded into nothingness as she stepped closer and let her soft body relax against the muscular strength of his. "Yes, Marc," she said, the glowing happiness in her heart making her voice firm with an unwavering certainty. "I want to marry you more than anything else in the world."

"Mrs. Marc Fremont," Marc said, sitting up against the lavender velvet headboard, curving her fingers around his hand and pressing the thin gold band to his lips. "I like the sound of it."

"Mmm, so do I," Megan said, pulling the white satin sheet up over her bare breasts and flexing her fingers as if she were trying to get used to the feel of the ring she had been wearing for less than two days. It was so small, yet it meant so much to her—a lifetime of love rather than a few stolen hours.

"I'll get you something nicer when we get back to Louisiana," Marc said. "That jewelry shop didn't have anything that really suited you. I think my grandmother's ring might fit you. Mother's been saving it for my wife." He smiled as his lips circled her fingertips. "It's part of the Fremont heritage."

"No, this is all I want . . . the ring I was married in. I'll never take it off . . . not ever . . . unless you ask me to."

"Forever, Meggie, forever," he said, pulling her up against his chest and devouring her lips with a raging hunger that flared and flamed until her body arched against his, demanding satisfaction. "That's how long I'm going to want you, just until forever."

Chapter Twelve

M arc's promise of happiness forever came to a shattering conclusion three days later when their brief honeymoon ended and they returned to Baton Rouge. They hadn't told Nora or Marc's parents about their marriage because Marc had insisted that the news was too important to be discussed over the phone. "We'll tell them in person," he'd said. "All together. After all, we're one family now."

"I can't stay there long, Marc. I have to get back to New York. I've got a deadline on my article."

"All right. I understand. You've got to complete it; you've given Butler your word. Besides, we need the publicity, but when that's done, you hand in your resignation."

Megan didn't answer him. Resigning from *Commerce World* was one decision she didn't want to face. Not now when they were so happy. Still, deep within herself she knew that much as she loved Marc, she needed her career too. But she couldn't tell him that, not today, not just yet. Later, when the time was right, she'd explain how she felt. If he really loved her, he'd want her happiness and understand her needs.

The flight to Louisiana was a journey of joy, replete with handholding, secret smiles and stolen kisses. But when they arrived at Fremont Oaks, the circular driveway was lined with expensive cars and the chauffeur explained that Mrs. Fremont was hostessing a dinner party.

"Just our luck," Marc said as the chauffeur carried their luggage into the house and they followed him onto the white-columned veranda. "Trust my mother to schedule a dinner party on the one night when I wanted our families to be alone."

The butler opened the front door and greeted them as they walked into the cathedral-ceilinged entryway. An eight-foot-round crystal chandelier radiated glimmering streaks across the gold-flocked walls and marble-tiled floor. Symphonies of flowers bloomed in tall china vases and wide silver pots. Fremont Oaks, beauty and elegance, money and power.

Standing beside Marc, in the center of all this splendor, Megan realized that in all the years she had spent at Fremont Oaks, she had never before entered the house through the front door, not until now, not until she had become Mrs. Marc Fremont.

A stately woman with gray hair and a fair, unblemished complexion walked through the door, handed her sable jacket to the butler, nodded to Marc and followed her tuxedoed escort into the drawing room. The carefully pressed elegance of her mauve peau de soie gown made Megan's hunter-green slacks and rust corduroy blazer seem even more creased and travel weary than they actually were. She nestled closer to Marc.

Marc smiled and curled his arm around her waist. "Why don't we go upstairs and change into something more appropriate for the occasion?" he said. "I'm sure mother can squeeze in two more dinner guests." He led Megan up the free-floating walnut stairway. "This might not be such a bad idea after all . . . a sort of belated wedding celebration." His smile broadened. "More public than the ones we've already had."

They changed in Marc's room, a masculine combination of burnished mahogany and blue damask. Half an hour later, when they went downstairs, Marc was wearing a charcoal-gray evening suit and Megan had on her black jersey gown.

"They must be in the dining room," Marc said, turning toward the back of the house. "Let's go."

Megan shook her head and moved away from him. "You go ahead. I want to see Nora first."

"I understand," Marc said, releasing her and smiling as she headed for the kitchen.

Nora, wearing a gray and white uniform, was standing by the stainless steel sink arranging some radish roses on twelve crystal platters of carrot curls, celery sticks and black olives. Two other younger maids were ladling lobster bisque into a gold-banded white china tureen.

"Grandma," Megan said, coming up beside Nora.

A radish tumbled into the sink as Nora turned to look at her. "Meggie, what a surprise!" She opened her arms and Megan, closing the distance between them, returned her embrace. "What are you doing here?"

"I've got some exciting news."

The dining-room buzzer sounded and Nora shook her head. "Your news is going to have to wait. I've got to get these relish platters on the table. Cook has the flu, two of the agency maids didn't show up and I've been having to cover for all of them." She shook her head. "I don't know how I'm going to get through the night. Look, you sit down." She pointed to the white enamel table. "I'll be back as soon as I can." She placed four platters on a tray and disappeared through the swinging door that led to the dining room.

Megan watched the two younger maids add a parsley garnish to the lobster bisque and set some white china bowls on a silver serving tray. They were too busy to bother with the relish platters. Nora would have to make two more trips to get them served. Maybe she could help. Why not? She'd done it often enough in the past, hadn't she?

Lifting a relish platter in each hand, she stepped into the dining room and handed them to Nora. Mrs. Fremont eyed her from the foot of the table, but Louis's seat was empty and Marc was nowhere in sight.

"I'll get the rest," Megan whispered to her grandmother.

"Thanks," Nora murmured.

When she turned back toward the kitchen, Marc was standing in the doorway blocking her way. "Just what do you think you're doing," he snapped, pulling her back into the kitchen.

Louis Fremont stood behind him, absolutely glowering with rage. "This is where she belongs," he mumbled.

"I was helping my grandmother," Megan explained. "Cook's sick and two of the agency maids didn't show up."

"So you're filling in for them?" Disbelieving shock laced Marc's words.

"I was helping Nora."

"You're my wife."

"She's my grandmother."

"Hmmph." Louis grunted angrily, then turned and left the room.

Marc motioned to the dark-haired young women who had finished preparing the bisque and were basting some cherry-glazed ducks. "I'd like you to set two more places at the table, please. The butler's arranging the chairs." Linking his arm with Megan's, he led her into the hall.

"I can't go in there," she protested.

"Why on earth not?"

"I can't sit there and have my grandmother wait on me."

"Don't be ridiculous. You're my wife, now. Nora will understand."

"Maybe she'll understand, but I won't be comfortable. I can't do it, Marc."

"Does that mean we're never going to eat together?" Marc asked coldly.

"Marc, I can't."

"Do you want me to fire Nora because you're uncomfortable having her around?"

"No. Of course not." Nora would be crushed if she lost her job. It meant everything to her; her career, although different from Megan's, was no less important.

"Then, let's go," Marc said, guiding her toward the dining room. "Stop acting like an infant."

Two extra chairs had been placed at the table, on either side of Marc's mother. And at the other sides of the two chairs sat the couple Megan had seen in the entryway. Marc sat beside the lady in the mauve gown and Megan sat next to her tuxedoed escort.

Nora and one of the younger maids began serving soup from a tureen. Her grandmother eyed Megan curiously, but said nothing. Megan had never felt more uncomfortable. Shadows from the past beckoned from the kitchen, but Marc and her present life insisted that she belonged in here with him. The tension was making her sick and she wished she could disappear.

"I'm a new grandfather," Megan's silver-haired dinner companion said, after he had been introduced as Leroy Pendergast, owner of a Kentucky thoroughbred farm. He pulled out a picture of a smiling young woman holding a sleeping baby. "Getting married was the best thing my son ever did; his wife's a wonderful little lady, the daughter I've always wanted. And now she's made me a grandfather." He beamed proudly as he studied the picture.

"Your daughter-in-law is a lucky woman," Megan said enviously. How wonderful it must be to have a loving father, something she had never known. Suddenly, she realized how desperately she had missed her own parents and how much she yearned to be welcomed into her husband's family, to have them love her and call her their daughter. But one sideways glance at Louis's scowling face told her just how hopeless those expectations were.

Nora hovered beside the table, checking to see that all the guests were content. One of the young maids removed Megan's untouched bowl of bisque, and when the duck was served, Megan's hands were shaking so that she knew, no matter what Marc said, she couldn't remain at the table. Quietly excusing herself, she left the room and fled upstairs.

Marc joined her a few minutes later. "Are you all right?" he asked, closing his bedroom door. "Nora's worried sick."

"I'm sorry, Marc. It's just that when we were in Las Vegas everything seemed so perfect, but now, I'm not so sure." She sat on the bed and covered her face with her hands.

"Okay," Marc said, sitting beside her on the four-poster and taking her into his arms. "I can see where the situation with Nora was uncomfortable. It was my fault for not understanding, but I just wasn't viewing the world through your eyes. I'll work something out; don't worry."

Megan snuggled closer and stroked the curve of his jaw. When they were alone and Marc held her in his arms, the world seemed completely in balance, but when their families and her career came into play, everything seemed to tilt.

"My parents will be up in a few minutes. As soon as the coffee is served, they'll excuse themselves."

They held each other quietly, stroking, nestling, caressing, until three raps sounded at the door and they sprang apart.

The door opened abruptly. "I won't have this going on in my house," Denise Fremont said, while Louis stood behind her and closed the door. "What you do on your own is one thing, but not here." She smoothed her black lace bodice and looked pointedly at Megan. "And how do you suppose Nora feels? How could you do this to her? After all she's done for you? Bad blood . . . just like your mother."

"We're married," Marc said, holding Megan tightly as she cringed against him. "We were married in Las Vegas."

"Good Lord," Marc's mother gasped and slumped into the oxblood leather wing chair by the fireplace.

"I tried to tell you, my dear," Louis said to his wife. "But you were too upset to listen." He straightened away from the door and glared at Marc. "You had no right to do this to us."

"Congratulate me, Dad," Marc said, ignoring Louis's obvious anger and smiling amiably. "Isn't this what you've always wanted, me married, grandchildren, continuing the Fremont heritage?"

"Our housekeeper's granddaughter," Marc's mother said, fanning her face with her white lace-edged handkerchief. "And her parents . . . Good Lord, we don't even know who her father was." Her arms fell limply to her sides and she leaned back as if she had fainted. "My grandchildren . . . Nora's . . . good Lord."

Shriveling within herself, Megan edged away from Marc. This was horrible, far more horrible than anything she had ever imagined. She couldn't accept

Denise's rejection, couldn't deal with her obscene implications.

Marc drew her closer, as if their physical proximity could keep his parents from driving them apart. "Watch what you say," he ordered, looking from his mother to his father. "Meggie's my wife. She's the one I married and I don't care a fig about her parents."

"You don't?" Louis snorted. "Well, maybe it's time you did some heavy thinking about your children and your heritage."

"I think we'd better leave," Marc said, turning toward the door. "I'm not interested in listening to your bigoted opinions about breeding and social class. I've had a lifetime of them, and by now you should realize that that's one subject we'll never agree upon. Meggie's my wife. I love her and, as far as I'm concerned, that's all that matters."

"She's been your wife for a few days while we've been your parents for thirty-four years. Now, suddenly, she matters and we don't." Louis's patrician cheeks lost their color. The dresser mirror reflected his silvery hair, highlighted by the glow of the burnished brass bedside lamp; his dismal pallor made him seem older and weaker.

"Dad," Marc said, his voice softening. "I'm sorry."

"Come on," Louis said, ignoring Marc and holding his hand out to Denise. "Our son no longer needs his parents." He helped his wife to the door and suddenly they seemed like two pathetically miserable people.

"I can't," Denise said as they reached the hall. "I can't walk. My chest." She crumpled against Louis.

Marc ran to his mother's side and lifted her in his arms. "Meggie, get Dr. Sloates. He's downstairs." Gently, he placed his mother on her bed.

For a while the entire house was in an uproar; everyone feared that Marc's mother had had a heart attack, but after Dr. Sloates had examined Denise, he said it was just a bad case of nerves. When the dinner guests had departed, Marc and his father hovered at Denise's bedside.

Megan looked on from the doorway. No one seemed to notice her, and she was certain that her bedside presence wouldn't speed Denise's recovery. They were fortunate; Marc's mother hadn't had a heart attack. But what if she had? Could Marc live with it? Could she? Could their marriage survive, and even if it did, would it be worth the price? She knew what it was to be without parents. How could she live with herself if she were the cause of Marc's losing his? She realized she couldn't do it.

Her high-heeled black silk sandals sank into the thick beige carpeting as she went downstairs. Nora was still busy in the kitchen, but Tim was in their cottage.

"I need a lift to the airport," Megan told Tim after he had recovered from the initial surprise of seeing her.

"Why? What's wrong? You look awful."

"Tim, remember, at your wedding, when we talked about keeping secrets and not asking questions?" Megan rested her hand on Tim's shoulder. "I need that now. Please," she pleaded, "just take me to the airport."

Tim nodded, got his coat from the closet and did exactly as she asked. Within minutes, they were driving through the gates of Fremont Oaks on their way to the airport.

The following afternoon, after a tearful, sleepless night, she was in Jerry's office telling him about the Las Vegas conference. A tan pigskin glove covered her left hand; despite her belief that her marriage couldn't survive the strains put on it by Marc's parents and her career aspirations, she hadn't been willing to take off her wedding ring. But she was in no mood to answer any questions the gold band was sure to provoke.

"You went to New Orleans after Vegas?" Jerry asked.

"Just for a short stop," Megan said. "I wanted to see my grandmother."

"Hmm." Jerry tilted back his black leather swivel chair and meshed his hands behind his head. "Fremont article about finished?"

"Nearly ready for your approval," Megan said, tossing an envelope onto his desk. Although she had spent a wakeful night, she hadn't wasted those sleepless hours; she had put them to good use and completed her article.

"That's what I like about you, Megan," Jerry said, reaching for the envelope. "All professional; I can always count on you to get the job done. No flimsy excuses."

"Well," Megan said, holding up her hand to halt Jerry's compliments. "There is one thing I still have to check out." She told him what Linda had mentioned about Louis's problem with the SEC.

"Check it out and get back to me," Jerry said. "It shouldn't be too difficult." Swiveling his chair, he checked the publication schedule hanging on the wall behind him. "And make it snappy, Megan. You're slotted for next week's edition."

Jerry was right. Checking Linda's story wasn't difficult at all, not when Megan had the prestige of *Commerce World* magazine behind her and not when America's monetary heartland was a mere taxi ride away.

New York's financial district was a world unto itself, where the importance of every natural disaster and political upheaval was rated solely by the effect it had on the stock market. People were rated similarly, and since a recommendation in *Commerce World* could send a stock's price up or down, depending on whether it was a buy or sell, Megan, as well as all the other staff writers, occupied a position of power. Most brokers were eager to supply any information she needed. After making a few discreet inquiries, she found that Louis Fremont had indeed sold, then repurchased, a large block of Fremont stock, but he had bought it back for Jacqui's son's trust fund.

"A corporate official can't sell and rebuy his own stock within a six-month period unless he reports it to us," the SEC attorney told her. "The thing is, Fremont didn't buy it back; his grandson's trust fund did, so he's claiming that it's okay because *he* no longer owns the stock. Still, he is a trustee of the fund. There might be a violation; we're checking into it. It's a technical question, but my own opinion is that while it's highly unethical, it's probably not illegal. If I were you, I wouldn't bother with it."

"Is anyone else involved?" Megan asked, still concerned about the consequences to Marc.

"You mean from the corporation?"

"Yes, or the family?"

"Well, Marc Fremont appeared in Washington to defend his father's actions and offer to return all the profits, but we don't think he knew anything about it until after it was done. He's totally different from the old man, but he's not about to let his father hang."

"Do you have the dates of the transactions?"

"I can't give you any more information. The case is still under investigation."

"I understand," Megan said. "Thanks for the off-the-record ruling." She shook hands with the attorney and left the office.

Unethical but not illegal. That certainly sounded like Louis Fremont. Could anything be more unethical than the method he had used to keep Marc from marrying her—from learning about her pregnancy? She looked down at her ring as her yellow taxi swiveled through the heavy New York traffic and beeped its way uptown, back to *Commerce World* magazine. But what about her own frightened reaction long ago at Fremont Oaks? In a way, it had been her own fear and uncertainty eight years before that had made all these bad things happen. From that very first moment in Louis Fremont's library she had known in her heart that Marc loved her, and had secretly refused to believe that Marc had deserted her. If she hadn't been so afraid of hurting her grandmother, and if she hadn't let herself be debased till she accepted Louis's offer out of bitter rage, she would have insisted on seeing Marc, they would have been married and none of this ever would have happened.

No use crying over what might have been, she decided as she paid the taxi driver and walked into the building. That problem had been settled. Last week Marc *had* married her, but the marriage couldn't survive, not with the demands his parents were placing on him as well as those he was placing on her.

After talking with Jerry, she spent the afternoon splicing the SEC information into the article, being very careful to report only what the attorney had told her. *Commerce World* readers would have the facts, but they'd have to reach their own conclusions. This was one instance in which she was determined to be absolutely unbiased.

Shortly before five o'clock, when she'd nearly completed her work, she called Jerry on the interoffice line. As she had expected, he told her that he'd see her right away.

"Is it finished?" he asked when she walked in.

"Just about. I have one or two problems I wanted to check out with you."

"Shoot," Jerry said, leaning back in his chair and twirling a pencil between his hands.

They reviewed the touchy sections and tossed ideas back and forth. Fifteen minutes later they had solved

Megan's problems. "Thanks," she said. "I don't know what I'd do without you."

"You'd manage," Jerry said, smiling. "You're a pro, Megan; you'd manage just fine. Now, why don't you go back to your office, finish things up and let me have the manuscript before you leave? With the stock battle between Fremont and Nessac, this is going to be the hottest item on the street. I want to get right on it and give it top priority."

Megan completed the article, reread it, made a few minor grammatical corrections, then dropped it on Jerry's desk and went home. At this point she was too exhausted even to think straight.

Her phone was ringing as she unlocked her apartment door, but by the time she had run across the living room and answered it, the line had gone dead. Had it been Marc? she wondered. Should she call him? No, she decided, what would that accomplish? "What's the use?" she asked, kneeling to pick up Tiger, who was purring against her leg. "Tell me, will you?" she repeated, nuzzling her cheek against the cat's soft fur. "What's the use?" Her article was finished, her marriage was finished, her life. . . . She poured some milk into Tiger's dish and headed for the bedroom. Sleep was what she wanted, pure, blissful sleep, but her hopes were in vain, and she spent another restless night dreaming about Marc, his touch, his love. Forever, he had said. Meggie, just as long as forever. But for them, at least, the sands of forever seemed to have run out.

At eight-thirty the next morning, red-eyed and exhausted, Megan went in to Jerry's office. He hadn't called her the night before and she was eager to hear his opinion about her article.

"It's good, Megan," Jerry said, getting up from his desk. "Really good. I especially like the way you started it, that human-interest angle on Fremont House is a super lead. Our photographer got some shots of the place and we're going to feature them as part of a collage. . . . Fremont Industries, the entire picture—chemistry and kids."

"That was Marc's idea," Megan said, almost to herself. "He loves children." She hadn't been wrong about that. Hadn't he said that he would have wanted their child even if she didn't? She bit her lip as she remembered Marc's anguished face. He had looked at his mother with the same devotion; people mattered to Marc. Maybe that was what she loved most about him, what she had always loved, even when she had been too young to know.

"I know, *he's* coming across super-good, but the old man . . ." Jerry shook his head. "A real robber baron . . . doesn't seem to care about anything except his family and his company. Two strong personalities, the old regime and the heir apparent . . . potent stuff." He snatched some papers off his desk and put them on the bulletin board. "This is a great article, Megan, and we're going to make it even greater." He pointed to a layout of two *Commerce World* pages, each with a square blocked out in the center. "We're going to do a sidebar. You know the family. I want you to give me a thumbnail sketch on Marc and Louis, profiles of the powers behind the company. Fast, Megan, I need it by this afternoon. We're going to press."

Returning to her office, Megan sat down at her desk and began typing out the profiles. Impartial, she told herself as she wrote, unbiased; remember you're a reporter. Her profiles were short and descriptive and, as she read them over, she realized that if her conscious mind hadn't registered the differences between Marc and his father, her subconscious certainly had.

Among other things, her profiles contrasted Marc's concern for his workers with his father's concern about social class; Marc's need to help the children at Fremont House was compared with Louis's need for an intimidating mural. Which was the real heritage of life? she asked at the end of her article. She left the decision to the reader, but made it perfectly clear that Marc Fremont was currently in charge and Fremont Industries would now be reflecting his values, his heritage of life.

At six o'clock, she handed Jerry the completed profiles and dropped into the brown vinyl chair opposite his desk. "I'm exhausted, Jerry. Do you think we could leave the rest for tomorrow?"

"Mmm," Jerry said, flipping through the papers she had given him. "Sure, take all—" Breaking off midsentence, he looked up and both he and Megan turned in the direction of raised voices coming from the hallway.

"You can't go in there," Fran said. "I'll have to check with Mr. Butler."

"I'm not interested in Butler," Marc replied firmly. "I'm here to see"—he strode into Jerry's office, then stopped and let his eyes flicker over Megan, a caressing possessive gaze—"my wife."

Chapter Thirteen

$\mathcal{F}$or several minutes a numbing silence shrouded the office and Megan felt as if they were all statues in a wax museum. Talk about open-mouthed shock, she thought wryly as she looked at Fran's startled face; the receptionist, like everyone else, seemed dazed.

Jerry was the first to recover. "Your *wife?*" he repeated, challenging Marc's statement.

"You heard me," Marc replied.

Crossing his arms over his chest, Jerry leaned back against his desk and turned to Megan. He didn't have to say a word; his "I'm listening and it had better be good" expression said it all.

Steepling her fingers in her lap, Megan looked down and tried to affect a calm she didn't feel. "I'm sorry, Jerry, I guess I should have told you," she said lightly. "I just didn't think it was very important." She crossed her arms over her breasts and shrugged. "You know, one of those spur-of-the-moment things, a quickie Vegas ceremony that didn't work out. Fortunately, it can be annulled just as easily." She now realized that she loved Marc too much ever to come between him and his parents. She could never live with that sort of guilt.

"No annulment," Marc said tersely as he grasped Megan's arm. "Come on. Let's get out of here. We need some privacy."

"I don't think that's such a good idea, Marc." She didn't want to be alone with him, to have him touch her and weaken her resolve.

Jerry cleared his throat. "What do you want me to do, Megan?"

"Stay out of this, Butler," Marc warned in a soft, clipped tone which brooked no interference. "It doesn't concern you."

"I was speaking to Megan," Jerry said, his hand edging toward the phone.

Megan saw Marc's body tense as his jaw tightened and he began walking toward Jerry. "It's okay, Jerry," she said, coming up to Marc and taking his arm. "Marc's probably right. We do have things to settle. I'll see you in the morning."

"Are you sure you want to go with him?" Jerry asked, leaving his desk and standing near the door. "There's no need to take unnecessary chances."

"Don't worry," Megan said. "He's not going to hurt me." At least not physically, she thought. "Let's go, Marc." She felt the tension rippling through his muscles as she gripped his arm and led him out of the office.

When Marc slipped his arm around her waist and drew her possessively to his side, Megan couldn't help but notice Fran's envious gaze. For a fleeting moment, she flushed with pride at the thought that he was her husband. Then, when she remembered his parents, her misery at the dining-room table and Marc's own repudiation of the importance of her career, the flush froze to a chilling shiver.

After they stopped in her office for her jacket and purse, they left the building. "Where do you want to go?" Megan asked when they reached Fifth Avenue.

"It's a nice night," Marc said, looking up at the dark, cloudless sky. "Would you mind very much if we walked for a while? Walked and talked?"

Megan shook her head and they started up Fifth Avenue. Marc caught her hand in his and for several minutes they walked silently. Most of the smart shops lining the street had closed for the day, but their wares were still clearly displayed in the brightly lighted windows—jewelry, clothes, furs—all the expensive and beautiful things Megan had always wanted. Yet now she barely noticed them because the man at her side meant so much more.

"You know," Marc said softly, breaking into the silence that surrounded them, "that first time we made love, I didn't want to."

Megan nodded. She remembered every moment of that first time, how she had risen to her toes and pressed her lips to his, how he had tried to hold her away from him, until . . .

"But I couldn't stop myself. . . . It really bothered me. . . . I'd never lost control before." Releasing her hand, his fingers stroked slowly up her back, cupped the nape of her neck for a few moments, then settled on her shoulders, drawing her to him. "When I couldn't keep from wanting you despite all my self-recriminations about your youth and innocence, I knew I was in love. I told my father that I was going to break my engagement to Deirdre so I could marry you. He tried to talk me out of it, but I wouldn't change my mind. When I returned from seeing Deirdre, my father told me that you weren't really interested in me, that you had schemed up our entire relationship just to get some money." His arm tightened around her shoulders. "I remembered how easily you had come to me that first time and everything my father had said made sense. I had been the seducee rather than the seducer. . . . I felt like a class-A fool."

"Your father told me you were marrying Deirdre . . . that you didn't want to see me. . . . Then when I found out I was pregnant . . ."

"What happened, Meggie? What happened between us? I know you haven't wanted to talk about it, but we have to, we really do."

Megan nodded. Marc was right. In halting, barely audible words, she told him about the ice, the pain, the horrible despair and the uncontrollable tears. "I felt so alone, Marc, so scared. No one to confide in, having to write my grandmother cheerful letters so she wouldn't worry. Remembering my mother . . . So afraid that something would happen to me." Her voice lowered to a tearful whisper. "I didn't know how you felt. I worried about what would become of my baby if I . . ."

An ambulance sped by, its sirens shrieking; Megan moved closer as the memories became too vivid and the events of the past too painfully clear. Not wanting to see the brightly whirring lights, she lowered her eyes and kept her gaze fastened on the sidewalk.

"At Nora's wedding," Marc said, "when I learned about our baby, I kept wondering if perhaps you really didn't want it because you hated my child, my father's grandchild, hated the baby because he'd be a Fremont too."

"Oh, Marc, I was upset, confused, scared, but I loved you, and I wanted our baby. I wanted it so much."

Holding her tightly to him, Marc caressed her upper

arm, tenderly, possessively. "I feel so empty, Meggie, such a meaningless sense of loss, a horrible helplessness."

Megan understood, she understood perfectly. Above them a cool autumn breeze fluttered the sweet shop's green- and white-striped awning. They continued walking silently. She was too upset to speak, and Marc seemed to be caught up in the privacy of his thoughts. Traffic whizzed by, a beeping, screeching parade of taxis, cars and buses. Attractive store displays gave way to the stately canopy and lighted windows of an elegant hotel.

Stopping for a moment, Marc held her to him, their now shared sorrows blending with the echoing pulses of their hearts. Megan sighed. Stepping away, Marc looked down at her and brushed a few stray hairs back from her forehead. "We're together now, Meggie, and whatever else happens, I don't want us ever to be apart."

The uniformed doorman standing near the potted juniper saluted them, but Marc shook his head and motioned to the hansom cabs lined up in front of the hotel.

"I've never been in one of those. They remind me of the surreys in the Vieux Carré. How about it, Meggie?"

Megan agreed, and a few minutes later they were comfortably settled in one of the black, horse-drawn carriages, a plaid wool blanket tucked over their legs.

Central Park was in the middle of the city, but to Megan it seemed like a world apart, a country forest, as lushly green as a Louisiana bayou. She made no effort to resist as Marc reached for her hand.

"How's your mother?" Megan asked. From speaking to Nora, she already knew that Denise had recovered.

"Much better, but Dr. Sloates has suggested a vacation, so she and Dad are leaving for the Caribbean later this week."

"I'm glad," Megan said, truthfully. "I'm glad she's feeling better."

"I want you to come home with me . . . back to Louisiana."

"Louisiana?" Megan straightened in her seat, shifting away from Marc. "I can't go back to Louisiana. Surely you know that."

"I know nothing of the sort. Why can't you go back? You've a right to be upset by what happened, but we're married and, despite everything, it's your home now, as well as mine. Where else did you expect us to live?" Framing her face with his hands, he turned her toward him and looked deeply into her eyes. "I was born at Fremont Oaks. My children, our children, will be born there, in the same bed where I was born."

Fremont Oaks, Megan thought, his parents' house, the parents who'd never accept her no matter what Marc said. She crossed her arms, clutched herself and shook her head despondently. "You heard what your parents think of me. I can't, Marc. I just can't."

"Okay," Marc said, his fingers slipping through her hair. "My parents don't approve of you. They're bigots . . . set in their ways. I won't argue the point. I'm hoping that in time they'll change. It would be nice if they did, but even if they don't, you'll still be my wife, and we're the ones who have to work things out. If you can face a creep like Regis Winthrop for the sake of your job, why can't you come to terms with Nora and my parents for the sake of our marriage?" Sighing, he closed his eyes, leaned back and shifted his arm to the back of the seat. "I never said it would be easy; nothing worthwhile ever is."

In the silent darkness, Megan turned to him, her heart melting with yearning at the sight of the man she loved so much. She couldn't bear the thought of losing him again, but neither could she endure the hatred and humiliation that awaited her at Fremont Oaks—the rejection of his parents, the split between them and Marc.

While she watched, Marc took a deep breath, sat up and opened his eyes. He seemed to have reached a decision. "I can't change my parents, Meggie, any more than you can change yours. You don't have to love them, but you'll have to accept them. They're a part of me and I'm not going to apologize for who I am any more than I'd expect you to. We'll just have to believe in what we have strongly enough to work things out. Unless you can agree to that, I can't see any future for our marriage."

"But, Marc, your parents."

"Are my parents. They're not me. We've been all through that."

Megan thought of living at Fremont Oaks, being with Marc's parents, knowing how much they hated her. And Nora, how could she be Marc's wife and sit in the dining room while her grandmother served them? She couldn't. No way. Not ever. She shook her head despondently. "I can't, Marc, I just can't."

"It's not that you can't, Megan. You just don't want to. I know there have been times when I've let you down and haven't been there when I should have, but that's over and you have to trust me, just as I've learned to trust you, otherwise it's no good, no good at all." The hansom cab stopped and Marc leaned forward to pay the driver.

Megan stepped out of the carriage and the horse whinnied as she reached up to pet him. Marc waited beside her, one hand on her shoulder and the other on the horse's neck. The simple gesture reminded Megan of all the times they had stood beside their horses just before they left the bayou. Her memories were so entwined with Marc's, the past such a constant part of the present; tilting her head back, she rested it on Marc's chest.

The hansom cab moved slowly down the street, disappearing into the park as a cool evening breeze ruffled through the trees. Megan watched the drying leaves waver, loosen and fall to the ground. Marc's arm tightened around her shoulders as he walked into the street and signaled for a taxi. She got in and slid across the seat, expecting him to join her. He leaned on the open door and shook his head.

"I meant what I said, Meggie. You have to accept me just as I've accepted you. Grow up, darling; learn who you really are. If you really love me, you can live anywhere, even Fremont Oaks. It's your decision." His jaw firmed as he pressed his lips together and took a deep breath. "You know where I'll be. I'll be waiting for your call." He closed the taxi door and walked slowly back to the curb.

Ten days later, Megan sat at her desk staring at the latest edition of *Commerce World*. Marc's face dominated the cover—a shadowy image of his father hovered in the background—and the bold black lettering beneath their pictures stated: FREMONT INDUSTRIES LOOKS TO THE FUTURE. A future that doesn't include me, she thought wryly.

Marc had made his feelings perfectly clear; she hadn't just married him, she had married a family and a way of life into which she could never fit, neither could her background nor the career that she had worked so hard to achieve.

She flipped the magazine open to page sixty-two, where her feature article began. BY MEGAN MAHLAR, it said right below the title. She ran her finger across her name as if it had some magical powers. Her name in print. It never failed to thrill her, but Marc's touch thrilled her too. If only there were some way she could have them both.

A feature article usually meant so much to her, so

why did she feel so empty this morning? Oh, she was proud of the well-written article, had worked to make it clear and informative, but somehow she didn't feel the boundless joy she had come to expect, like the thrilling pride she had experienced when she sat beside Marc in their wedding bed and he had lovingly kissed her ring—called her Mrs. Marc Fremont. What had Marc said about making their marriage as important as her job? About dealing with her insecurity, Nora, his parents.

Splaying her fingers over the article, she studied the burnished gold of her wedding band. How many times had she reached for the phone intending to call Marc, then changed her mind? Too numerous to count. Grow up, he had said. Learn who you really are. Well, she knew who she was and that person definitely didn't fit in at Fremont Oaks—except as a servant.

But she loved Marc so much. Wasn't he worth fighting for? Definitely, she decided. But how? The interoffice line buzzed her out of her reverie and she answered the phone.

"Get in here, Megan," Jerry ordered. "I've got some great news."

Great news, Megan thought as she closed the magazine, flipped it across her desk and hurried to Jerry's office. The only great news she wanted to hear was that Marc's parents loved and accepted her as his wife and that Marc understood the importance of her career.

Jerry's face was one big grin as he linked his hands behind his head and leaned back in his chair. "Guess who I just heard from?"

"The President. He's invited you to the White House to discuss the economy, an invitation exclusive to *Commerce World* magazine, a scoop so fantastic it will wipe out every other financial journal."

Wrinkling his nose, Jerry tilted his chair forward and

leaned his elbows on his desk. "You won't be so sarcastic when you hear what I have to tell you."

"So, tell me already," Megan said, slumping down in the brown vinyl chair. "The suspense is killing me."

"How do you feel about Houston?"

"Why? Are you shipping me there?"

"You guessed it," Jerry said, coming around to the front of his desk and patting her on the back. "The president of Lathrop International was so impressed by your article that he's finally agreed to that interview we've been after for the past six months. When can you leave?"

"Lathrop International?" Megan said. "He really liked my article."

"Said it was fair, unbiased, no sniping . . . when I told him it was written by a southern lady. . . ." Jerry rolled his eyes and looked at the ceiling. "Of course, I never mentioned that you were married to Fremont. . . . Well, that's water under the bridge . . . on to new and more interesting things. When can you leave for Houston?"

"Written by a southern lady, hmm? And he was impressed? Jerry, let me run an idea by you and see what you think." She settled herself comfortably and began talking.

When she had finished, Jerry nodded and said, "It's fine with me; in fact I think it's a great idea. Now, when can you leave for Houston?"

"Right away."

"Then what are you waiting for? Get moving."

When she returned to her office, the morning mail lay on her desk—envelopes, magazines, book cartons, a brown paper package from Elaine Akron in India and a long white box, a florist's box. Loosening the red satin ribbon, she lifted the lid. Roses, beautiful, long-stemmed roses. A small white envelope lay on the green tissue paper. She slipped out the card.

The article said it all. You're a fantastic writer.
Too good to quit. I love you, Meggie. I always
will. Come home, darling. We'll work everything
out.

                                        Marc

For several moments she stared at the card, and all
that muddled confusion became clear. Although she
rejected the misery of her past, she had no regrets
about going to New York and educating herself, just as
she had no regrets about marrying Marc. What had
Marc told her about growing up and learning who she
really was? Well, now she knew. She was Megan
Mahlar Fremont, writer for *Commerce World* magazine, Nora's granddaughter, Louis's daughter-in-law—
whether he approved or not—and, most important of
all, she was Marc Fremont's wife. And she belonged
with him. In the recent past, each time they had
argued, Marc had come after her, but this time would
be different; she had to show him that she had truly
changed and was confident enough of her own worth to
live anywhere, as long as they were together. Reaching
for the phone, she made airline reservations to Louisiana.

A heavy rain was falling as Megan turned off the
highway and began driving the winding bayou road
leading to Fremont Oaks. She hadn't told Marc or her
grandmother that she was coming. She'd surprise them
both, she thought, as a piece of Spanish moss hanging
from a cypress tree streaked across her windshield,
making Tiger hiss and lift a paw.

"Cool it, Tiger. It's only some moss. You're going to
have to get used to it if you want to live here."

Looking at her disdainfully, Tiger began licking his
paw.

Jerry had been unusually understanding when she'd

told him that she needed some time off before going to Houston. "Any way you want to work it out," he had said. "The assignment is yours and if you need to spend some time in Louisiana," he had added with a wink, "that's fine with me. I think your idea about basing yourself in New Orleans and concentrating on southern companies is great. Everything is workable, Megan. Everything is workable."

"I hope you're right," she had said, hugging and thanking him. Then, immediately after clearing the mail from her desk, she had gone home, put Tiger in his kitty carrier, packed and left for the airport. She had taken the brown paper package with her; Elaine had sent her a beautiful pink silk sari.

She turned the wheel to the left as the road curved and Fremont Oaks came into view. The stately two-story mansion with its thick white pillars hadn't changed—brick didn't have that ability. But she wasn't made of brick, so she had changed; now she knew that the successful woman she had become wanted more than anything to share that success with the man she loved.

She stopped the rented Toyota on the cobblestone cul-de-sac beneath the wide stone steps and looked up at the black-enameled front door with its shiny brass knocker. If she rang the bell, Nora would have to answer. Shifting her foot to the gas pedal, she drove around to the back entrance and parked her car.

Light from the kitchen illuminated the back door's curtained window and made the raindrops glisten as she ran up the narrow brick steps carrying Tiger. Without bothering to knock, she flung the door open expecting to see Nora.

"My goodness." A tall, angular woman turned from the sink, clutched her throat and looked at Megan in shock. "Who are you?"

"I'm Nora's granddaughter. Who are you?" She set

Tiger on the floor. He circled her feet for a few minutes, rubbed his neck against her legs, then took off to investigate.

"Nora doesn't work here anymore. I'm the new housekeeper." The woman wiped her gnarled hands on her white apron.

"Doesn't work here? But why? What about Tim?"

"Him neither. They're both gone. Working somewhere else."

"Gone? Somewhere else?" Megan couldn't believe it. Her grandmother had been with the Fremonts for more than thirty years. . . . And Tim. . . . What had Marc said about his loving his greenhouses? They'd never leave Fremont Oaks, not willingly. "Is Mr. Fremont here?" She'd have to speak with Marc—ask him what had happened. Surely he hadn't fired Nora because of that incident in the dining room.

"He's on vacation."

"Marc's on vacation?" What about the flowers? What about his saying that he'd wait for her?

"Mr. Fremont's on vacation. Mr. Marc's in New Orleans."

"New Orleans?" At Fremont Industries, no doubt. "May I use the phone?" Megan asked, walking into the hall.

Mrs. Jamison's response was pleasant and business-like. "Mr. Fremont's in conference," she said, "but he left instructions to put you through. Hold for a minute."

She clicked off and Megan toyed with the telephone wire as she waited for Marc. What was taking him so long?

"Meggie?" Marc said, coming on the line.

His tone seemed coldly formal, totally unlike the warm reception the roses had led her to expect. "Where's my grandmother?" Her voice echoed in her ears, as stiltedly hard as his had been.

"Your grandmother?"

"Yes, I'm at Fremont Oaks and the housekeeper says that Tim and Nora don't work here anymore."

"You're at Fremont Oaks? Let me speak with Mrs. Guntree . . . the housekeeper."

The housekeeper spoke to Marc for a few minutes, then handed the phone back to Megan.

"Wait for me," he said. "I'm on my way."

"Marc, where's my grandmother? What's happened?"

"She's fine. She and Tim are organizing a new branch of Fremont House in Baton Rouge. They're both so wonderful with kids, I thought . . ." His voice cracked and broke off. "Meggie, I'm at a board meeting. . . . It's difficult to talk. . . . Just wait for me and I'll explain everything."

As far as Megan was concerned, there wasn't anything for him to explain; Nora and Tim were all right and that was all that mattered. She smiled as she thought of Tim and Nora working with children. Marc was right, they were perfect. Hadn't they always been wonderful to her?

"I have the night off," the housekeeper said after Megan was off the phone. "I was just about to leave, but if you have any luggage I can help you upstairs before I go."

"That's not necessary. I'll be just fine." She smiled, certain that from now on *everything* was going to be just fine. There wasn't anything she and Marc couldn't work out between them, not when they loved and trusted each other.

Feeling chilled after driving through the rain, Megan poured herself a cup of coffee and sat down at the table. When Tiger returned to the kitchen and rubbed against her leg, she set some milk out in a saucer for him. Mrs. Guntree excused herself and disappeared into the small room off the kitchen that once had been Nora's. "I have to change," she explained.

A few minutes later a car horn sounded outside and Mrs. Guntree came hurriedly out of her room. "That's my lift," she said. "Will you be all right by yourself? Do you need anything?"

"I'm fine. I know where everything is. Remember, I grew up here. It's like coming home." *Coming home.* For the first time in her life, she felt that Fremont Oaks was her home, that she belonged there, belonged with Marc, wherever he was.

The storm's intensity increased as she went to the car to get her luggage, and by the time she returned to the house she was soaked through. Kicking off her wet shoes, she carried her suitcase upstairs into Marc's room, the room they would share, the room where their children . . . She flushed with desire as she thought of Marc and the children that were yet to be.

A curtained four-poster bed dominated the heavy mahogany furniture that filled the large, white-walled room. Heavy blue draperies covered the windows and logs had been laid in the fireplace. After lighting the logs, she ran some warm water into the claw-footed white enamel tub, stripped off her clothing and relaxed.

As she closed her eyes and leaned against the tub's curving back, she remembered Las Vegas, when Marc . . . Opening her eyes, she smiled to herself. This tub was barely large enough for her, let alone for the two of them. Enough of these romantic fantasies, she told herself, reaching for a thick white towel hanging on a wooden rack at the side of the tub. Marc will be here soon and then—*fantasies, Marc.* Drying herself quickly, she wrapped herself in Marc's robe and returned to the bedroom, now warmed by the crackling fire.

She set her suitcase on the wood and tapestry luggage rack, opened it and checked through her lingerie. Then, smiling confidently, she disregarded it, pulled out the sari Elaine had sent her and began tucking it around her. By the time Marc's car drove up to the house, she had taken the pillows from his bed and was lounging in front of the fireplace.

A key sounded in the front door. It opened, then slammed shut. "Meggie," Marc called, "Meggie, where are you?"

"Upstairs." She listened as he raced up the stairway, two steps at a time—swiftly down the hall. At last he was at the bedroom door, looking down at her, his hands resting on the doorjamb.

"Meggie," Marc said, his husky voice catching in his throat.

Smiling seductively, she got to her feet and beckoned to him.

"Oh, Meggie." Striding quickly toward her, he pulled her into his arms.

She pressed her hands against his chest, stepped away, shook her head, reached for his tie and began loosening it.

"Sweetheart." Marc's fingers combed through her hair, framing her face and lifting it toward him.

"No," she said, brushing him away. "Not yet. I'm not ready yet." Tossing his tie to the floor, she slowly unbuttoned his shirt, lowering it over his shoulders and dropping kisses along the bareness of his chest.

"Meggie," he growled, "I'm not made of stone."

"But, Marc, sweetheart," she said, urging him down onto the pillows, "don't you remember what you said to me about dancing for you . . . just for you?" Pulling back from him, she waved her hand over her face, undulated seductively toward him, then moved away. She smiled to herself as perspiration dampened Marc's forehead. Enjoying the effect she was having on him, she stepped closer, whirling as the sari flared around her bare feet.

Reaching out, Marc grabbed the hem of the sari,

pulled her down beside him, then leaned over her as she rested on the pillows. "Do you know what I remember most," he said, "promising that I'd take the veils off, one by one." He released the silk fabric and began slowly unwinding it. "You're like a package of joy," he said, "all wrapped in gauze . . . just waiting for me to get to the delightful inner core." His eyes darkened as the sari fell to the pillows and his lips caressed her flesh.

The rain beat against the window, pulsating, harder, a driving crescendo. Megan's body shifted, rising to meet Marc's, and the dance of seduction became a dance of love, whirling them, spinning them, carrying them back into that private world that had always been theirs and theirs alone.

"Marc, oh, Marc." She clutched his shoulders, needing him closer as she felt the ultimate exaltation of their love.

"Sweet Meggie, my own sweet Meggie. I love you so." Holding her tightly, he nuzzled his face into the curve of her neck and breathed a sigh of release.

For a few minutes they lay quietly in each other's arms, feeling the sweet joy of their bodies and the sweeter joy of their love. Then Marc lay back and nestled Megan against his chest. "I'll never let you go," he said. "Not even if I have to keep you locked in this room forever."

"I wouldn't mind," she said. "But there is the little matter of my job."

"You're staying here . . . there aren't any more excuses," Marc said firmly. "I had a long discussion with my parents and told them exactly how much you mean to me. If they ever upset you again, I'll walk out on the family, the company, everything. I can't change the way they feel, but they know I won't tolerate any mistreatment of you."

"But if we're living together in the same house . . ."

"We'll stay in New Orleans," Marc said. "It'll be much more convenient anyway. Besides, I'd never expect you to live in the same house with my parents, not after the way they've treated you."

"Oh, Marc, everything is wonderful. You're wonderful."

"These past few days have been hell for me. I'm useless without you, Meggie. Don't talk about leaving me for a job or anything else. Don't even think of it." His hand stroked slowly down the side of her body.

"Marc, my job is a part of me, just as yours is a part of you. Jerry is being very cooperative about letting me concentrate on companies in the South. I'm going to work out of New Orleans, and if you let me use your jet I should be home every night." She shifted her body over his and began rubbing her hands across his chest.

"Every night?" Marc repeated.

"I promise." She moved her hips seductively and nibbled his earlobe. Her dreams had finally come true; she had it all.

"If that's the case, sweetheart, then I support you all the way. I don't want you to give up your work—your writing. You're too good at it. Besides, I realize how much it means to you and I wouldn't do anything to make you unhappy. Just be sure that your daytime activities don't run into overtime." He grinned. "I wouldn't want anything to interfere with our nighttime pleasures."

"Why, Marc," she said, smiling up at him and running a tantalizing finger across his cheek. "Whatever do you mean?"

"Tease," he said, catching her finger between his lips and circling it with his tongue. "Do you have any idea of how much I love you?" Rolling her gently onto her back, he proceeded to show her exactly how much.

Silhouette **Romance**

15-Day Free Trial Offer
6 Silhouette Romances

6 Silhouette Romances, free for 15 days! We'll send you 6 new Silhouette Romances to keep for 15 days, absolutely free! If you decide not to keep them, send them back to us. You pay nothing.

Free Home Delivery. But if you enjoy them as much as we think you will, keep them by paying the invoice enclosed with your free trial shipment. We'll pay all shipping and handling charges. You get the convenience of Home Delivery and we pay the postage and handling charge each month.

Don't miss a copy. The Silhouette Book Club is the way to make sure you'll be able to receive every new romance we publish before they're sold out. There is no minimum number of books to buy and you can cancel at any time.

MORE ROMANCE FOR
A SPECIAL WAY TO RELAX
$1.95 each

2 ☐ Hastings	23 ☐ Charles	45 ☐ Charles	66 ☐ Mikels
3 ☐ Dixon	24 ☐ Dixon	46 ☐ Howard	67 ☐ Shaw
4 ☐ Vitek	25 ☐ Hardy	47 ☐ Stephens	68 ☐ Sinclair
5 ☐ Converse	26 ☐ Scott	48 ☐ Ferrell	69 ☐ Dalton
6 ☐ Douglass	27 ☐ Wisdom	49 ☐ Hastings	70 ☐ Clare
7 ☐ Stanford	28 ☐ Ripy	50 ☐ Browning	71 ☐ Skillern
8 ☐ Halston	29 ☐ Bergen	51 ☐ Trent	72 ☐ Belmont
9 ☐ Baxter	30 ☐ Stephens	52 ☐ Sinclair	73 ☐ Taylor
10 ☐ Thiels	31 ☐ Baxter	53 ☐ Thomas	74 ☐ Wisdom
11 ☐ Thornton	32 ☐ Douglass	54 ☐ Hohl	75 ☐ John
12 ☐ Sinclair	33 ☐ Palmer	55 ☐ Stanford	76 ☐ Ripy
13 ☐ Beckman	35 ☐ James	56 ☐ Wallace	77 ☐ Bergen
14 ☐ Keene	36 ☐ Dailey	57 ☐ Thornton	78 ☐ Gladstone
15 ☐ James	37 ☐ Stanford	58 ☐ Douglass	79 ☐ Hastings
16 ☐ Carr	38 ☐ John	59 ☐ Roberts	80 ☐ Douglass
17 ☐ John	39 ☐ Milan	60 ☐ Thorne	81 ☐ Thornton
18 ☐ Hamilton	40 ☐ Converse	61 ☐ Beckman	82 ☐ McKenna
19 ☐ Shaw	41 ☐ Halston	62 ☐ Bright	83 ☐ Major
20 ☐ Musgrave	42 ☐ Drummond	63 ☐ Wallace	84 ☐ Stephens
21 ☐ Hastings	43 ☐ Shaw	64 ☐ Converse	85 ☐ Beckman
22 ☐ Howard	44 ☐ Eden	65 ☐ Cates	86 ☐ Halston

Silhouette Special Edition

87 ☐ Dixon	101 ☐ Bergen	115 ☐ Halston	129 ☐ Rowe
88 ☐ Saxon	102 ☐ Wallace	116 ☐ Roberts	130 ☐ Carr
89 ☐ Meriwether	103 ☐ Taylor	117 ☐ Converse	131 ☐ Lee
90 ☐ Justin	104 ☐ Wallace	118 ☐ Jackson	132 ☐ Dailey
91 ☐ Stanford	105 ☐ Sinclair	119 ☐ Langan	133 ☐ Douglass
92 ☐ Hamilton	106 ☐ John	120 ☐ Dixon	134 ☐ Ripy
93 ☐ Lacey	107 ☐ Ross	121 ☐ Shaw	135 ☐ Seger
94 ☐ Barrie	108 ☐ Stephens	122 ☐ Walker	136 ☐ Scott
95 ☐ Doyle	109 ☐ Beckman	123 ☐ Douglass	137 ☐ Parker
96 ☐ Baxter	110 ☐ Browning	124 ☐ Mikels	138 ☐ Thornton
97 ☐ Shaw	111 ☐ Thorne	125 ☐ Cates	
98 ☐ Hurley	112 ☐ Belmont	126 ☐ Wildman	
99 ☐ Dixon	113 ☐ Camp	127 ☐ Taylor	
100 ☐ Roberts	114 ☐ Ripy	128 ☐ Macomber	

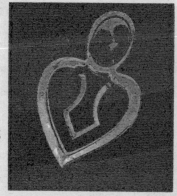